MARIE W. WATTS

TOUGH
TRAIL
HOME

Meredith;
Thanks for your support.
Enjoy!

Black Rose Writing | Texas

Mar W. Wan

ISBN: 978-1-68513-391-7
LIBRARY OF CONGRESS CONTROL NUMBER: 2023948138
PUBLISHED BY BLACK ROSE WRITING
www.blackrosewriting.com

Printed in the United States of America
Suggested Retail Price (SRP) $21.95

Tough Trail Home is printed in Minion Pro

*As a planet-friendly publisher, Black Rose Writing does its best to eliminate unnecessary waste to
reduce paper usage and energy costs, while never compromising the reading experience. As a result,
the final word count vs. page count may not meet common expectations.

For my mother, Mary Seibold Watson,
who gifted me the ability to tell stories

I would like to give a big thank you to all who have supported my writing journey including members of the Write Inmates of the Women's Fiction Writers Association, the Texas Writers League, past book coaches, family, and friends. Without your support, *Tough Trail Home* would never have been possible.

Lastly, many thanks to Mother Earth for creating the awe-inspiring ranch on which I live. After twenty years, I never tire of its beauty, vitality, and ever-changing landscape.

PRAISE FOR

TOUGH
TRAIL
HOME

"Marie Watts' *Tough Trail Home* opens the barn door on a very American way of life at a unique point in time. Grab the reins and settle into the saddle for an entertaining ride."
–Therese Gilardi, author of *Matching Wits with Venus*

"*Tough Trail Home* is partly a novel of relationships, but mostly a love letter to Texas. And this is Texas at its grittiest, with situations that would scare even the most enthusiastic of settlers. The relationships in the book are between the characters, but also between them and their environment. The author drew me in immediately, as a family of four leave the comfort and security of a life in Carolina, and are catapulted into a homesteading life in rural Texas, putting what might be an unresolvable strain on the parents' marriage. The second half of the book increases the pressure on everyone with a series of disasters that might have made weaker folk quit. With the help of their neighbors, these newcomers turn out to be tougher than they thought - true Texans at heart, and as the story progresses lessons are learned by everyone before a resolution is found. Recommended for book clubs."
–Gabi Coatsworth, author of *A Beginner's Guide to Starting Over*

"*Tough Trail Home* is a harrowing, motivational story of a woman's resilience and fortitude during extraordinary challenges and hardships when saving herself often collides with saving her marriage. Believable characters in a well developed setting add to the drama's plausibleness, leaving the reader guessing and speculating until the very end."
–Lucille Guarino, author of *Elizabeth's Mountain*

"Lisa and her husband are homeless and without jobs. In desperate need of housing and an income, Lisa receives an unexpected inheritance to solve their problems. *Tough Trail Home* engages the reader from the very first page as the family moves from a posh suburban lifestyle to a gritty ranch in Texas. As Lisa struggles to transition the children to farming life, Michael is determined to find work and move everyone back to a city. Raising cattle is hard work and there are trials at every turn, however, it's relationships that matter in the end. I thoroughly enjoyed this book."
–Iris Leigh, author of *Liza's Secrets*

"When life comes crashing down around LIsa, Michael, and their two kids, it tears the family apart. The novel pulled me into its pages to discover whether this once-close family could find their way back to each other. A bonus was the clearly drawn depiction of the dangers and joys of life on a Texas ranch. This book defines the true meaning of home."
–Kathryn Dodson, author of *Tequila Midnight* and founder of the Good Book Collective.

"*Tough Trail Home* is a delightful read about a family coming to terms with each other and their new lives. Just as Lisa and Michael and their two children lose their comfortable suburban lifestyle and all that comes with it, Lisa inherits a rundown Texas ranch. Will it bring the family together, or tear them apart?"
–Pamela Stockwell, author of *A Boundless Place*

TOUGH

TRAIL

HOME

CHAPTER 1

December 27, 2008
The Great Recession

The gloomy economic news and fighting in the Middle East left a pit in Lisa's stomach. Outside the Volvo's passenger window, the desolate swampland of murky water and leaf-bare trees streamed forth as the family headed west on Interstate 10 from Baton Rouge to their next place of residence.

After switching the satellite radio away from a recap of 2008 to an easy-listening station, Lisa closed her eyes, trying to unwind. But her inner self insisted on replaying what had been a personally brutal twelve months. Losing her accounting manager position…tightening finances… Michael's new gig in Houston…uprooted again…her great uncle dying…supervising the move alone…. *I can't take much more.*

"You OK?" her husband, Michael, asked.

"I'm worn out…and we haven't found a house yet…. I don't want to do this anymore. Promise me this will be the last move…. Not only that, I'm also feeling guilty about missing Uncle Joe's funeral."

"Relax. Everything will work out. I want to take our time finding the perfect house."

Michael's cell rang. He grabbed it off the console and answered. As he listened, his demeanor changed. He mumbled, "I'll be there as soon as I can." Ending the call, he dropped the phone into the cup holder, knuckles whitening from his ironfisted grip on the steering wheel as if a Mack truck had rear-ended them.

"What's wrong?"

"Dr. Cal's been charged with criminally negligent homicide."

"What?" Lisa's voice cracked. Dr. Cal Harris, the owner of Harris Cardiac Implants, was Michael's boss and would be Lisa's after the first of the year. "I don't understand."

Michael stared straight ahead. "The FDA's been real slow about approving the second implant device. We've been trying to rein in manufacturing costs on the first one, so we could hold out until the new one was approved. Apparently, with Dr. Cal's consent, production went to an inferior plastic. The cheap part cracked. Two people died."

Lisa stared at the full-diamond bezel of her Rolex, an overwhelming sense of dread mushrooming through her core. The stale air mingled with the roar of tires on asphalt pounded home the alarm. They were rolling, rolling, but to where? Her neck stiffened. The beginning of a new year usually held so much promise, but now....

Glimpsing into the back seat, she was relieved that their children, Jessica and Andrew, absorbed in DVDs, were oblivious.

***

Hours later, Michael turned into the parking lot of the corporate apartment in Houston where he had been living since starting his position on November 1. Jessica opened the door before Michael turned off the engine. Princess wiggled out and took off running across the grounds.

"God damn it! I've had it with that dog! Andrew, go get her." Michael said as he bounded to the second floor, leaving the door open.

Lisa cursed under her breath. *Annoyed with the dog? It was his idea.* He had offered it to ten-year-old Jessica as a bribe to move.

MARIE W. WATTS | 3

After a mad scramble, the trio cornered the long-haired miniature dachshund, and Lisa secured the puppy tightly in her arms. Tears dripped down Jessica's cheeks. Andrew appeared grim.

"Kids, your dad's stressed. There's some trouble at work. Everything will be fine. Let's go inside. I don't want her to get loose again…. Andrew, unload the car."

Andrew rolled his eyes. "Why doesn't Jessica have to help? Her fat booty could use the exercise."

"Mom!" Jessica said.

"I don't want to hear that kind of talk coming out of your mouth. Apologize to your sister. She needs to hold Princess while we're bringing everything in."

"Whatever." He sauntered off in the direction of the station wagon. Lisa bit her lip, staring at the once-darling pride of her life who had turned into a foul-mouthed, disrespectful sixteen-year-old who towered over her.

Princess fought and whined as they entered the apartment. While handing the bratty canine to Jessica, the red-haired devil squirmed loose, streaking through the rental and into the bedroom just as Michael was leaving. He jumped, banging against the door frame.

"I don't want to see any more of that damn dog!" Michael said.

Jessica burst into another round of blubbering. He bent down and took the child into his arms, smoothing her light-brown hair. "Oh, honey, I'm sorry. It's just stuff going on at work…. It's not you." Once her tears subsided, he kissed her on the top of the head, releasing her. Turning to Lisa, he said, "Not sure when I'll be back. I'll give you a call." After delivering a peck on her cheek, he headed out the door.

Jessica plopped on the couch. "I hate this place." I wanna go home…. Why does Daddy hate Princess so much?"

Surrounding the youngster with an affectionate embrace, Lisa wished they were back in Raleigh, too. Since their marriage, they had moved four times as Michael took more lucrative positions, her employer transferring her to their office in Michael's new land of opportunity. Raleigh was the longest they had stayed put—five years. *I made friends there, good friends. I'm too old for that. Never again.* "Honey, this is the last time, I promise. We're going to find a home and stay there forever."

Soon, Princess came slinking out of the bedroom, hopped on the couch, and put her head in Jessica's lap. The preteen brightened. "Momma, I love Princess so much!" Leaning down, she grasped the wriggling imp tightly. Lisa edged away gently to help Andrew with the luggage.

By the time their possessions were in the apartment, Lisa felt claustrophobic. If they had not moved, she would be chilling with wine by the fireplace in the sitting area of her Raleigh bedroom, watching the backyard's river rock fountain from her Barcalounger.

Glancing around, she noted there was barely enough space to walk with the children's "must haves" laying around. The only DSL outlet was in the living room; Andrew's computer equipment was strewn over the coffee table. Heavy curtains blocked what little light the cloudy day allowed. Arguing drifted from the bedroom her children were sharing. Bands of anxiety tightened around her chest, similar to consuming two Grande triple-espresso lattes prepared with whole milk and mounds of real sugar. She needed water.

The funk of leftovers struck Lisa as she peered into the fridge despite finding it bare. What had she expected? A bottle of that expensive Pinot Blanc 1999 Dr. Cal Harris had served while wooing Michael to work for him? Impatiently, she ordered Jessica to accompany her to the store.

***

Michael swung the Porsche into his reserved parking space, thankful he had not sold the 911 yet. A Mercedes, his company car by virtue of his position as vice president of sales and marketing, would not arrive for another couple of weeks. Perhaps his assistant, Delores, had everything wrong; maybe this was all a misunderstanding.

Delores glanced up as Michael strode in. "Mr. Dunwhitty, Mr. Schuster's been looking for you. He asked that you see him as soon as possible."

"Thanks." Michael ducked into his office, removed his suit jacket, and went directly to the CFO's suite. The man was on the phone but motioned him in. Easing into one of the overstuffed chairs next to the desk, Michael eyed his peer warily. The man appeared to have aged ten years in the last week.

Art hung up the phone as he gazed at Michael. "That was legal. It's bad. I'm sending everyone home except for a core group." Both men sat in silence. Art waved his hand at the company's stock price scrolling across the bottom of his computer screen. "The stock's been tanking all morning. We're down fifty percent."

Michael cringed. "Think we can hang on?"

"I don't know. I need you to call your biggest clients. See if you can save some accounts. I'm headed to a meeting with the bank in about fifteen minutes. They were about to approve a loan to float us through January, but they're balking because of the indictment."

"So, where's Dr. Cal?"

"He's out on bail. He wanted to go to his house in Cabo, but the DA put the kibosh on that. They agreed to let him go to his estate in Aspen."

"The son of a bitch! He's just left us high and dry to deal with this crap?"

"You got it."

Cursing, Michael set out for his office. Sending Delores home, he hit the phones. After an hour of fruitless calls, he jumped up, launching a sample of Dr. Cal's miniature heart implant device across the office. It hit the wall, shattering.

"What a piece of crap! You bastard!" Michael envisioned hurling the defective piece of shit at Dr. Cal. *You may be smart, you asshole, adding all those numbers in your head faster than a calculator. But you're an idiot. I could have made us billions, but you had to have money for those Bentleys and your house in River Oaks. You had a cash cow and you killed it.*

Sagging into his chair, Michael closed his eyes, allowing his mind to race through the options before him. For the first time in his life, he had no plan forward. *If only I could go back and undo everything.... What have I done to my family?*

He looked up as Art walked in and dropped wearily into the seat across from Michael. "You're not going to believe what's happened...."

CHAPTER 2

Brakes screeching from a late-night TV movie jarred Lisa awake. Shifting on the sofa, she glared at her Rolex—after midnight. Michael was not answering his phone. Her earlier anger had long since morphed into concern. Finally, around two, a key turned in the door. An inebriated Michael, tie ajar, coat over his arm, entered.

A chill permeated Lisa as she watched him disappear into the kitchen and return with two glasses of Crown and ice. Handing her one, he slumped on the couch next to her and took a long draw.

"It's over. That bastard Harris stripped the company bare, raided the bank accounts. He's filing for bankruptcy January 2." He took another sip and stared moodily at the TV.

"Will you have a job? Will I have a job?"

"I don't know about mine. You don't. We'll have to see how long I can last. I can't imagine anyone buying anything that bastard makes."

"I knew we shouldn't have moved. I had bad vibes from the start." Lisa slammed her fist on the cushion.

"What do you mean? You knew we shouldn't have done this?" Michael turned to her with a glare. "You were so happy to get the damn money and a job. You went right along with everything. You never complained or said you didn't want to move." He took a gigantic gulp.

Guilt silenced Lisa. In truth, she had been thankful for the plum accounting assignment offered by the company. Not having to claw and scrape for a new position when so many professionals were out on the street was a godsend. She hurriedly imbibed, impatiently willing numbness to overtake her.

"I guess it's good we've got the money from the sale of the house to live on for a while…. We do have that money, don't we?" Lisa's stomach churned.

"Not yet. We technically sold the house to Harris Cardiac Implants…. If they don't pay us before they file for bankruptcy, we'll have to file against them in court…. I guess I'll have to check with an attorney." Michael knocked back a slug of the magic elixir. "I knew we should've sold it ourselves like I wanted. But, no, you were too busy running around with your girlfriends to bother."

"It was as much your responsibility as mine! Besides, with the market the way it is, it would have taken forever to sell." This time Lisa took a long swallow, allowing the straight alcohol to burn a path to her stomach. "Sounds like we better find some other place to live quick. I bet the company won't pay the rent here…great…just great."

Michael put his empty glass on the coffee table. Taking Lisa in his arms, he said, "Sorry I'm such a grump…. I'm mad at myself because I got us into this mess…. We'll bounce back. We always do." He kissed her on the forehead and rose. "See you in the morning."

Draining her drink, Lisa got another, this time adding a dash of Sprite. Servicing their mammoth credit card debt would eat away at what little they had in their checking accounts. And then, how long would it take her to find work? Accountants were a dime a dozen with her former coworkers saturating the market. What about Michael? What if he kept working but did not get a paycheck?

Lisa could not process what was happening. Twenty-four hours ago, they were riding high. And now? Clearing the glasses from the living room, she deposited them in the dishwasher, then aimed for the bedroom in search of a state of unconsciousness.

***

The blaring TV and arguing kids woke Lisa. Head throbbing, she realized Michael was absent. Staggering to the bathroom, she swallowed two aspirins with a large glass of water. Back in bed, she tried putting a pillow over her ears, but further slumber eluded her.

"Andrew!" Lisa yelled as her cell phone rang. "Can you answer that?" The buzzing quit, and a few minutes later, Andrew popped in.

"Mom, it's Granny S."

"I'll take it." Lisa sat up. Andrew handed her the phone and disappeared, banging the door shut.

"Hi, Mom. What's up?"

"I got the most unusual call this morning. It was from a lawyer in La Grange, Texas. He said he was looking for you."

Lisa's mind fired on all cylinders. She hoped it was not someone suing her former employer and coming after her. "What did he want?"

"He said he was handling Uncle Joe's estate and wanted to talk to you. Joe put you in his will."

"Really?... I'm ready." Lisa scribbled down the number and spent a few more minutes chatting, carefully avoiding a discussion of Harris Cardiac Implants. Her mom spent most of her days socializing and playing golf, seldom in touch with business news. Her husband, Mel, had sunk all his money into bonds and CDs and did not routinely monitor the stock market.

Lisa took a shower and dressed. Then she faced the kids. Jessica was watching TV with Princess curled in her lap. Andrew had his earphones on, listening to music.

He jerked off his headset and said, "I'm hungry and there's nothing I want to eat around here. What a dump. How long are we going to stay here, anyway?"

Before Lisa could respond, Jessica asked if they could eat at Jack in the Box. "OK, but I have to make one phone call before we leave."

"Aw, Mom. Can't you make it in the car?" Andrew asked.

"I guess so. Get your coats and let's go." Lisa put on her jacket and secured her cell phone.

Once on the road, Lisa assigned Jessica to watch for Jack and had Andrew dial the number she had written.

"Mr. Bohac, this is Lisa Dunwhitty. You spoke earlier with my mother, Suzanne Perkins. She said you wanted to speak to me."

"Mrs. Dunwhitty. I'm so glad you called. I'm the attorney for Joseph Franks. He left you the bulk of his estate, and we need to discuss the matter as soon as possible. Your mother said you're in Houston now, is that right?"

By this time Lisa had pulled into a store parking lot, so she could devote her full attention to the call. The kids complained; Lisa motioned for them to be quiet. "You mean he's left me his ranch?... I don't understand. Why would he do that?"

Mr. Bohac laughed. "You made quite an impression on him. He told me you had visited him when you were a little girl and loved his ranch, said you wanted one like it when you grew up. He told me he thought you were the only one who would take good care of it.

"We need to discuss the conditions of the will. Since you're so close, I thought I would drive out tomorrow and speak with you. Would eleven work?"

"Sure. No problem. I'll have to call you back later and give you directions to where we're staying. We just got here, and I don't have any idea where we are." Lisa ended the call and pulled back onto the road.

When they had settled in with their food, she shared the situation, explaining that she would not have a job and that their dad might not either. "But we're going to be fine. Seems my great uncle has left us this big, beautiful ranch."

"Well, I'm not living there." Andrew crinkled his nose. "Not out in the boonies. Yuck. Let's sell it and move back to Raleigh."

"I want to live there," Jessica said. "Don't sell it. Are there cowboys and horses?"

Lisa smiled. Vivid memories came flooding back. After Lisa's father died, she and her mother spent a month with the Franks. The experience delivered the respite Lisa needed to set in motion the healing process. During her tween years, she would occasionally spend a week in their loving cocoon. As she grew older, the visits dwindled. It had been over twenty years since she had seen the place.

"No cowboys, sweetie, but the ranch is so lovely. There're cattle and large, lovely oak trees. I remember sitting on the porch in the shade. Oh, it was so hot that day. Aunt Ruby made a big pitcher of lemonade. And later that evening Uncle Joe took me fishing at the big pond. I remember the grasshoppers were everywhere and scared me, but he laughed and showed me how to catch them."

"How stupid," Andrew said. He had finished his breakfast and was gathering his trash. "What's so hard about catching a grasshopper?"

"OK, Mr. Smart Aleck. I'd like to see you catch one. It's not so easy." His teenage mouth annoyed Lisa. Andrew ignored her, wandering to the trash bin, then to the car. He leaned against it, listening to music on his iPhone.

"Momma, can I have some more hash brown sticks?"

"No, you've had enough. They're too fattening. Anyway, we need to get back, so we can do some laundry and take Princess for a walk."

"Sure, Momma. Would you go with me? Andrew is so mean when he goes."

"Yes, dear."

On the way, she called Michael to tell him about the inheritance, but he did not answer.

All afternoon Lisa daydreamed about the ranch and its promise of a breather from their perilous situation. She recalled the big red barn and the tack room storing the saddles. The smell of leather had always comforted her, the rich aroma of new cars and beautiful jackets! Then there was the pond. How gorgeous! She could picture Andrew bringing in a mess of fish to fry like her uncle had. How wonderful! And the oil well pumping near the road. How rich would they be?

Lisa called her friend, Olivia, to fill her in on the latest about Dr. Cal and the inheritance.

"Are you sure you want to live in the middle of nowhere?" Olivia asked. "I'd be terrified."

"I spent summers in the woods at Girl Scout camp and loved it."

"If you say so…. Well, before you know it, you'll be hanging out with Rick and Anita Perry." Olivia laughed. "Hey, are you going to fly me down on your big jet?"

"Very funny. But I will come pick you up at the airport in my Land Rover."

"Land Rover? I didn't know you had one."

"I don't, but I'll have to get one because my Volvo isn't built for the country."

***

Lisa barely noticed the haggard look on Michael's face when he arrived at the apartment later that evening. She tried to tell him about the call from the attorney as he was changing clothes.

"Michael, you're not listening. Aren't you excited? This could be the break we're looking for." Lisa was becoming impatient with him.

"Sorry." He slipped on a sweat suit. "It's all over."

"What do you mean?"

"Just that. It's over. I don't have a job." Michael turned and gazed into her eyes. "Worst part is I'm not getting any severance, not even a penny more than they owe me through today. The bonus is gone, too. I doubt we'll ever see the money from the house."

Lisa watched Michael carefully. Soon tears welled in his eyes.

"I'm sorry," he said. "I've screwed us." As he tried to stuff his tears, Lisa walked over and grasped him, taking in his aroma of cologne mingled with sweat.

"You know, sometimes things work out for the best. Who knows? We may even make more money by being ranchers and oil barons."

"I don't know, Lisa. It doesn't sound all that great to me."

"Well, the attorney will be here at eleven tomorrow to explain the will." She gave Michael a peck on the cheek. "Everything will be alright; I just know it."

***

That evening, after Michael had drunk himself to sleep and the children had turned in, Lisa bundled up and took Princess for a short walk. Stopping by the swimming pool, she settled into a lounge chair, talking quietly to the dog.

"You know what, Princess? I can't handle any more pressure right now. I'm tired of being strong and taking charge.... Some quiet time at the ranch will help us all regroup and figure out what we're going to do."

Princess crawled up Lisa's chest and licked her face, tail wagging. Lisa laughed. "I guess that means you approve. It'll be a lot better for you than an apartment." Lisa stood and gathered Princess in her arms, then turned back.

She climbed into bed and had wonderful dreams about parties in the country with her friends. For once, she slept better than she had in weeks.

***

By ten-thirty the next morning, Lisa had straightened the apartment, put on coffee for Mr. Bohac, and dressed in her favorite Ann Taylor slack and sweater outfit. She sat on the couch, trying to concentrate on the newspaper. Finally, a knock on the door.

Lisa opened it to find a tall, thin man who appeared ill at ease. He was holding a large briefcase. "Mrs. Dunwhitty?"

"Yes, I'm Ms. Dunwhitty. Please call me Lisa. You must be Mr. Bohac." Lisa smiled brightly.

The man grinned. "I'm glad I found the place, I wasn't sure. And, please, call me Herb."

"Come in, Herb, have a seat.... Would you like some coffee?"

"No, I'm fine."

The group settled in. The children, for a change, were paying rapt attention.

"As I explained on the phone, I'm Joe's attorney. I've known him for fifteen years. He was a wonderful man."

Lisa could feel her heart pounding and excitement mounting.

"Joe's put a number of restrictions on the will, however, that I wanted to discuss." Herb looked from Lisa to Michael. "The parcel is quite large, 4,263 acres, to be exact."

"That's a strange size," Michael said. His interest appeared to pique.

"Joe's family was one of the original settlers in Texas and got a land grant from Stephen F. Austin. The land is exactly a league."

"Wow, how cool!" Andrew said.

"At any rate, Joe specified that the land be kept intact and occupied by family. If it's not, the land's to be donated to the Lutheran church and used as a retreat and camp."

"What exactly does that mean for us?" Michael asked.

"Well, it means that you can't sell the property or any portion of it. If you have no interest in living on it or abandon its maintenance or upkeep, it goes to the church."

Silence hung heavily in the air.

Herb cleared his throat and began, "There's one other problem."

"What's that?" Lisa asked.

"As you know, Ruby died sometime back, and Joe's been ill for the last four years. It took all his savings and then some to pay the bills."

"I don't understand," Lisa said.

"Ruby had dementia and was in the nursing home for a good ten years. It drained all their savings."

"Why didn't they just sell off some land?" Lisa asked.

"Joe was adamant he wouldn't do that. The land's been in the family since the early 1800s. He wasn't willing to let a single acre go."

"What's your point?" Michael was becoming irritable.

"Well, there's quite a bit of back tax due to Fayette County. The land's getting close to foreclosure as we speak. The property's going on the auction block the first week of February."

"What do we need to do to keep that from happening?" Lisa asked.

"Well, you'll have to pay all the back taxes." Herb seemed uneasy.

"What are they?" Lisa asked, dreading the answer.

"Uh, $51,120, I'm afraid." Herb winced as if embarrassed to give them the figure. "It could have been worse. We had to sell all Joe's cattle to pay the nursing home bills. Some of his friends ran cattle on a portion of the land, so he could keep his ag exemption. The rest has been under a timber contract, but that expires at the end of this month."

"What's an 'ag' exemption?" Andrew asked.

"Oh, sorry, it's technically called an agricultural special valuation. Your taxes are quite a bit lower if you use the land for agricultural purposes, either crops or raising livestock."

Michael rose. "Mr. Bohac, thank you for coming. Personally, I can't see taking possession of the property if we have to make that sort of investment and live on it. However, Lisa and I will confirm that with you next week after my attorney's had a chance to look over the will. I want to see if there's any way we can get out of having to live on it."

Michael walked to the door, signaling the discussion was over. Surprised by the move, Herb stood and followed. "You'll let me know soon, then?" Herb asked. He handed his card to Michael.

"Yes, we will. Thank you for coming," Michael said. He then closed the door behind the scarecrow.

Before Michael could utter a word, Lisa jumped up, trying to control her anger.

"Andrew, Jessica, take Princess for a walk. Your dad and I need to talk." When they didn't move, she barked, "NOW!" The two rounded up the dog and piled out of the apartment.

"How dare you! You don't make decisions for me. This is my family land, my decision. Don't ever do that again!"

"You can't be serious. There's no way I'm living on a goddamned Podunk farm out in the middle of nowhere." Annoyed, Michael plopped down on the couch.

"Fine. You stay here. The kids and I are going. Where are you going to stay, anyway? We don't have a house. Or did you not notice? We couldn't even stay in this apartment if we wanted to because you...YOU are so money-grubbing and money hungry that you gave up a great, secure job. For what? We're ruined, Michael. RUINED! At least now we have somewhere to stay, somewhere to raise the kids, somewhere—"

"My God! You were all for the money, too. You act as if you and this uncle were like this!" Michael held up two intertwined fingers as he glared at Lisa, his voice becoming increasingly loud. "But you haven't seen him in years. Family land. Give me a break." Michael shot daggers at her, throwing up his hands. "You're crazy! You can go by yourself! The kids and I'll stay here." Michael left the apartment, forcefully shutting the door.

A feeling of helplessness overwhelmed her—the emotional lifeline of the inheritance crudely jerked from her grasp. Angry tears streaked down her cheeks. *Everything we've worked for has gone up in smoke. No jobs. The recession has wiped out our savings. Now what?*

Eventually, Andrew stuck his head in and let Princess back into the apartment. "Dad's taking us to a movie. Want to go?"

Lisa busied herself so Andrew could not see she had been crying. "No, hon, thanks for asking. I have a few things to do." After he left, she called her mother.

"Mom, Uncle Joe left me his ranch. Do you have any idea why?"

"Oh, my. That sounds like a lot of work."

"Yeah, but why would he leave it to me?"

"I'm not sure. Your father was one of his favorites."

"Hmm. I guess he wouldn't have wanted to leave it to Aunt Lena's kids. Is Bill out of prison yet?"

"I don't think so."

"If you remember anything else, let me know."

"Are you going to sell it?"

"That's the rub. I can't. I either have to live there or it goes to the church."

"So, are you going to let the church have it?"

"I don't know. I'll let you know." Lisa did not want to get into the job scenario. All Mom would do was worry.

Lying on the couch, Lisa weighed her options. Yes, she could continue her pity party—or toughen up and do something about it. Escaping to the ranch seemed like the practical thing to do. They could live there cheaply while looking for work; then she would not feel so pressured. At the rate they spent money, they might be penniless if they had to rent a place during the job search. Then, if they gave up the ranch, so be it.

Lisa formulated a plan to broach the subject with Michael, but the more she contemplated his dismissal of the attorney, the angrier she became. *This is my decision, not his. But the back taxes...*

In the bedroom, Lisa opened the briefcase with all their important papers. She leafed through, eventually finding the latest balance of her 401Ks. She had lost $70,000 in the last year. *Hmm.* There would be a hell of a penalty, but it would be worth it. She could ask for a loan, but who would loan money to two unemployed people with mounds of credit card debt?

A knock at the door made her jump. After stuffing the papers back into the attaché case and hiding it under the bed, she went to the door and cautiously asked, "Who is it?" Lisa stared through the peephole.

"It's Marilyn, the apartment manager."

Opening the door, Lisa let the woman in. The pleasantly plump lady seemed uncomfortable. "Uh, gee, I'm so sorry, Ms. Dunwhitty, but I need to let you know that the apartment owner has terminated the Harris Cardiac lease. I'm really sorry. You can stay here, but you'll need to put down a deposit and sign a new lease. The rent's paid until the end of December, so let me know as soon as you can. If you don't plan to stay, I'll need to rent it out to someone else."

"I understand. We'll let you know as soon as possible." Lisa turned away quickly so the woman couldn't see the pained expression on her face.

As Marilyn left, she looked over her shoulder. "I'm real sorry."

Lisa returned to her paperwork. *Well, at least Marilyn helped me make up my mind.* She would take the money out of one of her accounts and pay off the back taxes. *Why not? I've got sixty days to put it back.* After being on the telephone for what seemed an eternity, the final paperwork to remove half the money from the account was complete.

***

Lisa arrived at the apartment as darkness was falling.

"Where the hell have you been, and why didn't you answer your cell phone?" Michael said. "You've had us all worried."

"It's done." Lisa ignored Michael.

"Done? What do you mean, done?"

"I've raised the tax money and had the bank wire it to the county. The property is now free and clear." Lisa did not stop talking for fear Michael would launch in on her. "We have a place to stay."

Jessica jumped up and down, clutching the dog. "Yahoo, Princess, we're going to live on a ranch! We can play with the baby cows and have chickens and see their eggs hatch and—"

"Mother, how could you?" Andrew said. "I'm not going to live in the middle of nowhere around all those shitkickers."

"Andrew, shut your mouth. That's not polite." Lisa took her eyes off Andrew and dared a peek at Michael. His face was stone, no emotion showing. Without a word, he disappeared into the bedroom, shoving the door tight. Sullenly Andrew sat down at the computer and surfed the Internet.

Lisa steeled herself. She had been on such an emotional roller coaster. Owning the property free and clear, liberated her. As much as she liked to think of herself as a woman of the world, it was the first time she had ever made an important decision like that without Michael's advice and consent. Now, fear enveloped her. What if Michael decided not to go?

"Jessica, get your bath. We've got a big day tomorrow. We've got lots to do before we head to our new home." Lisa busied herself with supper.

After a tense meal, the children went to bed. Michael and Lisa sat on opposite ends of the couch. Finally, Michael broke the silence. "Lisa, you had no right, no right to spend that much of our money without talking with me first. I can't believe you did that."

"It was my money, not your money. My money, Michael. I didn't touch a single penny of your money. It was my 401K. I didn't know I needed your approval to do anything with my own money."

Michael started to respond but stopped. The hush was chilling.

"Honey," Lisa reached out and took his hand. "Please, let's not fight over this. Honestly, I felt backed up against the wall. The apartment manager said we either had to sign a lease or leave. Besides, we couldn't buy a nice place to live around here for $50,000. You know that. It'll buy us some time to find jobs. I also pulled out enough to tide us over for a month or two till we can get on our feet."

Michael jerked his hand out from hers. "You don't get it, do you? You decided. Not about the money, but about where we're going to live. And I wasn't even consulted."

Lisa looked intently at Michael. "Do you realize that every time you interview for a job and get an offer you want to accept, I've moved? When did you ever consult me about where we were going to live?"

"Not fair. Not fair. I always ask you before I say 'yes' to the job. You know that."

"Fair enough. But living there temporarily makes sense. We've nowhere else to go."

"OK, point made." He pulled Lisa to him and kissed her. "You're right... I'll see if I can get the old house back, but that's not a given."

Lisa cuddled against him, the warm spicy aroma of his cologne sending shivers through her. "Things will work out, you'll see." Soon she arose, grasped his hand, and said, "Come on."

Michael followed Lisa, who closed the door quietly behind them. He took her into his arms and nuzzled her neck. Her excitement mounted. Looking up, his gaze cocooned her. It was as if he saw into the very depths of her soul, there was nothing to hide from him. He knew her, accepted her, and loved her unconditionally.

Lisa reached up and leisurely caressed his cheeks, pulling his face down to hers. Unhurriedly they began exploring the depths of their mouths. Michael put his arms around Lisa's waist as he continued probing.

Eventually, Michael released her, pulling back slowly. "I'll start the shower."

After luxuriating in the warm water, Michael focused on the bar of soap. Lathering up mounds of citrusy suds, he methodically washed her back and then massaged her shoulders. He worked his way down, applying light pressure to her taut muscles. Unable to stand the tension any longer, Lisa moved his hands to her breasts. As he gently kneaded her nipples, she felt waves of ecstasy overwhelm her.

"You know, babe," he breathed heavily into her ear, "I always said I'd take care of you. I intend to." He rotated her gently and gathered her in his arms. Lisa felt his hardness against her stomach and the gentle undulation of water on her back. The steam rose; her body shuddered.

CHAPTER 3

New Year's Eve, 2008

Driving through pouring rain had Lisa on edge. She clutched the directions in her right hand and steered with her left, slowing to peer at the street signs. "Andrew, is that Dog Run Road?"

"What?"

"Take those things off. Now. I need help."

Andrew removed the headset and produced a big sigh. By this time, Lisa had slowed, pulling off on the shoulder. A small sign identified an unpaved path heading east. "Dog Run Road." Lisa looked at her GPS and back at the marker for one last confirmation.

"Mom, you mean we're going to live on a dirt road? That sucks." Andrew pouted as Lisa maneuvered the Volvo on the muddy, rutted thoroughfare.

"Can it. I'm not in the mood." She glanced at Michael's Porsche in her rearview mirror and winced. Imagining the expression on Michael's face made her thankful she was not in his vehicle with Jessica and the dog. No doubt he would come unglued when gravel knocked a hunk of paint off that precious shrine to his manhood.

Lisa's mood darkened as she crept along the twisting, potholed, reddish-tinged path lined with a mixture of dense oak and cedar trees. An occasional barbed-wire cow pasture interrupted the gently rolling terrain. Twelve miles of this! They'd never get there. It was more off the beaten path than she remembered.

They passed a run-down farmhouse, the first sign of life since leaving the highway. Much of the white paint had peeled off the clapboard siding long ago, exposing weathered wood. The tin roof had rusted in spots. Beside the dilapidated barn were four Oldsmobiles in various states of disintegration. The owner had driven them until they died and parked them neatly in a row. Near the barn were three ancient, rusted tractors arranged in a circle around a tree, their steel wheels bogged in goop. At least the barn was standing. Another outbuilding had literally imploded. A few skinny cows and a donkey or two meandered through the wreckage, nibbling at the sparse grass among the spiny plants that littered the area. A few large, leafless trees complimented the barren, desolate landscape.

Horror crept through Lisa. *What have I gotten us into? These are our neighbors? This is more remote than I remember.* Andrew began to speak, but Lisa cut him off. "I don't want to hear it. You keep an eye out for the ranch."

Despair deepened as they inched forward. An unmaintained fence bordered this section of Dog Run Road. Trees and brush pushed up around the cedar poles strung with barbed wire, causing the fence to lean crazily. Numerous strands were gone altogether or drooped so low as to be useless.

In the thirty minutes they had painfully made their way along the twists and turns, not another car had passed. The rain, mercifully, eased to a light mist, improving her vision.

"Andrew, my mileage counter says we've been eleven and a half miles. We should be there." She slowed, looking for a turn-off to the right.

There it was! The old *JF Ranch* sign had seen better days. Barely readable, it swung in the wind. Just past the sign, Lisa spied an oil well. Its gigantic torso, flecked with rust, stood idly as if frozen in time. Further down, weeds clogged the sides of the gravel driveway that led to the gate.

Across the street from the entrance was an old, but well-maintained house with pink vinyl siding and tin roof. Several small buildings and sheds dotted the complex; goats and chickens roamed the yard. At first, Lisa thought it was vacant but then noticed smoke rising from the chimney.

"We're here." Lisa's attempts at being cheerful were becoming increasingly difficult.

"Oh, boy, Dad's going to love this."

"Open the gate. After your father drives in, close and lock it. Here, take my umbrella so you won't get wet." Lisa reached behind the driver's seat and produced a red collapsible.

Andrew ignored the offer and climbed out. After a few minutes of struggling with the latch, he removed the chain and swung open the gate. Lisa eased over the rickety cattle guard, Michael and Jessica behind her. With Andrew back in the car, she edged toward the house.

Dog Run Road had been a challenge, but it was passable. The driveway was another issue. House in sight, Lisa pulled forward steadily, attempting to avoid a yawning mud hole between her and the house. As she moved off the beaten path, her tires spun, throwing gook on the windows. She became quickly mired in muck.

Seconds passed. Andrew said nothing. Michael pounded on the window. Tears streamed down Lisa's cheeks.

"Happy New Year!" Michael snarled. Lisa lowered the window. "I'm sorry," he said. "We'll just call a tow truck. No harm done."

As he spoke, the sky opened, and rain poured through the window. Lisa hurriedly rolled it up as Michael sprinted back to his car.

After the downpour subsided, Lisa and Andrew climbed out and sloshed through the mess to a patch of grass. Michael climbed out of the Porsche and pulled out his cell phone. "God damn it!"

"What's wrong now?" Lisa asked. By this time, tears were again welling in her eyes. The dull winter sky bursting with musky humidity matched her mood. All she could hear was the rain dripping from nearby branches to the sodden mounds of leaves below. *This isn't the safe, warm place I remember.* She shivered.

A screeching howl pierced the country silence sending a frightened look across Andrew's face. "That sounds like a wolf, just like in the movies. Are there wolves out here?" He moved closer to Michael.

Michael's look of frustration crumbled as he licked his lips. "I think we all better go inside. It's going to be dark soon and the cell phones don't work out here. It'll be tomorrow before we can have someone pull the car out. Andrew, bring the suitcases up to the house."

"I'm not walking up there by myself."

"We'll all walk together." Michael looked around warily.

Lisa heard barking and turned to see Princess loping toward Michael. She jumped and left a muddy streak down the leg of his new Tommy Hilfiger jeans. Jessica, hanging out the door of the Porsche, wailed. "Daddy, I'm scared. I wanna go home!"

Michael waded over to the car and lifted her out, snuggling her. "It's OK, sweetie. We're going to have fun. It'll be like a camping trip. Momma's car got stuck in the mud, that's all." He turned around and shot Lisa a dirty look, then retrieved a towel from his gym bag to wipe off his pants.

The bedraggled party unloaded what they could, locked the doors, and struggled to the house.

A large porch about six feet deep ran the length of the early twentieth-century farmhouse. A few of the boards appeared worn, but otherwise, the footing was sound. Two old rocking chairs, badly in need of scrubbing, sat by the door. Leaves exuding an earthy smell had pooled in the porch's corner, held in place by the banister.

Lisa fished around under the welcome mat, finally producing the key. "Seems like we should have some kind of ceremony or something. Just think, we're Texas ranchers." She ventured a brave smile. A look at the gloomy faces forced her to back off. "Jessica, hold on to Princess. I don't want her to get the house muddy."

"Here," Michael said. "Let me have her." He scooped up the squirming dog, wrapping her with the towel, and tucking her under his arm.

Lisa unlocked the door, gradually pushing it open. A damp, stuffy chill assaulted them.

Mom!" Andrew said, "We can't live here. It smells gross."

Lisa stared. "Enough." Numb, she looked around, thankful she had at least thought to ask Herb to have the utilities reconnected. He had also hired someone to clean and put fresh sheets on the beds as well as leave enough provisions to last for a couple of days.

***

Michael flipped on the light as the family piled into a small entry room that ran nearly the width of the house. An austere wooden bench sitting atop old, distressed linoleum greeted them. Piling their luggage on the bleacher, they explored their new digs.

To the right was a bathroom, and to the left the kitchen; straight ahead appeared to be the living room. Michael entered. Ten-foot ceilings and white paneling made it more inviting than the entry. An old La-Z-Boy rocker with weary green Naugahyde sat facing an ancient console television. A couch of similar color ran against the wall, directly across from the fireplace; an oval braided rug warmed the scarred wood floor.

A door at the far end of the living room led to the largest of the bedrooms. That bedroom, in turn, had a door that opened to the back porch. The space was Spartan, with an armoire and a chest of drawers. On top was a picture of what must have been Joe and Ruby in front of a big cake—no doubt an anniversary, probably fifty years. Stuck in the frame was a photo of Lisa atop a pony her mother was holding. Behind Lisa, Michael recognized the farmhouse.

He walked back into the living room and took a right turn into the second bedroom. Reaching a third sleeping area required passing through the second bedroom or an exterior exit. As they toured the house, Michael shook his head. All his life he had worked hard to provide for his family, and now, they were in a rathole even more desolate than the one in which he grew up.

The kitchen, accessed from both the second bedroom and the entry room was the last stop. It contained an electric stove, a big sink with washboards on the side, and a small pantry. Although it had plenty of cabinet space, it was minuscule compared to their Raleigh kitchen.

Jessica picked up a scrapbook sitting on the small dining table. "Look, it's an old photo album. Look at this picture. Doesn't the house look nice?"

Peering over her shoulder, Michael eyed the white structure with black trim. Potted plants covered the porch, giving it a welcoming feel.

"Jessica, we can look at these later. Let's get Princess cleaned up. Here, hold her while I take my jacket off."

Jessica got a firm grip, but Princess struggled and popped out of her arms, streaking through the living room, leaving filthy paw prints on the frayed rug. Screaming and yelling, they chased the red imp into a corner of the bedroom where they managed to grab her collar.

Michael grimaced. "I'll get her. You start the bath water."

"I'm sorry, Daddy. Princess, you're a bad girl!" Jessica scurried to prepare the bath.

"DAAAD!" Andrew yelled. "There's no Internet and the TV only gets two stations! What are we going to do?"

"Andrew, I've had enough of your mouth. Put your suitcase in the very back bedroom and your sister's in the other. Your mom and I will take the big bedroom."

Not willing to risk losing Princess again, Michael shut the door to the bathroom before letting go of the perky puppy. Opening a cabinet, he found a stack of well-used bath towels that exuded a funky odor. *At least they're good enough for the dog.* He quickly sniffed the flimsy ones dangling on the towel rack. Thank God they weren't rancid.

"Daddy, the water's not getting hot. I don't know what's the matter."

"I do," Lisa said from behind the bathroom door. "Herb left a note. He couldn't get the hot water heater running."

Michael started to explode, but hesitated, realizing Jessica was again close to tears. "Don't worry, honey. We'll clean her off with a washrag. She'll be fine until tomorrow."

As Lisa's footsteps receded, he knelt and held Princess so Jessica could wipe her paws. She then picked off a bit of mud clumped stubbornly in her friend's long-haired tail. Princess began to squeal and lick Jessica's face, chasing away her frown. Michael's heart warmed.

"Sweetie, that'll do. Princess really looks like a princess, don't you think? You do, too, for that matter." Michael put the animal down and grabbed Jessica, giving her a peck on the cheek.

"Oh, Daddy, you're so silly!" Jessica playfully took a swipe at him. They both laughed, and Michael rose to open the door. As he did, Princess raced out to explore her new world.

Michael tramped into the living room as Andrew and Lisa were struggling with armloads of firewood. He observed Lisa stacking the split oak next to the fireplace, her face dour. She arose, picking scraps of bark off her new BCBG sweater. "Herb couldn't get the guys out to fill the propane tank, so he made sure we had plenty of firewood. They should be here on the second, though."

"If they can get past a car up to its floorboards in mud," Michael said. Observing the anguish on Lisa's face, he quickly changed the subject. "Andrew, let's see how much you learned in Boy Scouts." Michael crouched beside his son, who was working feverishly to start a fire. In no time the toasty flames were dancing brightly. "Good job." He gave him a pat on the back.

Michael eased himself into the ragged Naugahyde chair. Jessica had curled up on the couch with Princess and was thumbing through the photo album while Andrew had retired to his room to unpack. Michael sipped a scotch and water while gazing at the fire.

All his life he had worked hard to come up in the world, and now…. A primal urge to lash out overtook him. *How did I let Lisa talk me into this? We can't live out here, a million miles from nowhere. What would I do? Rope cows? Plant corn? Wear a cowboy hat and drive a tractor?* Twitching, he envisioned himself in overalls, picking his teeth with a piece of straw and jawing over the fence with the neighbors. *This isn't going to work. I don't care how much money Lisa sunk into this hellhole; we're not staying.*

"Dinner's ready!" Lisa said.

Michael swallowed the rest of his drink and entered the kitchen. The aroma of steamy bowls of chicken noodle soup Lisa was ladling out brought back buried memories of the hearty meals his mother served on snowy days. Stomach growling, he collapsed into a rickety chair at the pockmarked table.

One taste and a smile spread on his face. "This is good!"

Lisa laughed. "Sure is. Herb's wife made it. She thought we might arrive too late to cook, so she left it in the fridge."

The four laughed and chatted for the first time in months. They gathered later around the fire and tried to watch the old television, but the reception was fuzzy. Andrew began poking through the drawers and found a deck of cards. Michael suggested a game of blackjack, using a jar of old buttons Lisa had spotted on a closet shelf.

As they collected around the kitchen table, Jessica, with coaching from Michael, agreed to be the dealer.

Jessica dealt the cards and the game turned serious. Soon Lisa's tokens were gone. She poured herself a glass of wine and returned to the table to observe the competition. Michael's pile of chips grew. Occasionally, he would give Andrew pointers to improve his game.

Eventually, Andrew pushed the rest of his stash into the kitty.

Michael studied his cards, then flipped over an ace hidden under the jack. With both hands, he swept the last of Andrew's buttons into his massive pile.

"You lose, Andrew!" Jessica said as she gathered the cards.

Slamming his fist on the table, the surly teen stalked off.

"Gee, that was fun," Lisa said. "Jessica, get ready for bed, I'll be there in a minute."

Lisa washed her glass, ignoring Michael.

"What's wrong now?"

Lisa turned and stared at him. "Why are you so competitive? Everything you do with him is like a contest. Can't we just have fun?"

"Did you want me to let him win? He's sixteen. He needs to learn how to lose gracefully."

"You're right…. Maybe you should talk to him about it."

After pouring himself a drink, Michael settled in the recliner, frowning. What a New Year's Eve. Despite everything, he had been enjoying himself until Andrew blew up and stalked off. *I have a hard time losing, too. I guess it's in the Dunwhitty blood. I need to talk with—*

BAM. "Shit!"

Michael jumped at the sounds of Andrew's scream and Princess's yelps, tearing through Jessica's bedroom, flipping on lights as he ran. Michael flung open Andrew's door only to find him lying on the catawampus bed. The frame had collapsed on the far corner near his head.

Relieved, Michael laughed.

"What's so funny?"

"I knew the furniture was old, but didn't know how old," Michael said.

By this time, Lisa, Jessica, and the dog were in the room, staring at Andrew, who was crawling out from under the covers.

"Are you hurt?" Lisa asked.

"No." He stood in his briefs but quickly scrambled into jogging pants.

"So, now what? Where am I going to sleep?" Andrew asked.

"Lisa, get me a flashlight," Michael said.

Lisa eventually returned empty-handed. Sighing, Michael made his way to the far side of the room where Andrew was standing, squeezed by him, and knelt. Lifting the sheets, he peered under the bed.

"Looks like the bed frame broke. No big deal. It shouldn't be hard to fix," Michael said.

"Are you going to fix it now?" Lisa asked.

"No. We'll probably need some nails or something. It's made out of wood."

"I'm not going to sleep on it like that." Andrew crossed his arms on his bare chest and scowled.

"You can sleep with me," Jessica said.

"Absolutely not. No way in hell—"

"I don't want to hear that language," Lisa said.

Andrew sulked and stared.

"Let's just put the mattress on the floor. Andrew, you get that end." Michael grabbed the sunken corner.

"Duh, Dad, there's not enough room for both the mattress and the bed frame on the floor."

"Sure, there is. Come on. I'm tired. Just move it."

Andrew pulled while Michael pushed. It migrated off the box springs but could not quite clear the frame.

"I told you so."

Michael ignored Andrew and pushed one end of the mattress under the bed, leaving about seventy-five percent of it sticking out. "There."

"I can't sleep like this."

"Just try it."

Andrew plopped down and slid his feet under the frame. They barely fit. He tried to turn over, but his legs knocked the underside. "See, I told you it wouldn't work."

"Well, I guess you can sleep outside."

"That's not funny," Lisa said.

"So, here's your choice. You can either sleep in here on part of the mattress or sleep on the couch in the living room."

Glaring, Andrew said, "I'll sleep here."

"Good night, then."

The three of them backed out of the bedroom, leaving Andrew muttering under his breath as he tried to get comfortable.

"Jessica, honey, go back to bed." Lisa tucked in the dog and daughter, kissing her youngest on the forehead.

The two returned to the living room where they sat in silence. After draining his glass, Michael rose and put more wood on the blaze. "That ought to keep us warm till morning. I'm going to bed." He leaned over, kissing her goodnight.

"I'll be in soon."

***

Seeking a distraction from the relentless self-recrimination reverberating in her head, Lisa grabbed the picture album on the floor next to the couch. Fascinated, she leafed through the panorama of Joe and Ruby's life. One picture dating to the nineteen sixties highlighted a young African American couple with small children. *Strange. I wonder what else I don't know about Joe and Ruby.* With each flip of the page, she watched the couple age; the depth of feeling between them growing steadily with time. The African American man appeared in several of the later pictures. Thinking back, Lisa remembered a Black man occasionally helping Joe with the chores. *Hmm. Is this the same person?* Closing the memories, she sat back, staring at the fire. An energy of well-being surged through her that she wanted to embrace forever.

CHAPTER 4

Windows rattling from gusts of wind caused Lisa to stir—the night's comforting aura replaced by the reality of their situation. She knew Michael had left early because the sagging mattress had forced them together. At least she had managed a few hours of sound sleep since he departed.

Rising with Michael was not an option. She did not want to hear the "I told you so's" he would inevitably sling at her. *What a fool I've been! Cashed in my 401K—and for what? To live in a dilapidated house out in the middle of nowhere?*

Listlessly she rose to face the consequences. Pulling on her robe and locating her slippers, she padded to the bathroom and then into the kitchen. The stillness indicated she was alone. Fortified with an uninspiring cup of Maxwell House, she stepped out onto the front porch. A strong northerly blast accosted her, sending chills through her body, and scattering dead leaves through the grass.

Near her car, Lisa spotted Michael and Andrew talking to a tall, slim man whose cottony white hair contrasted with his ebony skin. *The man in the pictures!* He calmly smoked a pipe as he inspected the Volvo. Dressed in overalls and tall rubber boots, he seemed unperturbed by the brisk air or the muddy driveway.

She rushed inside to dress. While combing her hair and putting on makeup, she steeled herself. *I can't admit to Michael he was right. Not now. I've invested too much in this.*

By the time she arrived, the bumper of the Volvo was hooked to an old-fashioned tractor. Michael was in the car with Andrew standing nearby, dodging the muck spinning off the tires. The elderly man looked over his shoulder as he inched the auto to higher ground. Lisa scowled. She had waved off the salesperson when he had tried to sell her four-wheel drive, thinking she would never need it.

Michael hopped out and unhooked the chain from under the bumper, then drove the vehicle to the main road. Lisa walked to the tractor.

"Hi," she said, "I'm Lisa Dunwhitty." She offered her hand and gazed into the kindest face she had ever seen.

"Hello, Mrs. Dunwhitty, I'm Carl Turner. I live across the street." He waved his hand toward the quaint pink cottage spewing smoke. Lisa pasted on her plastic, corporate grin. How could someone so close to Joe and Ruby live in a place like that?

"Thanks so much for pulling me out, Mr. Turner. I'll have the driveway fixed as soon as possible so it won't happen again."

Carl nodded as he shifted his tractor into gear. "It's no problem, really it isn't. We all help each other out here. If there's anything else I can do, let me know. Here's my telephone number." He pulled out a scrap of paper and handed it to Lisa, seven digits written in pencil. "I'll be on my way. You have a good one." With that, Carl eased his tractor toward his place, waving to both Andrew and Michael. They returned the gesture while continuing to wipe mud off the car windows.

Lisa trudged to the Volvo, watching her men as they worked.

"Looks like I'll have to take it to the car wash tomorrow," Lisa said.

"Duh, Mom, why?" Andrew gave her an irritated stare. "The car will look like this by the time you get home. He turned back to the headlights, which were now down to a thin film of gray.

"Happy New Year." Michael smirked. "I hope you're enjoying yourself. I am." He shook out his towel and turned to Andrew. "Come on, we need to see if we can get the Porsche turned around and out, so it doesn't sink, too." Without looking at Lisa, he stomped back to his car and, turning the ignition, gunned it until the engine whined, interrupting temporarily the whistle of the wind.

Lisa stormed into the house, slamming the door behind her. Raging, she fell across the bed, pounding her fist into the pillow. *What have I done to deserve this? Where will we go? What will we do?* She gazed over at the photo of her on the pony, wondering how she had ever loved this Godforsaken place. Her eyes drifted upwards to the picture of Ruby and Joe. She picked it up, examining it closely. While studying Ruby's face, she felt the woman was trying to tell her something. But what, she had not a clue.

"Mom? Hey, Mom!" Lisa lifted her head as she heard Andrew yelling.

She wiped her nose with the back of her hand and said, "I'm busy, what is it?"

"Hey, have you seen Jessica?" Lisa managed to stand and pretend to be gazing out the window as he stuck his head in the door.

"No. I thought she was outside with you."

"Uh, she was, but I haven't seen her in a while. I'm going to help Dad bring in some more firewood. Mr. Turner says they won't be bringing any propane until at least tomorrow, holiday and all."

"That's fine. I'll be out in a few minutes." Lisa went to the bathroom, washed her face, repaired her makeup, and walked out as Michael struggled up the porch with a load of kindling.

"You find Jessica?" She held open the screen door for him.

"I thought she was with you."

"I'll see if I can find her," Lisa let go of the door. Walking into the yard, she yelled, "Jessica! Princess! Where are you?" After calling several times, she marched around the homestead, out to the cars, and shouted again. Re-entering the house, she searched the bedrooms and peered into the bathroom.

Cleaning excess ash from the fireplace absorbed Michael and Andrew. Not panicked but becoming increasingly concerned, Lisa said, "Michael, I'm not finding her. When did you last see her?"

"She's not anywhere around here? It wasn't that long ago that she was outside playing while we were messing with the Volvo." He stood and wiped his hands on his Tommy Hilfiger pants.

"Hmm. Come on, Andrew, let's go look for your sister," Lisa said.

"Do I have to?"

"Now, Andrew." Lisa menaced, hands on hips. She followed him out. "I'll check the barn if you'll try that other building over there. Michael, why don't you go over and check around the pond?"

Lisa walked to the barn and squeezed through a door that was slightly ajar. The interior exuded the pungent odor of dirt and rust but offered a welcome break from the stiff breeze that had become downright nerve-wracking. Sunlight cut through the slits where the wood slats did not meet, providing enough light for Lisa to check the area. Sporadic clumps of hay littered the tightly packed earthen floor.

"Jessica, are you here?" Only the wind responded. She gazed at the paraphernalia of country living—rusted washtubs, an old two-handled saw, a rake, license plates from the 40s to 60s nailed to one wall. *We'll have a good time exploring this.* Then, she peered into an undersized room to the right. A small saddle—shriveled, dusty, and stiff—sat pommel down, against the wall. *The one in the picture!* A tangle of brittle leather reins hung on a rusty nail while a pile of what must have once been saddle blankets sat in the corner. A vision of Uncle Joe calming the pony, cooing to it as if it were a baby, and preparing to saddle him so she could ride emerged.

"Mom!"

Lisa jumped. "Andrew, you scared me!"

"Uh, sorry, Mom. Mr. Turner's got his horse out. We can't find Jessica anywhere. He's gonna ride down that trail back behind the barn. Dad saw some footprints going back there, but it's awfully muddy. Mr. Turner says he can see better from the top of his horse."

Lisa rushed out of the barn in time to see her neighbor astride his mount.

"There's a creek down there, Zink's Creek, Mrs. Dunwhitty," Mr. Turner said. "She could have gone down there; I don't rightly know.

We'll find her though. Old John, here, knows the area. I'll bring her home shortly. Meantime, why don't you and Mr. Dunwhitty wait in the house?"

Not knowing what else to do, Lisa, tight-lipped, paced. With no telephone connection and a cell phone that did not function, the family could not call for help. Even her Volvo was a useless piece of crap out here. Thank goodness Mr. Turner was nearby. He had bailed them out once already.

After about thirty minutes, the alarmed parents heard Jessica's voice and saw her nestled on Old John's saddle in front of Mr. Turner as he made his way to the house. She had Princess tightly in her arms. "I'm here, Momma and Daddy! The creek is so pretty! And I saw the most beautiful woodpecker. What kind was it, Mr. Turner?"

"A pileated woodpecker." Jessica handed the dog to Michael, who passed it to Andrew. She reached out and clutched Michael's neck securely as he gently pulled her off the horse.

"Old John, you're a good horse," Jessica said. "Mr. Turner, can we ride some more? It's so much fun!"

"Jessica, you scared us to death! You should never wander off like that!" Lisa said.

"Mr. Turner, thanks so very much," Michael said. "Where'd you find her?"

"Oh, she'd wandered a bit down past the creek chasing after that woodpecker. I guess she walked after it as it flew from tree to tree. I'll head on home. Now remember, if you need anything else, let me know. I suppose getting used to the place will take a bit." Mr. Turner shook the reins and clucked. Old John plodded past the Dunwhittys and disappeared out of sight.

"Can we get my bed fixed now?" Andrew asked. He had procured a rusty hammer and an assortment of nails while waiting.

"Sure, we might as well," Michael said.

"Come on, Jessica," Lisa said. "Why don't you play inside for a while? Leave those filthy shoes on the porch." Lisa followed them into the house. The vibes emanating from Michael signaled he was near a volcanic eruption, so she joined the work crew.

Andrew stripped the sheets, and Lisa deposited them in Jessica's bedroom. The area was a wreck. "Jessica, come get this mess cleaned up," Lisa said.

"I'm busy. I'll do it later."

Lisa hoofed it into the living room. "Now."

Jessica threw back her shoulders, exhaling an exasperated sound, but left her dolls on the floor to do as told.

"We need to take the bed springs off," Michael said. "Let's get this mattress out of the way first."

The two struggled to stand it upright and dragged it into Jessica's room. Then they tackled the bed springs. By this time, Michael was breathing heavily.

Lisa monitored Jessica as she cleaned, but soon became distracted by a quarrel that erupted.

"This isn't rocket science. Just hit the head of the nail with the hammer. It's not that hard," Michael said.

"It's not that easy. The nail keeps bending," Andrew said.

"Here, let me do it." Michael jerked the hammer out of Andrew's hand. Andrew moved out of the way.

Michael sat cross-legged, hammer in his right hand, nails in his left. He hesitated.

"OK, hold those two pieces together for me."

Andrew squatted across from Michael and grabbed the two ends of the bed frame as instructed.

Michael took a few practice hits. "I can't get good leverage. I don't have enough room to swing." He reared back and took a swipe at the nail.

"God damn it!" He dropped the hammer and stuck his left thumb in his mouth.

Andrew snickered. "See, it's not that easy."

Before Michael could respond Lisa said, "Are you hurt? Do you need an ice pack?"

"No." He took the hammer again, this time swinging timidly. The nail would not budge. "That old wood's really hard."

"Shouldn't you use a drill and some screws?" Lisa had spent a good amount of time with her stepfather building shelves and other things, becoming proficient with power tools.

"Maybe that would work better. Andrew, see if you can find a drill and screws." Michael continued to nurse his digit while Andrew disappeared. When he did not return in five minutes, Lisa went to check on him.

As she neared the barn, she could see him rifling through the drawers.

"I don't see a drill here," he said.

Lisa glanced at the wall. "There it is." She pointed out a device with a rosewood knob atop a metal shaft hanging on a nail. The shaft curved out, flattened, and then turned back in. At the bottom of the shaft was the mechanism that held a drill bit.

"That's a drill?"

Lisa lifted the rusty tool off the nail. "See? You turn it like this." She grabbed the knob with one hand and the wooden sleeve that wound around the flattened portion, rotating the shaft.

"It doesn't have a drill bit," Andrew said. He looked around the workbench. "Maybe Mr. Turner has a drill—a real one with a motor."

"This is a real drill and 'no' we're not going to ask Mr. Turner for any more help today." Lisa glanced around. "I see a pile of bricks against the wall. Let's just take some of those and we can prop the bed up until we get time to fix it."

"This better work. I'm not spending another night on the floor."

They gathered an armload and made their way to the back bedroom. After some yelling and finagling, Andrew pronounced it fit for sleep.

***

Monday morning Lisa pulled into Zink's Corner, a small grocery three miles past the JF Ranch. Examining it closely, she realized she had been there with Ruby. Recollections of the cherry popsicle she always received when visiting made her smile. Upon exiting the Volvo, a large red merle Australian Shepherd came loping up, throwing himself on his back, and waving his paws in the air. Grinning at his expectant look, she leaned down and gave him a good belly rub. Eventually, she side-stepped the animal and swung open the screen door, tentatively sticking her head inside, meeting that old-building smell head-on.

A slender woman with silver-flecked hair pulled into a ponytail looked up from the counter and said, "Hi, welcome to Zink's Corner. I hope Scotty didn't bother you. I've been working with him. Got him from the shelter. He wants attention, that's all."

Lisa threw a bewildered look at the woman who continued nonstop. Glancing at her Rolex and down to her Ann Taylor slacks, a wave of self-consciousness swept through her.

"I'm Edith Cooper, by the way. My great-great-granddaddy founded Zink's Corner way back in 1830. The family's been here ever since. You must be Lisa Dunwhitty. Herb told me you'd be moving in. He's a great guy, isn't he?"

"He sure is."

"I really miss Joe. He was a regular here.... I hear you met Carl, too," Edith continued. "Good as gold that man is. He'll give you the shirt off his back. Lots of folks around here don't like Black folks, but he's a fine, fine man."

At that moment, the telephone rang, giving Lisa a chance to lose herself in the aisles. Looking around, she marveled. The grocery had not changed since her visits as a child; worn, slick wooden floors and light fixtures barely throwing out enough illumination to read the labels. A tiny selection of fresh vegetables, mostly carrots and potatoes, sat in a box near the bread. The meat counter held some hamburger, pork chops, a chicken or two, and steaks so thinly cut that Lisa, at first, did not realize she was looking at rib eye. She gathered a few things and went to the counter.

Edith disengaged from the telephone and rang up Lisa's order. "Need anything else today?"

"No, this will do, thank you very much.... Have you lived here all your life?"

"Oh, honey, gracious, no. I grew up here but moved out after I graduated from high school. Wanted to go to the big city. I lived in Dallas for about thirty years. Then it got too big and crowded. I decided to come home." Edith put the groceries in a bag and shoved it across the counter.

"So, what did you do in Dallas?" Lisa put the change in her purse and secured the bag.

"Oh, I owned a public relations and marketing firm. The business got too cutthroat. Nothing was fun anymore."

Fortunately, Edith turned her attention to a new customer entering the store, giving Lisa time to mask her surprise. *This lady in jeans and a T-shirt was a CEO? How crazy can you be to leave a sweet setup like that?*

"Hi, Fred. How's Susan doing?" Edith turned back to Lisa and said, "Glad to have you in the neighborhood. Hey, drop by the store tonight about seven. Just knock. A few of the other U.R.s will be here. We'd like to have you join us."

"U.R.s?" Fred asked. "What's that?"

"Urban refugees. It's a get-together of all us ladies who escaped to the country for some peace and quiet. We meet every Monday night."

"I'll try and make it," Lisa said, loneliness enshrouding her. Edith continued to jaw with Fred about who was running for county commissioner and the price of beef, so Lisa scooted out the door, gave Scotty a quick pat on the head, and climbed into the auto. Cranking the motor, she turned the heater on full blast, then tried her cell phone. A signal! She dialed Olivia.

"Oh, how wonderful to hear your voice. How's life on the ranch?"

"Oh, Olivia." Lisa sobbed.

"What's wrong? It can't be that bad, can it?" Lisa was grateful for the concern in her friend's voice. Sniffing, she continued, "Well, let's just say things didn't start off well. Cell phones won't work at the house. There's no hot water, no heat, and Jessica got lost in the woods."

"Oh, and you haven't even been there a week."

"And to top it off, the store only sells Folgers coffee, and the meat counter's truly pitiful.... I thought living here was the right decision, but now I'm not so sure. My brain is telling me to run like hell."

"But what does your heart say?"

Lisa thought a moment, recalling that overwhelming sense of security that penetrated her being New Year's Eve. "It says not so fast."

"Lisa, sugar, you need to trust your instincts. When will you get phone service?"

"I'm hoping sometime this week. I'll give you a call and let you know."

Lisa felt better after their conversation. She always did. The woman was out there but seemed to have practical advice for her.

As Lisa pulled out of the parking lot, her mind drifted. The looming confrontation with Michael filled her with dread. She assumed he would rebuff her plan to live happily ever after at the ranch. And rightly so. Making the house habitable would take extensive work, not to mention property upkeep. Broken fences, overgrown pastures, and rusty equipment—the list was endless. Besides, they knew absolutely nothing about farming or ranching. Everyone was miserable except for Jessica and Princess.

They could go back to the city—but which city? Returning to North Carolina would cost a fortune. Unfortunately, the furniture was already on its way to the ranch. Houston was unappealing, memories of Dr. Cal too fresh in her mind.

School! I'd forgotten all about that. I need to enroll them now. Moving, finding a place to stay, and setting up a house would take time and money. And what if their new jobs were in another city? That would mean another quick pivot, disrupting their lives again. No, staying put until one of them found work was the only realistic option.

Lisa's eye caught a movement off the road to the right. Slamming on the brakes, she stared. A large buck with a full set of horns eyed her warily and then trotted off through the underbrush. Her mind raced, full of wonder. The last time she had seen a deer in the wild had been at Girl Scout camp. What a gorgeous creature! How could anyone shoot them?

Quickly throwing her car into park, she shut off the engine, climbed out, and stood in the middle of the rutted, rocky road, searching. The whitetail was long gone. Deep breaths allowed the fresh, frosty air to fill her lungs. The gentle hum of the breeze in the trees and the call of unseen birds serenaded her, more soothing than the dull roar of city traffic. Unbelievably, she discerned a noise that sounded like "gobble, gobble." Standing motionless, she closed her eyes, concentrating on the sound. Seconds passed; the telltale chatter returned. Dense vegetation blocked Lisa's attempt to wander toward the din. *I swear that's a turkey!*

A tingling surged within her. *I've been so busy feeling sorry for myself, I've blocked out any positives about this place.* She lingered, glowing in the moment's serenity. Fond memories of the slow pace of the out-of-doors lingered. Soul refreshed, she reluctantly continued to the ranch.

Not willing to take another chance as she neared the house, she parked on the road and walked up the driveway. To her amazement, the area resembled a construction site. The telephone company connecting lines; the propane tank filling. Lisa heard an engine droning behind her and jumped out of the way, only to see the satellite television truck lumber past her.

"Wow!" She walked up to Michael. "I can't believe they got here so fast."

"Me neither. I'm not complaining, though. As soon as the Internet is hooked up, I can start my job search. You won't believe it. We're getting DSL."

"DSL? Out here? I'm impressed. Let me put up the groceries." She headed to the house, balancing the bags in her arms. How amazing. You can be out in the middle of nowhere and get the same services you would in the middle of the big city. Now if she could just get her cell phone to work.

Lisa returned to the yard and watched along with Michael. Every few minutes she glanced at Princess and Jessica, determined not to disturb Mr. Turner again.

The telephone man came over with papers to sign. "Mr. Dunwhitty, you're all fixed up. Your information to access the Internet is right down there, and we have a twenty-four-hour help desk if you need anything."

"Thanks. Oh, by the way, we don't get cell service out here. Any suggestions?"

"What service do you have?"

"Sprint."

"That's the problem. AT&T works out here."

"Thanks. I appreciate you being able to come out on such short notice."

"Not a problem, Mr. Dunwhitty," the man said. He headed for his truck.

***

By early afternoon, the amenities were working. Lisa made calls to friends and parents while Andrew and Michael sat at the kitchen table, surfing the Internet. Jessica and Princess were napping on the couch.

Lisa brewed a cup of Maxwell House, wincing after breathing in its anemic smell. *I've got to get some decent coffee tomorrow when I switch cell phone providers.* Walking over to the fireplace, she put on another log, stirring the embers until the flames danced. Even though the heat was on, she did enjoy a good fire.

Settling in the recliner, she popped the chair back, absentmindedly sipping her coffee. That comfortable, contented feeling relaxed her. Soon Jessica stirred and crawled onto Lisa's lap.

"Oh, Momma, I love it here. We won't have to go back to that apartment in Houston, will we?"

"Sugar, I don't know what will happen. Daddy and I have to earn some money. We'll have to wait and see. In the meantime, you need to go to school…. Michael," Lisa raised her voice, "Look on the Internet and see if they have a website for the school district. We're going to have to get the kids in school."

"Oh, Mom." Andrew entered the living room. "You're not going to make me go to school here, are you? I bet they have a one-room cabin and hold class by candlelight."

Michael called out from the kitchen, "Andrew, you have to start school, it's the law. As soon as I find a job, we'll move you to a decent one."

Lisa said nothing, continuing to cuddle Jessica and running her hand through her daughter's hair. Lisa was not so sure she wanted to forget the idea of making a go of the ranch. However, Michael appeared disengaged.

CHAPTER 5

Michael pulled back the curtain and glared at Lisa as she directed the movers to unload their furniture into the barn. Irritated, he dropped the drape and pulled out his suitcase, slamming it on the bed. She could be so goddamn stubborn sometimes. Jesus!

He had desperately tried to talk her into putting their belongings into storage, to no avail. Moving all that expensive furniture into a leaky old barn full of dust, hay, and rodents—what a way to pour thousands of dollars down the drain! By the time they found a decent place to live, it would be water-stained and full of rat shit.

Appointments tomorrow with several Houston headhunters were the only bright spots in an otherwise dismal start to the new year. Confident about landing a job shortly, he planned to remain in the city for the duration of his search. Besides, the farmhouse put him in the dumps; a reminder of a childhood he assumed was behind him. The tumult of the big city energized him, keeping him focused.

His decision led to Lisa's tantrum. She accused him of wasting their savings and insisted he could job-hunt from the ranch. After reminding her it was his 401K to spend how he chose, she quit speaking to him. *Now she knows how I felt when she pulled the same stunt.*

Stuffing the last of his clothes in the suitcase, he zipped it shut. He found the children in the living room, sitting silently. Even Princess, who generally squiggled everywhere, was lying quietly in Jessica's lap, apparently aware her mistress was bearing a heavy burden. An attack of guilt overwhelmed Michael. *I should have checked out that damn Dr. Cal closer. I'll make it up to them, I promise.* He put down his luggage and stretched out his arms.

"Bye, guys." The children reluctantly rose and held him tight.

"I still don't see why I can't go with you," Andrew said. "I don't like it out here."

"Daddy, you won't be gone long, will you?" Jessica looked worried. Michael realized she must have heard the entire argument with Lisa through the paper-thin walls of the house. He cradled her tightly.

"No, I won't, sweetheart. As soon as I find a job, we'll all be back together."

Michael grabbed his jacket and suitcase and rushed out the door, not even bothering to tell Lisa he was leaving. In all the years they had been together, they had never had a disagreement of this magnitude. They had always had a plan and worked toward it. And now, because of his carelessness, there was no plan. He found himself adrift, on edge. *I just can't stay here any longer.*

As Michael started his car, he examined the dwelling critically. Poor, neglected, pathetic. He would not have that for his kids; he would find a good job and give them the life they deserved. While pulling out of the driveway, he saw Mr. Turner in his front yard, splitting wood. Michael watched in awe as the elderly man lifted what must have been a twenty-pound sledgehammer over his head and brought it down with a crash upon the top of the small metal wedge buried in the log. The piece split in what appeared to be an effortless manner. But Michael knew better. He had tried it the other day; it was not that easy. *I'm out of my comfort zone.*

"Mr. Turner!" Michael stuck his head out his window. "I'm heading to Houston. Shouldn't be gone long.... Could you check in on the family now and then? I'd sure appreciate it."

Mr. Turner put down the maul and gave Michael a long look. "I'd be happy to. Sure will. Don't worry about anything." Michael waved and then concentrated on steering his Porsche around the potholes that imbued Dog Run Road with such character.

***

When Lisa heard the car start, she did not bother to turn around. Michael was no longer the kind, sensitive man she had known. A snob! A real jerk! Everything had to be so upscale. He could not even stay in the house for a couple of months while looking for work. She understood he could not earn the money they needed at the ranch. However, he did not seem concerned that he had moved the kids all over the country, never allowing them to develop roots. It was time they had a stable life, a—Lisa stopped; afraid she would start sobbing. But she was terrified. This was the first time they could not work out their difficulties.

"Ms. Dunwhitty?" Startled, she looked up to see one of the moving crew standing beside her with a handful of papers. "I need you to sign here, ma'am." She took the stack and flipped through it quickly, then affixed her signature. "Ma'am, if I were you, I wouldn't leave all that nice stuff in that barn too long. You know the heat and humidity can do a number on the furniture."

"Yes, thank you, Bruce." Lisa had seen the name on his shirt. "I'll see that it gets taken care of. This is only temporary storage."

With the movers out of the way, Lisa roamed through the barn, squeezing around boxes piled a good ten feet high. The thought of unpacking overwhelmed her. Fortunately, she had parted with quite a few of their belongings during the move, expecting to buy new furniture.

Her wanderings took her into the tack room. She examined it critically. The place was filthy; the dusty odor setting off a sneezing fit. *I love the kids, but they get on my nerves. I need my own space so I can think.* Unexpectedly she envisioned an oasis. The room had a door that led to the outside and one closing it off from the barn. The wooden plank floor felt sturdy beneath her feet. Lisa flipped the light switch, but nothing happened. At least the room had electricity at one point—the line to the barn simply needed reworking and plugs added for her electronic equipment and a reading light. A space heater would do the trick. She would place her computer desk under the only window and Wi-Fi her Internet from the house. It might work.

Lisa slid to the floor, leaning against the wall. Closing her eyes, she worked to clear her mind. Taking deep breaths…. Concentrating on the steady in-and-out of her breathing…. Feeling the sensations of her body…. The cool air numbed her cheeks, the motes continued to tickle her nostrils. Abruptly she envisioned the children. *They've got to be hurting as much as I am.* Determined to be upbeat, she turned back to the house. Andrew met her halfway.

"Hey, Mom, Granny Ellen called. You're not going to believe this! She and Papa Sam are coming here to help!"

Lisa's eyes widened and panic set in. "Help? What do you mean?"

"She called and Jessica answered. I guess Dad had given them the number. Jessica told her this sad story about how the house needed fixing up and all. Said we were so poor we couldn't afford to get things fixed. Granny Ellen told her not to worry, that they were on the way, and that everything would be OK."

Through her consternation, Lisa realized Andrew delighted in telling the story. He thought Jessica was going to catch hell. And he was right. Lisa stormed past a snickering Andrew and threw open the front door. "Jessica! Come here this instant."

The child had a frightened look on her face. Lisa tried to calm herself. "Honey, exactly what did you tell Granny Ellen?"

"Mom, Daddy had told her he was on his way back to Houston. She asked me a lot of questions, and I answered. She's so worried about us. Then she said she and Papa Sam were coming here. Won't that be fun?" Jessica brightened.

"But Jessica, where would they sleep? There's barely enough room for us in this house." Lisa was on a roll now; she had some good excuses to cut them off at the pass.

"They can stay in Andrew's room." Jessica glared at her brother.

"No way. Not my room!"

"Quiet." Lisa nipped the brewing quarrel in the bud. After a quick telephone call to Ellen, Lisa returned to the room. "Well, kids, she wouldn't take 'no' for an answer. She says we need her now and she's coming whether I want her here or not. I guess we better start getting ready for them. They're driving so they'll be here in about three days."

After some argument, Lisa agreed to relinquish her room and sleep with Jessica. Lisa, overwhelmed with squabbles about who went first and who stayed too long in the bathroom, negotiated a school-day schedule. She had never had to deal with this problem; there had always been enough facilities for everyone.

After the children were in bed, Lisa sat down at the kitchen table with a glass of wine. She would not tell Michael his parents were on the way. While he adored his mother, he despised his father. *Not my business.* Lisa could not understand what his problem was; she got along with his parents well.

Lisa started a list. So many things to do! Well, at least if they were coming, she would take advantage of their help.

<u>House</u>
Repair bad boards on the side of the house
Patch shingles on roof
Need to add more plugs and circuits for all electrical equipment
Re-wire?
New bathroom?
Insulate doors and windows
<u>Barn</u>
Patch roof
Clean out tack room for my personal space
Install decent light fixtures and extra plugs
Hook up electricity
Grounds
Mow
Fence repair
Buy cows?

Lisa thought about her last entry, remembering Herb had said something about tax deductions for livestock. And keeping taxes low was a priority. *But how would I take care of them? Where's the money for all this coming from?*

A funk enveloped her. No, depression was a better word. Sometimes she hated the thought of money, but you needed it. *And it does make me happy.* Opening a CPA practice was a possibility, although the thought did not interest her in the least. But it would bring in cash. Maybe she should take Edith up on her invitation to join that group of ladies; they could give her some feedback. *Oh, well.* She put down her pen. Nothing she could do about it tonight.

***

The next day, steeling herself, Lisa slid on her sunglasses and pulled her Smith & Hawken floppy straw gardening hat down on her forehead. Being seen in Walmart was embarrassing even though she did not know anyone in La Grange. However, she could not stomach the idea of ruining her designer jeans while working outside. *I'll just have to get over it.*

Grabbing a cart, she eased her way into the women's section and hurriedly loaded several pairs of Faded Glory jeans, Hanes sweatshirts, and crew socks into the basket. A pair of cheap tennis shoes followed.

Then on to the cleaning supplies. *When was the last time I cleaned the house myself?* At once, she found herself caught up in the Swiffer collection. *Hmm.* Pricy but a lot easier to handle than one of those sponge mops or stringy thingies. She loaded the cart with a Swiffer mop and refill bottles as well as a package of dusters.

The diamond bezel of her watch glittered in the *fluorescent* lighting, catching Lisa's attention. Self-consciously she slid the Rolex off and stuffed it in her purse. *I can't wear this at the ranch, it'll get trashed.* At the jewelry counter, she found a sturdy Casio with a plastic band.

By the time she finished cruising the aisles, the basket could hold no more. Flexing her plastic, Lisa made it through checkout in record time. Safely into the Volvo, she eyed the next chore on her list, then eased out of the parking lot.

Staring at the door of the Laundromat, she sat in the car as it idled, prickling with anxiety. It had been years since she had washed clothes and had not gone to a washateria since her college days.

Unexpectedly, she pitied the children, wondering how school was going. The campuses were inviting enough, certainly not the one-room schoolhouse Andrew had predicted. The district had a good rating from the Texas Education Agency, which was encouraging. If she was worried about going into the Laundromat, she could only imagine how they were feeling at school.

Grabbing the roll of quarters, Lisa took a big breath and made a beeline in. *How stupid. I've dealt with CEOs of major corporations, and now I'm afraid of a silly washateria.*

Once inside she looked around, relieved to be the only customer. The television, perched on a shelf near the ceiling, blared in Spanish. The cost of detergent from the coin-operated machine irked her. Next visit, she would bring her own. In no time, six washers hummed. *The kids are going to have to wear only one outfit a day and reuse their towels. I'm not doing this more than once a week.*

For a while, Lisa sat on a graffiti-marked wooden bench, the scent of fabric softener mingled with the whir of the machines and canned laughter from a game show. A Formica-topped table nearby held copies of old People magazines. Idly flipping the pages, her gaze wandered out the window, a used bookstore catching her attention. She hesitated; afraid someone would steal the clothes. *To hell with it.* She bounded across the parking lot.

Minutes later she emerged with a pile of books, including a dog-eared copy of Danielle Steele. *How long had it been since I've read anything for fun? Ages.* Usually, poring over the Wall Street Journal or the latest issue of Forbes consumed her reading time. Engrossed in the juicy novel, she reluctantly put it down to fold the laundry.

The grocery store was the next stop. Its size reassured her she would have many more choices than at Zink's Corner. However, her hopeful bearing sagged at the meat counter. Sam liked a good piece of beef, but the thin-cut steaks were unappetizing. She passed them up and chose a pork tenderloin. At least it looked yummy. Fortunately, she found Starbucks whole beans in the bag. She was prepared to do without many high-end things but drew the line at coffee.

Sticker shock struck a blow at checkout. *One hundred seventy-five dollars' worth of groceries? You've got to be kidding.* She briefly scanned the register tape while pushing the cart to the car. When you had money, you never noticed how much you spent. But now....

As Lisa wound down Dog Run Road, her indignity mounted. She did not deserve this. *I've worked so hard. Now I'm nearly broke. I own 4,000 acres. So what? I can't sell it and don't know how to make any money off it.*

She held back the tears until she neared the oil well. The fence along the corner rippled like the United States flag in a stiff breeze. It might not be strong enough to hold cattle. In one place near the pond, the first strand of wire was gone altogether, making it easier for the deer to clear the barbed strands. Overwhelmed by the stagnant air in the Volvo, she crumpled. Then, anger overtook her. *I can't just sit here feeling sorry for myself...be strong.*

As she approached the driveway, she noticed Mr. Turner in his yard feeding the chickens. He followed her up the driveway and was nearby as soon as she turned off the car. Wiping her tears away, she stepped out and said, "Hi, Mr. Turner."

"Please call me Carl. I see you've been to town." He motioned to the grocery bags piled in the back. "Let me help you with some of that."

"Oh, Carl, thanks, but it's not necessary,"

Carl opened the rear hatch and gathered an armful of sacks. "Oh, I like to be useful. It's no problem, really."

"Well, truthfully, I'd appreciate the help." She wrestled with the laundry. After several trips, everything was inside.

"How about a cup of coffee?"

"Oh, no, ma'am, I don't want to intrude."

"Carl, I could use the company right now." Lisa turned to him in all the earnestness she could muster. There was something about this old gentleman that intrigued her. Without his help, they would not have found Jessica so quickly. "I could use a friend."

"Don't mind if I do." Carl pulled out a chair and sat as Lisa dug her treasured beans out of a grocery bag. She had not had a cup of Starbucks in some time and was looking forward to it. Eagerly she busied herself with the Bunn coffeemaker she had located in one of the boxes stashed in the barn.

Soon Lisa poured each a mug, breathing in the satisfying aroma of the rich brew, and sat across from Carl. She said, "Michael has gone back to Houston to look for a job. I'm not sure how long he'll be gone."

"I knew that. I saw him when he left. I told him I'd look after you all for him. Why didn't you and the children go, too?"

"All this moving back and forth is too much. The kids are already enrolled in school, and I would have had to withdraw them and then re-enroll them in Houston. Then, no telling where Michael or I would find a job. I decided it would be better if the kids and I stayed here until Michael found work.... I saw pictures of you, Joe, and Ruby. I guess you knew them well."

"Yes, very well."

"So, why did he leave the ranch to me?"

Carl leaned forward in his chair, face clouding. "This property has been in Joe's family since the early 1820s. They've fought to keep it through war and drought and the Boll weevil. Joe just couldn't let it go to strangers. Not on his watch."

"That's deep."

"I understand where he's coming from. My property's been in the family since after the Civil War. I want it to stay there."

"I don't know if I'm up to the task."

"I suppose he wouldn't have picked you if he thought you weren't.... So, any way I can help, let me know."

"Thanks." Lisa poured herself another cup, unnerved by the faith a man she hardly knew had put in her. "Michael's parents are on the way here. They say they're coming to help. His dad's a retired mechanic and can fix almost anything."

"Well, that's good. I don't mean to interfere, but the first thing you need to do is get that tractor up and running. And if you plan to run cattle, the fences need to be fixed. There's a man near Smithville that's looking for some timber land." Carl paused and then said, "If you don't do something soon, the taxes will eat you alive."

Lisa could feel the blood draining from her face. "There's so much to do. I don't know where to start, but I've got to do something." Her lip trembled; she refused to cry. Instead, a flash of irritation with Michael intruded.

"Lisa, there's only so much you can do." Carl took a sip and leaned back in the chair. "You know, one day at a time, one day at a time."

Both sat in silence. Finally, Carl continued, "I don't mean to get all into your business, but if I were you, I'd call that timber man and give him the rights to 4,000 acres. There are only about 200 or so acres around here that's cleaned off enough to feed the cows. That means you'd only have to worry about a little bit of the fence and clearing a small portion of the land. There's an auction at Flatonia where you can pick up some good cattle to get started."

"How many cows do you think I need?" Lisa was relieved to hear she did not have to repair all the fencing at once.

"Oh, I'd say no more than sixty head at most. You could start with thirty. Did you know I used to work for Joe and Ruby? I'd help them with chores around the farm all the time. They sure were good people, the Franks."

A bit of optimism surfaced as Lisa's mind raced. "Carl, would you help me? I mean, I need a plan of action. I need to know what to do first. I can't pay much 'till we get started."

"Lisa, I'd be happy to. Why, get you some paper and a pencil, and we'll get to work. And the pay—don't worry, it'll work itself out." Carl took another swallow and the conversation turned to bringing the JF Ranch back to its glory days.

When they finished, Lisa said, "I saw pictures of you and some children in Ruby's photo album. Were those yours?"

"Yes, ma'am, I have five of them."

Stunned, Lisa said, "Five?"

Carl stared at the countertop. "When they were little, their mom took 'em away from me. She said she didn't want them to be raised in the country. I tried to find them. Her sister refused to tell me where they'd gone…. They never liked that we got married and moved her away from her family…. I even spent one solid week in Houston just driving around looking for her car." He rose, putting his coffee cup in the sink. "I need to get back home; chores to do."

***

A few days later, Lisa gazed through the window, watching as brown leaves swirled around the trunks of the bare trees. To the far right, she examined what used to be a garden brimming with vegetables. According to Carl, the patch had sustained the Franks through good times and bad. Lisa had to admit she loved a good tomato, but the thought of all the work to rid the area of debris and weeds was daunting. But what was worse, weeding or talking to irate customers who could not understand why their taxes were so high? She shivered. *But how else am I going to raise money to get the ranch going?*

An approaching vehicle drew her attention. Must be Sam and Ellen, as the school bus was not due for another hour. Putting on her best host smile, she hurried out only to see Ellen carrying a large bag of groceries. Sam, short and wiry, followed with two suitcases.

"Now don't start in on me, honey," Ellen said. "I picked up a few things at the store. You know how much I love to bake. It's never the same cooking for two. I can't wait to have that kitchen smelling of apple pie. I haven't had one in so long my mouth is watering!"

Lisa greeted them and suggested they settle in while she put the groceries away. In no time, Ellen, a trim woman with short dark hair, was in the kitchen, packing the room with her loving warmth. Lisa felt reassured.

They chatted as Ellen peeled the apples. Sam sat silently, barely getting a word in edgewise. "Sam," Lisa said, "I know you recently retired and all, and if you don't want to do any work out here, don't feel like you have to. I—"

Ellen's hearty laugh interrupted Lisa. "Oh, I wouldn't worry about that. I haven't seen Sam so bored in ages. I figure having something to do will be good for him."

Lisa looked at Sam; she received a big grin. "Ellen's right. I do miss having something regular to do. What all around here needs fixing?"

Relieved, Lisa told him everything Carl had said.

"Let me take a look at the tractor," Sam said. The spark in his spirit reminded her of Michael when he got excited about a new venture. Funny, she had seen no resemblance between the two before. Michael physically resembled his mother's side of the family.

"Let's go out to the barn. I'll show you where everything is." Lisa stood, grabbed her coat, and Sam followed.

The tractor was located under a lean-to attached to the barn. "It has to be at least forty years old," Sam said. "They call them poppin johnnys because of the rhythm the two-cylinder engine makes."

The distinctive green and yellow veneer of the Model 430 John Deere was dull and pockmarked with rust from scratches and dents accumulated throughout the years. Sam walked around the machine, knocking off cobwebs and piles of brush, most likely nests for the neighboring creatures, he explained. As he opened the gas tank, the nauseating aroma of diesel fouled the air.

Eventually, Sam crawled up on the seat and gave the tractor a crank. Nothing happened. "Hmm," he said, pushing a shock of salt and pepper hair off his forehead. "We definitely need a new battery and fresh gas. Probably need to change the spark plugs and clean the carburetor, too. Tires are bad. Meantime, I'll poke around and figure out all the work that needs to be done. You go on in, Lisa. I'll putter around here. You know where the tools are?"

Lisa led Sam to a corner in the barn. He browsed through the heavily rusted mounds of equipment. Shaking his head, he said, "It's going to take a lot to get the tools back in order. They need cleaning and oiling. They've rusted something awful." He picked up a crescent wrench and knocked it against the heel of his work shoe. "Looks like it's only surface rust. The tool seems pretty sturdy. It'll be fine."

Lisa entered the tack room, leaving Sam engrossed in the task ahead. She wearily leaned against the wall. How could Sam ever get the tractor running? The parts would probably be expensive. The tires had dry rot, and the seat… it was down to bare springs. At least she had Sam because leaning on Carl too much bothered her—she should pay him for every bit of work he did regardless of what he said. Despite her concern, a path forward emerged.

Lisa heard Jessica squeal and run to greet Sam. Andrew mumbled a hello. To her astonishment, Sam put them to work. Jessica was responsible for sorting the tools, putting the screwdrivers in one pile and wrenches in another. When Andrew balked, Sam emanated an authority she had never heard from him before.

"Young man, you think you're so smart because you can build a computer. Well, are you smart enough to fix a tractor? We need it running so we can fix things up. Otherwise, you'll have to do the hauling, carrying, and digging by hand."

"Oh, Papa Sam, we're going to be out of here soon." Andrew did not sound as confident as Lisa would have expected.

"You may well be, but learning to repair more than computers won't hurt you a bit. It's something your father never learned to do."

That was all it took. Lisa snuck out as Sam began giving Andrew an overview of how a combustion engine worked and how they were going to ensure all systems were functioning properly.

Before returning to the house, Lisa walked to the mailbox. She saw Carl on his porch. "Carl, come over and meet Michael's mom and dad. Sam's out back with Andrew looking at the tractor."

Lisa watched Carl's face brighten. "I'd love to meet them. Let me get my tools, and I'll see if I can give them a hand. It's been mighty lonesome around here since Joe died."

Lisa escorted Carl to the barn, and soon he and Sam were deep in conversation. Andrew was paying attention and asking questions while Jessica, bless her heart, had piles of tools sorted. Carl showed her how to clean them and put them back where they belonged.

Feeling like a fifth wheel, Lisa went to the house. Opening the door, she took a deep breath, smiling. The oven emanated the aroma of apple and cinnamon.

"I'm so glad the two of you are here. I don't think I could have tackled everything without you," Lisa said.

Ellen grinned. "Honey, don't say that too soon. A week of us and you'll probably be ready to run us out on a rail. It's fun for us, too. Getting away from the house and seeing some different country is wonderful." She came over, enveloped Lisa, and continued, "The house is pretty clean. You know all this old furniture in here and your good stuff out in the barn—that makes no sense at all. I tried out that bed back there you saved for us. It's pretty bad."

"Well, if we got enough help, we could move our mattresses in and get rid of these old ones. But mine is king-size, I'm not sure it will fit in that room. I guess we'll have to measure it. It would be nice to put Jessica's twin beds in the room where she and I are. She's a tough one to sleep with."

***

After dinner, Jessica entered the kitchen where Lisa was reading the newspaper online. "Momma, the teacher says you need to sign this paper." Jessica held it out.

Lisa grimaced. A fifty-eight! She looked at Jessica. "You failed your math test."

"It was hard. I tried; I really did. I'm just not good at math."

Lisa shuddered. Jessica had always had trouble with numbers, but she had never made a grade this low. What was going to happen when she got into high school? Lisa scanned the problems Jessica had missed.

"Go get some paper. Let's work the first one together."

Jessica sat down with a pencil and paper while Lisa read the problem aloud.

Nina made cookies. The recipe required less than a cup of nuts. Which of the following fractions is less than 1/3?

A. 1/2

B. 3/4

C. 2/5

D. 1/6

"Are there some answers you can immediately eliminate?" Lisa asked.

"No, I have to first convert all of them to the same denominators before I can tell which one is smaller."

"No, you can eliminate two answers without doing that."

"But that's not how my teacher said to do it." Jessica pouted. "I want Daddy to help me. He knows how my teacher says to do it."

Lisa began explaining how answers one and two were obviously wrong, but Jessica tuned out. Sobbing, she ran to her room.

Ellen entered. "I'll go talk to her."

Lisa stewed. The child either did not have a brain or did not want to use it. Every time she tried to lend a hand with lessons, things went downhill fast. *How in the world do people homeschool their children?* Michael usually helped, but since he was not here, Lisa would have to hire a tutor. Just thinking about how he had abandoned them made her head ache.

After getting Jessica to bed, Lisa moved to the living room where Andrew and Sam were playing a video game. Soon Sam begged off and leaned back in the recliner with a book. Andrew surfed the Internet.

"Hey, everyone. I found out about that old tractor," Andrew said. "They only made about 15,000 of them; the last one was February 1960. It's a real antique." He then showed Sam everything he had found.

"Speaking of the tractor, Lisa, we've got a long list of things to buy…. It's not going to be cheap." Sam hesitated and then continued. "You're going to have to do something about that car of yours."

"What? The Volvo? What's wrong with it?"

"How are we going to bring back tires? I don't think you want to be paying people to bring all that stuff out."

"Oh, I hadn't thought about that. I guess we do need a truck. Are they very expensive?"

Sam laughed. "Depends on what you get, but yes, you can spend as much for one as you do for a car. Carl tells me you can get special discounts for farm use. You need to look into that. Meantime, be thinking about what you want to do. I can use Carl's truck tomorrow but from the looks of it—"

"I know," Lisa said. "I thought it was Jed Clampett's truck when I first saw it."

"Who's Jed Clampett?" Andrew asked.

"Never mind, I'll explain it to you later. Andrew, could I ask you a favor?"

"Maybe," he said.

"Do you mind looking online and seeing what you come up with in the way of a truck?"

"Sure."

Sam moved to the kitchen and began making the shopping list. Lisa joined him, watching uneasily as it grew. Restless, she opened an inexpensive bottle of chardonnay. Pouring herself a glass, she asked if he wanted anything. Never looking up, he declined with a nod. Lisa settled next to him, took a sip, and looked around. The kitchen could use a coat of paint. Andrew's voice interrupted her thoughts.

"Hey, Mom, Papa Sam. This is way too cool. They recently came out with a brand-new Dodge Ram that is so macho. If you get it, I could drive it to school. One of the guys in my class, Eric, already has his license. He says I can get one if I take a driver education course or you can teach me to drive."

Andrew showed them the truck on his laptop screen. "Oh," Lisa said. "That's neat."

Andrew was more excited than she'd seen him since they left Raleigh. "Yeah, Mom, it's a Laramie Longhorn with a Hemi V8, Nav system, leather seats, and a pretty good audio. We could probably get by with a 2500, but it needs to be two-toned."

Sam looked up from his list and stared at the screen. "How much is this truck, anyway?"

"Oh, about $55,000. It's a real bargain compared to mom's Volvo."

Lisa's mood hit rock bottom. Finally, Andrew showed some real excitement about the move, and it was over a truck that was not only impractical but terribly expensive. There was no way she could afford it. As Andrew explained all the finer points of the truck to his grandfather, her heart sank. How was she going to bring herself to crush his dream? Guiltily she realized they had always driven nice, expensive automobiles, and Andrew was only reflecting her and Michael's tastes.

"Andrew," Sam said, "Don't you think it's a bit impractical? Do you really need such a fancy interior?"

"Why get something plain?"

Lisa could sense Sam was about to reply so she spoke up, "Andrew, I tell you what. Why don't I pick you up after school tomorrow and we'll go look at trucks? Don't get your hopes up about that one, though." Andrew tried to object, but Lisa curtly said, "We'll discuss it tomorrow. You need to get to bed." She reached out and gave him a peck on the cheek and, for the first time in a long time, Andrew leaned down, kissing her.

"Night, Papa Sam," he said, retreating to his room.

"Boys and their toys," Lisa said. "Don't worry, Sam. We won't get that truck. I'll get something practical. It's my job to bring Andrew back to earth on this one."

Sam shook his head. "Not giving kids everything they want can break your heart." He sat staring at the ceiling. Then he asked if she needed the bathroom. If not, he was going to clean up and head to bed. The fresh winter air and all the work outside had worn him out.

***

Lisa sat in her Volvo watching students stream out of the high school. Jeans were the order of the day. T-shirts, hoodies, boots, tennis shoes. Everyone seemed to make their fashion statement. Finally, as she was about to go into the building in search of Andrew, he appeared. She watched as he limped to the car and eased in.

"What's wrong?"

"Nothing."

"Look at me." Andrew turned to face Lisa. She could see a red place welling on his right cheek.

"Have you been in a fight?"

Andrew did not respond but turned back to look out the car window.

"Answer me or I'll go into the school and talk to the principal."

"It's no big deal."

"Yes, it is. Look at you, you're hurt." Lisa touched his arm lightly.

"Look, Mom, just let me take care of it. I don't want you to get involved. Please."

Lisa heard the pain in his voice. Then she realized he looked downright dorky in his chino slacks, long-sleeved polo shirt, and Sperry Top-Siders. It had never occurred to her he would not fit in.

Grimly she started the car and eased out of the parking lot. "Tell you what. I don't feel much like looking at trucks. Why don't we get you some jeans and T-shirts? You'll need those for helping Papa Sam around the ranch."

Andrew did not react but did not object. Lisa thought a moment and then headed to the department store where they bought enough outfits to last a week. At least Andrew's mood seemed to improve.

"You know, working outside, seems like you need a pair of boots," Lisa said. "What do you think?"

"Yeah, I'd like that. Eric has a pair of Ropers."

"Where can we get some?"

"I think Tractor Supply has a pretty good selection."

Lisa drove straight to the store. The sign "For Life Out Here" surprised her. *Awesome. They must have seen me coming.* Andrew picked a pair of boots, and Lisa chose some as well. Nothing fancy. She also bought Andrew a hoodie and a camo baseball cap. Several pairs of work gloves rounded out their purchases.

Before going home, Lisa stopped at the bakery to buy kolaches. She forced Andrew to go inside with her. They got a drink and enjoyed one of the Czech pastries.

"Andrew, I don't like this at all. I won't say anything this time, but if it happens again, I will. If you need me to go up to the school, just tell me."

Andrew picked at his treat. "Mom. I said I got it. If you do anything it'll just get worse. And please, don't tell Dad."

"Fine, just this once."

CHAPTER 6

Michael waved at the hotel bartender. "Another." Jason dutifully mixed a scotch and water. The two had gotten to know each other far too well, Michael mused. *Thank goodness I don't have to drive home.* As he sipped the bitter concoction, he replayed the events of the past week. For the first time in his life, recruiters had been cool, hinting that the 'good doctor's' behavior had tainted him. Michael tried his best to explain that he was brand new and had not been privy to company secrets. In response, he received what he felt were placating looks. Between their "don't try to play dumb" expressions and the ongoing recession, he was worried.

The process was taking longer than expected. The Hyatt and eating out every night were draining his bank account fast, forcing another 401K withdrawal. Briefly, he toyed with the idea of moving back to the ranch or a cheaper hotel, then quickly dismissed it. The depressing living conditions would shove him into the dumps. Being upbeat and positive was vital to landing a position.

Hitting the bottom of his glass, he paused, aching for his family. Although he spoke regularly with the children and his mother, he and Lisa had not communicated. Her silence both worried and angered him. She had always been his sounding board for work-related issues, giving him fresh perspectives on sticky situations. His biggest cheerleader. Fingering his cell, Michael thought about calling her. *Damn it. I'm in the right. Why can't she see that? And my parents…. I'm glad they've been there to help, but...* his mother had been hinting that she was worried about the family being alone, stoking his guilt and irritation at Lisa. He frowned. Finding a job had never taken this long before. *Maybe I should move back....*

As he pondered, his eyes wandered to a woman sitting across the horseshoe-shaped bar. She was young, in her twenties, dressed conservatively, petite, curvy, with shoulder-length blond hair...so unlike the tall, slim woman who had captured his heart.

As he stared, she gazed at him. Rubbing his thumb over his wedding ring, he started to glance away, but bleakness stopped him. Neither blinked.

Fortunately, Jason approached Michael, blocking his view.

"I'm sorry, what?" Michael responded to the bartender.

"Want a refill?"

"Yeah, and give the lady over there another drink and put it on my tab." Michael motioned to the blond.

Jason glanced over his shoulder and grinned. "Sure thing, Michael."

As he watched, the bartender made introductions, pointing to Michael while he produced another white wine for the woman. After raising his glass, Michael nodded, and, seeing her smile, sauntered over to speak with her. *No big deal; just some conversation. Anything to keep my mind off Lisa.*

Thirty minutes later he excused himself, lying that he had an early morning. Alone in his room, he tried to sort out what had occurred. The woman was intelligent and well-read, her personality immediately reminding him of his wife. Sharon, a pharmaceutical rep who had just transferred to Houston, would begin making hospital rounds Monday. But first, she wanted to see the city, relax a little, and look for a place to live. Did he want to join her in seeing the sights? *Was she feeling me out or just lonely?* He had become unnerved.

In the bathroom, Michael scrutinized himself in the mirror. *I look like crap.* He ran his fingers along his cheeks. *Too much booze lately.* His eyes were red and puffy; he had put on weight. Michael stared at his belt notched one hole farther out than usual. *I'm going to have to start on a workout program, skip the drinks....* Testily he brushed his teeth. Abruptly stopping, he glared at himself in the mirror. *Quit whining. You got yourself into this mess. You can get yourself out.*

Back in bed, he flipped on the TV, trying to brush off the situation. Soon as he settled on a basketball game and relaxed, his cell phone rang.

"Daddy, I miss you. When are you coming home?"

"Hi, sweetie, I miss you, too, but I've got to find a job."

"Daddy, my class is having a concert next Wednesday. You've got to be there. We're singing patriotic songs. We've been studying the presidents. Please come; please say you'll be there. Momma and Papa Sam and Granny Ellen will be there, but it won't be the same without you."

Michael took a deep breath and squeezed his eyes tightly. *Something's got to give.* "Sure, honey, I'll come. What time are you singing?"

"Oh, Daddy, I love you!" Jessica sniveled. Michael's heart cracked. What had they done to the poor children? It was all because Lisa was so stubborn.

"We start at one in the afternoon."

"OK, sweetie. I'll be there. I promise." Grimly, Michael hung up the telephone and tried to zone out.

***

Lisa cautiously opened the door to Zink's Corner and peeked in before deciding to enter. Finding her mouth dry, she wished for a bottle of water. Edith appeared just as Lisa had decided to leave.

"Lisa! How wonderful to see you. I'm so glad you finally decided to join us." Edith waved to her. "I was about to put the closed sign on the door. I hate to be interrupted when we're getting together."

As Lisa neared, Edith clasped her arm. "I know you've been having a tough time out there. Carl said there's a lot to do. I bet you need to kick back. Come on, don't be shy."

Edith led Lisa into her living quarters attached to the store. Two other ladies were lounging in the shabby chic room, a cinnamon aroma emanating from a three-wick candle. Comfortable pillows covered an ancient leather couch partially disguised with a green and brown throw sporting a rabbit motif. The coffee table was a gorgeous hunk of cedar, sliced lengthwise and polished, giving the appearance of a fine sheet of ice. A tall lamp, wearing a shade decorated with sparkling clear spangles, stood to the side of the couch. Lisa hurriedly sank into the sofa's vacant corner.

"Hi, I'm Rachael," a frumpy woman with dishwater blond hair said. "And this is Dorothy." The tall, lean woman known as Dorothy was sitting to Lisa's right and leaned over to shake her hand.

"What'll it be, Lisa?" Edith asked. "We have wine, beer, or I've got some gourmet coffee. I've got one of those new machines that does it by the cup so you can have an Ethiopian Sumatra, or I've got a great cinnamon snickerdoodle brew. Uh, let's see, the wine is a red Ménage à Trois, and I've got either Heineken or Corona. Sorry, I seem to be out of domestic beer. My order's late."

"I'll have wine."

Dorothy, it turned out, was a local veterinarian who specialized in horses. Lisa discovered that Andrew's new friend, Eric, was her son. Dorothy reminisced about how hard it had been to get the respect of the men in the surrounding area when it came to the ability of a woman—especially an outsider (Dorothy had grown up in Lubbock)—to care competently for equines.

"But," Dorothy said, "It's turned out to be a good move for us. The kids are happy and love school and John has a good job at the bank and volunteers with the La Grange Fire Department. It's a nice place to raise a family. It's not such a cutthroat place, not like the big cities."

Lisa leisurely twirled the glass with her fingers, eyeing it closely. This was no cheap goblet. Definitely not. And the wine was one of her favorites.

"I know you inherited the ranch from Joe, but how did you and your husband end up with no jobs?" Dorothy asked.

Startled, Lisa looked at Dorothy and then at Edith.

"Hey, it's a small town," Edith said. "Everyone knows everything."

"Well," Lisa said, "I used to work for Benson Bart as an accounting manager. About the time the company went under, Michael, that's my husband, got a job with Harris Cardiac Implants."

"Benson Bart? Isn't that the accounting firm that went under when the mortgage industry tanked?" Edith asked.

"Uh, yeah, but it wasn't the office in Raleigh that did anything wrong. The problem was in the Houston office."

"Then Harris? Ooh," Rachael said.

"You know the company?" Lisa asked.

"Sure do. I'm a radiologist over at the hospital. One of the physicians who practices there knew Dr. Harris from med school. He told us all about it."

"Yeah. The worst part of it was that Dr. Harris—he was the president— wanted Michael so bad that he offered me a job to sweeten the pot. We stupidly sold our house to the company and moved to Houston. It was too late to go back."

Lisa felt herself on the verge of crying, so she took a long, slow sip of wine.

"You know," Edith said. "Things always happen for the best."

"I'm not quite convinced of that right now," Lisa said. Eager to change the subject, she asked, "Did any of you know Uncle Joe?"

Edith nodded and Dorothy said, "I took care of his cattle. He was quite a man."

"Any idea why he wanted to leave the property to me?"

"Joe loved the land so much. It'd been in his family since the 1800s. He wanted it to stay in the family," Edith said.

"Wasn't there anyone else to leave it to?" Lisa asked.

"Not from what he told me," Dorothy said. "One afternoon I was out vaccinating calves. We had a long talk about it. He'd wanted to leave the land to Carl, but Carl refused, saying it belonged to the family. Joe'd thought about it a long time. You were the only one who seemed halfway interested. So, he picked you."

"He and Carl were that close?"

"Like family."

"I didn't realize that…. The thing I mostly remember about my visits to the ranch was riding the pony and how fun it was," said Lisa.

"Do you like to ride horses?" Dorothy asked.

"Gee, I haven't been on a horse since then, but I'd like to learn."

"Wonderful! I can't get these two couch potatoes out to do anything fun." Dorothy scowled, giving Edith and Rachael an evil look.

"You're crazy if you think I'm getting on one of those wild mustangs of yours again," Rachael said. She then told the story of her riding adventure with Dorothy that ended with the horse throwing her into an expansive mud hole, bruising her derrière so badly she could not sit for a week. Lisa laughed. She had not let loose like this in weeks. These ladies were fun!

Edith supplied another round of drinks. As soon as the bottle cap of Rachael's Heineken popped off, the foam spewed. "Quick! Quick!" Rachael yelled as she dropped the bottle opener and stuck her hand under the container, trying to keep as much of the brew as she could off the exquisite table.

"I got it." Edith briskly cupped a dishcloth under Rachael's hand, the remains of the foam spilling onto the cloth. Then Edith wiped up the sticky mess.

"What's with this beer, anyway? That's the second one that's done that." Rachael settled into her chair and took a long sip out of her frosted mug.

"Oh, they have a new driver, and he must have dropped the case coming in, that's all I can think of."

"Well, I'll change my order, then. Is the Corona foaming?" Dorothy asked.

"I hope not." Edith then turned to Lisa. "Oh, by the way, I can order almost any beer, wine, or coffee, you want. Let me know by Monday, and I'll have it for you in time for the weekend."

"Really?"

"Yeah, sure." Edith gave her a critical glance. "I don't stock too much of the high-end stuff since the locals don't buy it, and I want to keep my supplies as fresh as I can. Are you surprised?"

"Uh, yeah, I guess so." Lisa squirmed. "It's just that everything out here is so different, you know…"

"Boy, isn't it?" Rachael shook her head and took a sip of beer. "I came out here to care for my grandfather about ten years ago. After he died, I stayed on. You'd be surprised, though. There's a lot more of us 'foreigners' than you'd expect."

"Foreigners?" Lisa said, puzzled.

"Oh, when I say foreigners, I mean those not born and raised in the county. It seems some natives don't care for all the newcomers and their newfangled ideas."

"Really, Rachael." Dorothy shook her head. "You know that's not true of everyone. Most people in Fayette County have a good heart and welcome anybody who's willing to work."

After another glass of wine, Lisa felt quite comfortable with the women. They were quick to give her advice on everything from shopping to starting her own business. Dorothy even recommended a tutor for Jessica. When the ladies heard the dilemma about the furniture, they immediately offered assistance. Dorothy said she would bring her son and a group of his friends to help.

As they were breaking up, Lisa dug in her purse, pulled out some scraps of paper, and hastily scribbled her telephone number and e-mail address for each woman. On a larger piece of paper, she left Edith a list of precious coffee and wine that would make her exile more palatable.

After hugs all around, Lisa promised to return to the group's next meeting.

Walking to the car, the sky was so light you could read a book. *A full moon!* She never noticed the rhythm of life in the big city. No craziness here; just the fullness of new friends and the quiet countryside.

Backing out, she drove carefully, having consumed too much wine to be behind the wheel. Realizing she could only go about twenty miles per hour and had little likelihood of meeting anyone on Dog Run Road eased her misgivings.

The idea of riding horses grew on her. She could explore the far reaches of the property, check fence lines, and hunt for Jessica if Carl were not around. *I'll be more comfortable not having to depend so much on others. Maybe I can rent one.*

Lisa latched on to her first feelings of belonging. Simply having a place to talk to women who were like her and being able to order her favorite beverages made a great deal of difference. She especially wanted to know more about Dorothy, a strong, determined woman who knew what she wanted in life. Lisa desperately needed to draw on that strength to rebuild her own. Michael invaded her thoughts. *I miss him. He's the one I always turned to when things weren't going well.* Where was he now? What was he doing? *I'll have to back down and call him. I don't want our relationship to slip away.*

WHACK!

The Volvo lurched to the left and stalled, piercing squeals shattered the night air. Jerking open the door, a pungent odor mixed with a coppery smell assaulted her. Lisa ran around the hood and came face to face with a giant boar, blood flowing from its shoulder, drenching its scraggly black coat. Bile gathered in her throat, causing her to puke. Petrified, she jumped back into the car, threw it in reverse, and jammed down the accelerator. No movement. The scent of burning rubber quickly permeated its interior. Lisa threw the Volvo into park and turned off the engine.

Unable to stand the screeching, she took off, dashing up the road. A rustling sound just to her left sent her into shock, causing her to stumble. Wiping herself off, she looked around warily, but could not discern what had made the noise. Breathing deeply, she sat off at a brisk trot. Thankfully Carl's house came quickly into view, his living room lit. Shaking and breathless, she banged on the door. Within an instant, he peered out.

"A pig! I hit a pig! It's still alive!"

He disappeared, only to return with his rifle. "Get in my truck."

They drove the short distance to the scene. The swine's bellowing had turned to low moans. Closing her eyes, Lisa took a deep breath. *I've got to get out and see what he's doing. I can't depend on him so much. It isn't fair. What if it happens again and he's not around?*

Lisa forced herself to exit the vehicle. She watched as Carl put the muzzle of the rifle between the animal's eyes. Dropping her head into her hands, tension seized her as the thunder of the shot reverberated through the air.

Carl walked back to the truck, stowing his gun behind the seat. "That's a big one, alright. Lucky it only dented the fender." He then backed the truck up to the hog.

"What are you doing?"

"No sense letting all that meat go to waste. Makes some mighty good sausage when it's mixed with deer meat. Let me get the hog loaded, and then we'll see about your car."

Lisa watched as Carl quickly set up a winch and then donned rubber gloves. He looped a nylon rope around the hog's hind legs and hooked the rope to the winch, lifting the carcass into the truck bed.

She turned away, then forced herself to watch. "Do you need help?"

"No. Don't want you touching it without any gloves on. These animals have a bad disease, something called brucellosis. You need to be careful."

Lisa stepped back, shivering as Carl swung the monstrous heap of flesh into the bed of the pickup. He then removed a crowbar and flashlight from his toolbox.

"Now, let's see what we can do with the car." He studied the fender pressing against the tire. With a bit of elbow grease, he managed to free the wheel. "Alright. You should be able to drive now. You just go on. I'll follow you to be sure you get home OK."

Lisa slid in and eased her foot onto the gas pedal. Thankfully, the car crept forward. She pulled into the driveway and parked next to the house. After inspecting the damage, she made a quick trip to the bathroom and then went to thank Carl.

As she neared the road, Lisa could see the lights from his truck casting long shadows into the trees. Closing in, she spied the beast hanging from a high branch by its back haunches. Blood was running into a plastic bucket nestled underneath. A large aluminum tray containing a hacksaw and a cleaver sat on a wooden table nearby. Carl was standing next to the beast, sharpening a butcher knife.

Lisa fled.

***

Nursing her stiff neck, Lisa leaned over to shut off the alarm clock, more convinced than ever that a full moon brought out craziness. Last night seemed bizarre and surreal. The brutality of nature arising amid the beauty had haunted her dreams. Letting out a deep breath, she steeled herself for the day ahead.

"Jessica, honey, get up. It's your morning in the bathroom first." When Jessica didn't move, Lisa poked her. "Come on, come on. I'm going to the bathroom, and you better be ready when I get out."

Lisa donned her bathrobe and made a quick trip to the toilet before the line formed. She could already hear Ellen bustling in the kitchen. Yelling once more at Jessica, Lisa made a beeline to the coffeepot and poured a fresh brew. After grabbing some aspirin, she sat at the table savoring the rich flavor.

Sam entered the house, depositing his coat on the rack just as Jessica sat down.

"Whatever happened last night?" Sam asked.

"Oh, it was awful. I hit a pig."

"Well, it sure tore the car up. I'm surprised the airbags didn't deploy."

"Hmm. I wasn't going very fast."

"You had a wreck?" Andrew asked. He was passing through the kitchen on his way to the bathroom.

"Yeah, a big, black, ugly pig. Ugh."

"I want to see the car," Jessica said.

Ellen turned off the bacon and the group trooped out to view the damage. Carl was in his yard feeding the chickens and sauntered over.

"Wow," Andrew said, "It must have been some big pig. The whole fender is crumpled."

"I wonder whose it was," Ellen said. "They shouldn't be so careless as to let their animals run wild. You could have been hurt."

Carl chuckled. "The varmint that did that was wild. A feral hog is what they're called."

"They're like feral cats? Pigs that got loose?" Andrew asked.

"That's right. And they're a mess. They tear up pastures and cause erosion."

"So where is it? I want to see it," Andrew said.

"Well, it's in my freezer right now, but you can come see it after school if you want."

"You mean you put the whole pig in the freezer? Why?"

Carl laughed. "No, I cut it up for meat. I put the meat in the freezer."

Lisa, tormented by the macabre scene, quickly changed the subject. "Andrew, the bus will be here soon. Go get ready." Turning to Carl, she said, "Come on in and have some breakfast."

"Thanks, but I've already eaten."

"Then just come have coffee," Sam said.

After breakfast was over and the kids were on the bus, Sam asked Carl what he had done with the entrails of the hog.

"I just dumped it out in the back of my property."

"Won't it start smelling?" Ellen asked.

"Not at all. In fact, I suspect wild animals have already eaten the leftovers. I've seen the body of a full-sized cow disappear within a week between the coyotes, buzzards, and other creatures."

Lisa felt ill. *I've got to come to terms with the circle of life. But how, I've no clue.* "Please excuse me. I need to make some phone calls and see about getting the Volvo fixed. I can't sell it the way it is."

***

Michael paid his hotel bill and asked the attendant to bring his car. Easing into the Houston traffic, he sipped on a Starbucks Americano while singing along to his Steve Miller Band CD. Not even the backed-up traffic on I-10 West could dampen his spirits.

His leather messenger bag held a ticket for a 10 p.m. flight from Austin to Kansas City. An interview! The company was eager to fill the position according to the headhunter, and Michael was on the shortlist. His mind scanned the positives. The salary would never match what Harris Cardiac Implants paid, but it was equivalent to his compensation in Raleigh, and the rapidly growing company would cover moving expenses.

Recognizing he would have to give Lisa a sales pitch, Michael had perused the Internet, reading everything about Kansas City he could find. *Hopefully, she's tired of the country by now and getting her buy-in won't be hard.* He planned to stay over to house hunt. Lack of money for a down payment would force them to settle for a smaller house. He made a mental note to call the attorney and see if they could do anything further to get the Raleigh house back or at least take Harris to court.

The traffic eventually thinned allowing Michael to put the Porsche through its paces. His life was back on track. Michael had not felt this positive in weeks. A new job within his grasp, seeing the family—the week was turning out better than expected.

Michael stopped at a flower shop near the school and bought a single red rose for Jessica. The woman had wrapped it in crinkly green paper, tying a shiny red bow around it. Minutes before the program began, he inched into the back of the room, just in time to see Jessica's class walk on stage and arrange themselves on the risers. He could see her in the second row, scanning the audience. Their eyes locked; an expression of relief— then happiness—crossed her face.

The singing began, but Michael was not listening. Instead, he panned the crowd for Lisa. First, he spotted his father, then Lisa and his mother. Stiffening, he flashed back to the many school programs he participated in that his father never attended.

Restless, he leaned against the wall to listen, watching Jessica intently. After the last song, the crowd gave a standing ovation. They clapped, and the students filed out. Michael edged to the exit and, as Jessica passed, blew her a kiss, and handed her the rose. She squealed. After a brief, affectionate embrace, he urged her to follow the class. "I don't want you to get in trouble. See you after school."

Michael waited outside, relieved his mother and father were exiting in front of Lisa. He held his mother close, shook his father's hand, and smiled at his wife, shyly nodding.

"Mom, Dad, could you excuse us? I'd like to take this beautiful woman for coffee."

"Sure," his dad said. Sam turned to Lisa. "We'll take the car back to the house. You guys come on when you're ready."

"Thanks," Michael said. He hooked Lisa's arm and gently led her to the Porsche. "Where can we get coffee?"

"There's a wonderful coffee shop downtown." She provided directions. However, the chilliness in her voice unnerved him. Michael parked and scurried to open her door, but Lisa had already climbed out. She found a table near the entrance while Michael bought two cups.

When setting hers down, Michael noticed she was not wearing her Rolex, but some cheap plastic watch. Easing into the seat across from her, he gave her his most seductive smile.

"I'm sad and scared, Michael. I haven't heard from you in weeks. You never told me you were leaving, and you haven't called. What's happening to us?"

"We'll be OK. Just a bump in the road…. You didn't call, either. You know I love you. I'm just trying to find a job." Desperation engulfed Michael as he struggled with his shame at being jobless. He shifted, gathering all the bravado on hand, explaining his job prospect in Kansas City as well as about the schools, neighborhoods, and job possibilities for her. As he was speaking, Lisa turned to stare out the large plate glass window. He glanced in that direction but could see nothing of interest. Abruptly he stopped talking. An eerie silence punctuated the atmosphere.

"So, you're asking me to drag the kids to a place we've never even been before so you can take a job you may or may not like. If you don't like it, we'll be on the road again."

Looking down, Michael mumbled, "I've got to find work. We can't live without an income."

"Did you even look for anything around here?"

"I'm looking everywhere. This job is the only bite I've had since I started looking."

"A move right now would be terrible for the kids. Jessica's struggling with math, and I've finally found a tutor who works with her and her teacher. Besides, they've started to make friends." She stared at him. "Hell, I'm even making friends." At this point, Lisa crossed her arms over her breasts and glared at him. "You really don't understand, do you? I'm at my limit."

Lisa dropped her arms and gazed out the window. Michael could see a tear rolling down her cheek. Anguish morphed into anger. *Damn her! She's trying to manipulate me, make me feel in the wrong.* Muscles quivering, he wordlessly finished his coffee. Now was not the time to make a scene. Besides, he might not get the job.

"We better get to the house," he said. "I want to visit before I catch my flight out of Austin."

Michael interrupted the silence only when asking for directions. By the time they arrived, the children were home. Jessica ran out of the house and jumped into his arms, babbling nonstop about Princess and her new friend at school who was coming over on Saturday to play.

"Daddy," she said, "Granny Ellen has a cake for our snack. Her cakes are sooo good." She grabbed his hand, dragging him into the house.

Glancing over his shoulder, he saw Lisa climb out of the car and wander toward the barn.

Inside, the aroma of his mother's world-famous coconut cake engulfed Michael. Seeing her brightened his spirits. She insisted on giving him a large glass of milk with his substantial slice. He thought about resisting but then relented. His diet and waistline would have to wait. Once he had a job, he could hire a trainer and work on the growing tub around his midsection.

Jessica joined him at the table. Michael glanced at her. *I can't understand why Lisa thinks she's overweight. She looks just fine. It's probably just a bit of baby fat she'll grow out of…. She doesn't look like she's struggling.*

"Mom," Michael said. "I thought you were going home last week."

"We planned to," Ellen said, joining them with a cup of coffee. "But there's so much to do here. Sam's so much more relaxed and enjoying the challenge…. Besides it's so cold at home…. I'm loving getting to know Jessica and Andrew better."

"It's so fun having them here." Jessica spoke although her mouth was full. Meanwhile, Princess roamed at their feet licking every crumb from beneath the table.

"Michael," Ellen said, "Jessica has some math homework tonight. I thought you could help her."

"I'd love to."

He and Jessica wrapped up the problems in about thirty minutes. As Jessica was putting away her papers, Michael asked, "Where's Andrew?"

"He's out in the barn working on the tractor with Papa Sam. His friend, Eric, is here. They're doing the, uh, something with the motor, I think," said Jessica.

Surprised, Michael said, "Well, let's go see!" They donned their jackets and Michael opened the door. Before he could react, Princess scooted between his feet. He began cursing and yelled, "Go get the dog before she gets lost."

Jessica glanced at him with a funny look. "Daddy, Princess always comes back to the house. I've been letting her wander around since you left."

"Oh." Michael's mood darkened. "Let's go see Andrew."

As Michael approached, he could hear laughter drifting from the barn. He spotted Andrew and another boy squatting next to a big tub.

They had grease on their forearms and were swirling something around in the vat.

Andrew glanced up. "Hi, Dad." He quickly turned his attention back to the tub. Andrew then used a long pair of tongs to fish out ball bearings. He handed them to the other boy who began scrubbing the part furiously with an old towel.

"Well, hello," Sam said. "These boys are quick learners, that's for sure. Pretty soon they'll have the tractor all squared away and ready to go."

Michael gaped. He had not seen his father so relaxed and talkative in years. The boys peppered Sam with questions as he coached them to reinstall the bearings and apply a coat of grease. Michael felt invisible, walking into the middle of a play but having no part; he did not know what to say or do.

come with me. I want to show you the birdhouse Mr. Carl made me." Michael reluctantly followed her several hundred yards down the path to the creek and then to a small clearing. At least his Berluti loafers were not sinking in the mud.

"Look. It's a bluebird house. Mr. Carl says there are lots of them here. Momma even bought me a book of Texas birds so I can look up their names when I see them." Michael listened patiently as Jessica went through the inventory of her common sightings.

They strode back to the work area, where Jessica agreed to be the gofer for tools. Andrew caught Michael up on the latest school happenings with his friend, Eric, chiming in. The young man seemed nice enough, and Michael was relieved that his son had someone to hang with. Making friends in Raleigh had been tough for the teen.

As he watched the interaction between Sam and the boys, turmoil brewed within him. *Why didn't Dad ever treat me like that?*

Eventually, he said his farewell. All called a cheery goodbye and returned to the task at hand.

Michael backtracked to the house to announce his departure. Lisa was in the kitchen with his mother. They were laughing and talking. Lisa was making a list.

His mother said, "We're having a moving party Saturday."

"What?" Michael asked.

"Lisa's new friends, Carl, and the children's new friends are coming over to help us move some of the old furniture out of the house and the new furniture in. It's going to be like the barn raisings you used to hear about. We're providing the meat and Carl is barbequing. You'll be here for it, won't you?" Ellen gave Michael a pleading look.

"No, Mom. I'm staying in Kansas City for the weekend." Michael avoided her eyes and turned to Lisa. "I'll call you after the interview." He bent down and kissed Lisa on the cheek. She sighed.

He glanced up, only to see his mother's raised eyebrows. After squeezing her, he stepped onto the porch; she followed him out.

"Michael, I don't mean to get into your business. I understand you need to find a job, but you need to come home for the weekends."

Michael looked down; his gleaming shoes covered in a light sheen of dust. He missed the family, but his hurt over Lisa's lack of empathy regarding his situation gnawed at him. Why was she incapable of understanding?

"It's complicated."

"Family's important. The kids need you. Lisa needs you."

"I know…. But I have to earn money to take care of them."

CHAPTER 7

Lisa propped open both doors to the tack room, itching to begin work on her retreat. Ellen and Sam were at the store, the children at school. What a great time to get in some uninterrupted cleaning. She started by moving the saddles and bridles out. Dust swirled, setting off a sneezing attack. Within minutes, perspiration was dripping between her breasts. The saddle blankets looked pretty torn up and not worth keeping. Picking one up from the pile, she eyeballed a nest of pink, hairless mice whose eyes had not yet opened, greeting her with squeaks, the mother nowhere to be seen. Dazed, she threw the ragged material back down.

Lisa stepped backward deliberately, watching for the mother. *Are mice mothers aggressive? Will she attack me?* Reaching the outside door, she turned and ran straight into Carl. Lisa shrieked.

"Oh, sorry. I didn't mean to scare you."

Lisa put her hand across her heart. "You scared me, but the mice scare me more."

"Mice?"

"In the saddle blankets. Look." Lisa pointed to the pile in the corner of the room.

Carl poked his head in. "I see."

"Any suggestions?"

"You need to call Sam and Ellen and tell them to pick up some rat poison. I'll take care of them." Carl entered the barn and returned with a shovel.

When Lisa reached into her pocket for her cell phone, Carl said, "You better go to the house to make the call."

"What are you going to do with them?"

"Don't ask. Give me ten minutes and come on back."

Lisa had learned enough to do as told. As she scurried away, her mind churned. The babies were too small to eat poison...if you left them there, they would grow to be big mice and have more babies. You could move them to another area, but Mom may not find them, and they would starve.... Once inside she made her call and lingered awhile.

By the time she returned, he had the saddle blankets piled in a heap in front of the barn, pouring diesel on them. He threw in a match. "WHOOSH!" Flames shot into the air.

Lisa shivered. *Thank God Carl's here.* They looked cute in cartoons, but she knew they could overrun the place. She was dying to know what Carl did but was afraid to ask.

"Could you use some help cleaning up?" Carl asked.

"Oh, I sure could. I'll probably see a mouse under everything I pick up."

Carl laughed and began to move the rest of the odds and ends. At his suggestion, Lisa found the garden hose, and Carl washed down the room. She swept out the standing water.

Exhausted, Lisa sat on one of the benches she had removed from the tack room and wiped her face with her sweatshirt. "Why did Uncle Joe let this place get so bad?"

Carl sighed and sat on the bench. He leaned down, his hands on his knees. "It's hard to explain. After Ruby took sick, Joe tried to keep her here, but she was just too much for him. I'm the one who finally convinced him she had to go to the nursing home. It ate up all their savings. Since he wouldn't sell the land, he had no choice but to do without. It takes money to keep things up. After she died, it's like he just gave up. He got too sickly to do any of the work himself and refused to let me do much of anything."

Lisa thought about Joe, alone. Ruby had been with him all those years. She hoped she was the first one to go. Living by herself frightened her. Her thoughts turned to Michael. While she understood he needed to find employment, his refusal to work from the ranch confused her. *Doesn't he miss me as much as I miss him?*

"Let's get this finished," Carl said. He started piling all the salvageable tack in the back of the barn. Within an hour they had the tack room ready to receive Lisa's furniture.

CHAPTER 8

Lisa woke as the sky turned from black to gray. Quietly she crawled from beneath the covers and donned her bathrobe and slippers, allowing Jessica and Princess to sleep. The day was going to be busy.

She relished stealing into the bathroom, leisurely showering, and fixing her makeup. The mascara and rouge were impractical, but she wanted to make a good impression on her new friends.

Feeling confident in her Wal-Mart jeans and sweatshirt, she wandered into the kitchen. Funny. Six months ago, she would not have been caught dead dressed in anything from the discount giant. Now it seemed perfectly normal. A peek out the window assured her at least one thing would go right today. The weather was perfect! The sun was edging over the trees, revealing a brilliant, blue sky. The forecast called for a bit of wind, but it would not cause too much discomfort.

Settling into one of the front porch's rocking chairs, she sipped a Columbian Breakfast blend, warming her hands around the steaming cup. As the sun's illumination brightened the landscape, Lisa could feel hope arising within her. The rich freshness of the air held a sense of excitement. If Michael were here, the day would be perfect.

She had let him walk away the other day. Why? If he had met her halfway, she might have been willing to move. But he did not. His whole pitch was all about him and what he wanted. He had expressed no concern for her or the children whatsoever. Were they supposed to pick up and tag along blindly like ducklings following a momma duck?

Before Lisa lost her sense of optimism, she forced herself to push Michael out of her mind. *I'm going to enjoy today. My first guests!*

Lost in her thoughts, a noise on the driveway jarred her. Looking up, she saw Carl in his old truck. Pulling level to the porch, he called out, "Good morning. I'm just bringing over the pit. I want to start cooking early. The chickens need a good two hours, and I can't start until the coals have burned down good."

Lisa warmed. Carl was not your typical suburban neighbor, but he was a dear, dear man. "Fine. Why don't you come get some coffee before you unload?"

"Sounds great."

Carl parked and followed Lisa into the kitchen where the aroma of sausage frying indicated Ellen was hard at work. Issuing a hearty "good morning," Ellen insisted Carl eat. They enjoyed a wonderful breakfast of hash browns, sausage, biscuits, and eggs. Carl politely asked whether Ellen ever fixed grits, to which she admitted she had not. Carl promised to bring some over soon.

Lisa leaned back in her chair, took a swallow of coffee, and listened to the pleasant banter. How long had it been since she had sat around the kitchen like this? Her food preparation areas in her previous homes were large, sterile affairs that did not have the cozy ambiance this one had. Sheepishly, she admitted her meals involved Eggos or Pop-Tarts for the kids. They ate most family breakfasts out.

Carl rose. "Ellen, that was a mighty fine meal. There's nothing like a good breakfast to get a person going in the morning. I'm going to get that fire started. I've got some mesquite wood to smoke those chickens with. We're also having some of the link sausage from the hog Lisa nailed." Carl picked up his plate and mug, and despite protests from Ellen, carried them to the sink. Sam followed suit and left to help Carl with the pit.

"Ellen that was truly wonderful." Lisa hugged the bright-cheeked woman. "I need to take biscuit lessons, those were fantastic."

Ellen laughed. "It's great to have people to cook for." She turned to start cleaning and, as Lisa began to pitch in, Ellen said, "Go on out now.

You've got a lot of work to do before everyone arrives. I'll see to it that the kids get up and eat. Then I'll send them out to help."

Lisa needed no more urging. Once outside, she began assembling the tables Sam had fashioned with sawhorses and several long boards he had found behind the barn. The red and white checkered oilcloths Ellen had discovered hid the imperfections of the makeshift tabletop. One would hold mounds of food. Her friends were bringing coleslaw, potato salad, and a pot of pinto beans, and Edith, bless her heart, was bringing two pies from that restaurant in Round Top.

Lisa had just finished putting the beer and wine in the ice chest when Edith arrived. She climbed out of her Explorer and Scotty followed, quickly sniffing the area, particularly where Princess liked to do her thing. He then ran to Lisa, promptly lying on his back and impatiently waiting for a belly rub. Laughing, Lisa leaned down to oblige.

Edith opened the back of the SUV and produced three bags of ice. "I thought you could use this."

"Oh, thanks. I was about to go up to the store to get some."

After safely hiding the pies in the kitchen (Edith insisted they not stay outside as she was afraid nibblers would polish them off before lunch), Lisa showed Edith around the place.

"Oh, it's so good to see some life in this old ranch again. So, this is where you're going to put your office?" Edith pointed to the tack room at the end of the barn.

As they walked over and entered, Lisa said, "Yeah, I think so."

"You don't seem very excited about opening your own firm. I thought you had your heart set on it?"

"Well, I don't know what else I can do. A long time ago I burned out on accounting, but not on the money." Lisa sighed and stepped back outside and into the sunlight.

"You know, moving out here is like getting a second chance at life. It's cheap living compared to the city. I've learned to get along on a lot less than I used to, that's for sure. You should do what you want. Life's too short not to."

"Easy for you to say. You don't have to save for college tuition."

Lisa looked up in time to see Dorothy and her husband, John, arrive with Eric and a crew of teenagers. She was glad for the interruption. Her thoughts turned to Michael and his interview. A small piece of her hoped Michael got the job; she could stop shouldering the burden of family and opening a business would not be necessary. But…would he be happy? Would the kids be happy? *Will I be happy?*

By 10 a.m., everyone had arrived, and work began in earnest. Dorothy had insisted they take Joe and Ruby's belongings to the church resale shop, so the crew emptied the house and loaded its contents on John's trailer. A vigorous discussion then ensued over what would fit in the tiny dwelling. Edith finally took a measuring tape, determining the sizes of the rooms. Then Rachael sketched a drawing of each space so Lisa could figure out which pieces of furniture she wanted to move. Bit by bit, the house assumed the Dunwhitty ambiance.

When satisfied she had sufficiently unpacked, Lisa declared a moratorium on the effort. The boys gravitated to the yard and began a game of flag football. Jessica and her friend went inside to play with Jessica's dolls, which she had not seen in a while. The adults gathered their lawn chairs in a circle and relaxed. As the beer flowed, the talk babbled like a brook.

Lisa swigged a Shiner Bock, feeling the tension leave her neck and shoulders. As she inhaled the earthy smell of the mesquite-smoked chicken, her stomach rumbled. The sun had taken the chill out of the air and was shining through the cedars, leaving a dappled pattern on the ground around her. *God! Have I become a Steel Magnolia?*

Up to this point, the situation felt as if it were temporary. Now that she had unpacked, things were more permanent. Today was like Christmas. Opening boxes, finding things she had not seen in a while. With the help of the crew, she had organized the barn so she could get to those items that would not fit in the house. They had even put the office furniture in the tack room for her. After carefully wrapping the other furnishings to prevent damage, Rachael suggested renting climate-controlled storage in town to protect her belongings as much as possible from the creatures and the elements.

Carl served a plate of sliced sausage, each piece stuck with a toothpick. John took a bite. "Hey, Lisa, this road kill's mighty good. Next time you nail a porker, give me a call."

"No seriously," Edith said, "This is really good. Carl, what all did you put in it?"

"I mixed the pork with venison and used some secret spices."

"And you're not going to reveal the spices?" Dorothy asked.

"No ma'am. It's a family recipe that's been handed down for generations."

Lisa hesitated when Carl waved the plate under her nose.

"Try it, you'll like it," he said.

Thoughts of the squealing swine spurting blood and Carl's butcher knife intruded. About to refuse, memories of the numerous times she had demanded the children *try it just once* sparked her guilt. She grabbed a piece, shoving it in her mouth before her brain could protest further.

Her tenseness waned upon realizing the morsel was delicious. "This is good," she said, helping herself to another piece.

"See, told you," Carl said.

Shortly, he announced the chicken was ready and that it was time to bring out the food. Commotion ensued. The teens happily carried bowls and trays brimming with everything from pickles to freshly baked bread. They ate until they could eat no more. The children hurriedly finished their desserts and drifted away to entertain themselves while the adults swapped stories of other moving experiences. Leaning back in her chair, Lisa listened happily to the idle chatter.

If this is being a Steel Magnolia, I like it. In Raleigh, she had not even known her next-door neighbors. Oh, she had seen them a time or two, but could not tell you anything about them, only the type of car they drove or perhaps what time in the evening they pulled their luxury vehicles into their home fortresses. Soaring wooden fences and automatic garage doors which snapped shut like a drawbridge as soon as the inhabitants entered their castle shielded each citadel from the neighbors' watchful eyes. She had been on Dog Run Road only a few weeks but felt like she had friends—good friends—who would help her with any emergency life might throw at her.

And Michael's father, how wonderful he was! She had never spent much time around him but found him to be gentle and caring. Lisa was so glad the children were getting to know him. She briefly wondered why Michael felt Sam had been such an inadequate parent; he certainly was not a poor grandparent.

The conversation soon turned to when Lisa was going to open her CPA firm. Dorothy gave her a rundown of everything she had heard about the number of people in the county doing this kind of work.

"I don't know," Lisa said. "Frankly, I don't have my heart in it. It seems so boring. I'm ready to do something else, you know."

"So do something new," Edith said. She then poured herself a large tumbler of wine. Taking a deep swig, she said, "You're starting a new life. Start a new career. Why do we always keep doing the same thing? After all, I took over the grocery store."

"Easy for you to say. I've got kids to raise and put through college. This place needs a lot of work. That takes a lot of money."

"What about the oil well?" Ellen asked. "I thought you made lots of money that way."

Lisa made a face. "The oil's played out here. The well's practically worthless. I get enough royalties a year to buy Jessica a Happy Meal."

Carl said, "At first it paid off big time. Now it runs only a couple of days a month. One of the men who comes by and turns it off and on told me that oil seeps into the bottom of the well, it's pumped out, and then they have to wait for it to fill up again."

"The timber lease brings in some money," Lisa said, "but not enough for us to live on."

"Well, what about the cattle business?" Sam asked. "I see lots of cows around here."

John chuckled. "You're lucky if you break even with ranching. Folks have cattle these days for the tax exemption."

"I beg to differ. There's a new cattle market that's hot right now—miniature cattle," said Dorothy.

"What do you mean?" Carl asked. "I never heard of any such thing."

Dorothy put her beer down and spoke about the mini cow business. The more she talked, the more animated she became, gesturing wildly as she explained the cows could be as short as thirty-six inches at maturity and weigh between 500 and 900 pounds.

Lisa listened carefully, taking it all in. As Dorothy expounded on the pros and cons of the twenty-six different breeds, Lisa became uncomfortable. It had been a long time since she had been ignorant about a topic under discussion. She was undeniably out of her comfort zone.

"Excuse me, Dorothy, but why on earth would you bother with this size animal?" Sam asked. "You know, I'm a city guy myself, I don't know that much about cows."

"Well for one thing, because they are so small, they're easier on the ground. Heavy livestock can tear up pastures. Also, you don't need as much land to raise them as you do for large cattle. You can put ten of them on the same amount of land that you can put two normal cows on, and they only eat about a third of the feed that the full-sized ones eat. They're also a plus when it comes to selling the meat. These days, most people don't have room in their freezer for a regular-sized butchered cow."

"Hmm," said Carl. He removed his pipe from his mouth. "Probably easier to deal with, too. I know that old white Angus bull Joe had used to scare me nearly half to death. One day I was out working on the fence, and he got upset with me. He came toward me, and I got behind a tree. He'd move one way; I'd move the other. After about ten minutes of that nonsense, he got tired and left."

"Yeah, and they're also easier to load in trailers and tend to medically," said Dorothy.

As Carl and John traded "bull" stories, Lisa's mind drifted. She saw herself sitting astride a horse in the pasture that abutted Zink's Creek, watching the herd of miniatures intently as they grazed. Later that night by the campfire down near the creek, she and Michael would drink cowboy coffee and sing songs to the cattle.... Lisa sat up quickly, furious with herself. How stupid of her. The idea that she and Michael could live here happily ever after was a bunch of bullshit!

"OK, Dorothy, I hear what you're saying," said John. "But why would you make money with small cows when you can't make money with big ones?"

"The meat," Edith said. "The meat."

"The meat? What's so different about the meat?" John asked.

"What I mean is you would want to go natural beef—you know— no hormone stimulants—natural feeds, grass, hay, that kind of stuff. I've been reading up on market changes and organic's big, especially in Austin."

"Now that's the first sensible thing I've heard all day," John said. "You could sell small lots to specialty stores at top price. Besides, this land's been vacant for so long most all the pesticides must be gone."

Now Lisa was all ears. Her friends in Raleigh had been into organic foods with a vengeance and were very particular; not wanting to eat anything that might be tainted with pesticides. From her years of accounting, she was familiar with the financial side of the agricultural business. It certainly seemed more interesting than preparing tax returns.

"Now that's something I might be able to sink my teeth into," said Lisa.

"Wow," said Rachael. "Now that's a big change: from CPA to MCO."

"MCO?" Lisa asked.

"Yeah, Miniature Cattle Owner. You need to put that behind your name on your business card—Lisa Dunwhitty CPA, MCO," said Rachael.

Lisa laughed.

Cleaning up from the party consumed the rest of the afternoon, with Ellen insisting on sending the remaining food home with the guests.

***

After everyone retired, Lisa opened her laptop at the kitchen table and began serious research on the miniature issue, the market for natural beef, and the projections for beef sales. When she looked up, it was 2 a.m. Shocked, she closed her computer and put it away. How the time had flown! What a thrill to be learning something new. That had not happened in so long. This cattle thing just might work.

Crawling into her own bed rather than sharing with Jessica made her feel like a queen. A review of the day left her with a warm feeling inside. As she nodded off, she realized she had not missed Michael for twelve hours.

***

Michael tightly wrapped his overcoat as he hopped into the car. Tiny ice pellets whipped his face and clung to his body. Closing the door, he ruffled his hair with his gloved hand and brushed the frosty particles off his coat, wishing he had brought a hat. Cranking the engine, he heaved a grateful sigh when it caught. He had stopped for lunch before beginning a driving tour of Kansas City residential neighborhoods, but glancing at the darkening sky, he returned to the hotel.

Easing up to the bellman, Michael thankfully abandoned the automobile. Once inside, he zoomed over and grabbed the Saturday newspaper, taking it into the bar area. Irish coffee is exactly what the doctor ordered. While sipping the gut-warming drink, he glanced through the local newspaper.

This town is too cold and bush-league. I can hear the kids now. His mood plummeted; he ordered an extra shot of whiskey to pour into his coffee. He knew they would offer him the job, but should he take it?

The fight would be hellacious, he could hear Andrew's livid shrieks, see Lisa's angry stare boring into his soul, and feel Jessica's wet sobs as he held her close.

But if he did not take it, then what? The recruiter had warned Michael that Harris's problems had tarnished him and not to be too picky. He motioned to the bartender. "Whiskey—neat."

No, nothing doing. I'm not going to live in this Eskimo village. I'll have to keep looking. Sighing, Michael gathered his coat and newspaper, signed the tab, and returned to his room. He moved his flight to Sunday morning and sent the recruiter an e-mail. Then he lay on the bed and dozed, still a bit relaxed from the alcohol.

In no time, he began to daydream. The woman he had met at the hotel lounge popped into his mind. He wondered what she was doing. How attentive she had been, unlike Lisa. Leaning over, he opened his wallet and took out her card, studying it intently. Sharon Wilson…Sharon Wilson. He felt himself tremble. *Am I crazy?* He had never cheated on Lisa in his life. *I won't cheat. I'll ask her for a simple dinner—nothing more.* It would be good to have someone to talk to…. As his mind turned to Lisa, he returned Sharon's information to his wallet.

Michael put his head back on the pillow and thought about the first time he had met his wife. They had been in the same first-year Spanish class in college. His attraction had been immediate— not just to her looks—but to the way she confidently responded to the professor's questions. Completely mastering the language, she rolled her r's as if she had grown up in Guadalajara. He asked her to coach him and then to a football game. They had been inseparable ever since.

Rather than wait for the love of his life to come to her senses, he would stop at the ranch on the way back to Houston and plead his case for her to join him.

CHAPTER 9

Lisa flipped on the lights in her office and plugged in the electric heater. Looking around, she kept her coat on. Her modern Ikea desk looked bizarrely out of place in the corner of the tack room. Not having more windows was irritating, but at least it kept the room warmer. Hmm, she would have to get a rug so it would seem cozier.

She started her laptop and tested the Wi-Fi. Success! Having a computer geek in the family was so nice. Andrew had set it up this morning before Ellen had driven him to Eric's house. Thank goodness he had found someone to pal around with. Hopefully, this friendship will last. At least it did not appear he had gotten into any more fights.

Lisa glanced about. Ellen was such a sweetie pie. She had picked up a small, cheap coffeepot at the store and set up a refreshment area. Since there was no running water in the barn, Ellen had brought in several jugs of water. Lisa laughed. Gourmet snickerdoodle coffee served in a tin mug in a tack room! She would have never imagined herself here in a million years.

Something was missing. Lisa went into the barn and returned with the small saddle. Removing her gloves and dampening a dishcloth, she cleaned off the dust. Then she arranged it, pommel down, on her filing cabinet. With some leather cleaner, it would look almost new.

Coffee in hand, she settled into her recliner, only to hear a phone ping—a text from Michael.

Declined job. Family wouldn't be happy here. I miss you and the kids. Will be at the ranch around 2 to discuss. Boarding plane now.

Dread and excitement welled within her. She missed Michael terribly.... Closing her eyes, she imagined a family business. Michael, with his sales and marketing skills, could round up all the customers the mini cow business could handle while she took care of day-to-day operations, accounting, and finance. The children could stay in this nurturing environment, and all could develop lasting friendships. Eventually, they could build a state-of-the-art house and turn the farmhouse into their corporate headquarters. Once they started, Michael could expand their enterprise in any way he wished.

But can I convince him? Lisa began plotting her pitch.

By one, she had showered and dressed in her favorite slacks outfit. After working diligently on her makeup, she chose Michael's favorite perfume, rubbing a bit on her wrists as well as on her throat and behind the ear lobes. Rifling through her jewelry, she chose the diamond studs Michael had given her for Valentine's Day last year. Spying the Rolex, her mind shifted to her former life. Some part of her longed for the high-end restaurants, high-stakes corporate meetings, and the elation at purchasing something she felt she had to have. But another part.... She snapped the watch onto her wrist and sat impatiently in the den, thankful that Ellen had noticed the fact that she and Michal needed some alone time.

A knock at the door startled Lisa. *Knock? But he lives here?* Her skin tingled at the realization of how far apart they had grown in recent weeks. As she approached the door, he opened it and timidly stepped in. Lisa's heart did somersaults. *How I've missed him.* He gathered her in his arms, giving her a slow leisurely kiss.

"I've missed you so much," Michael said.

Lisa reluctantly released herself from his grasp and, grabbing his hand, led him into the den. "What do you think?"

"Wow! It looks so different with our furniture here. Almost seems like home."

"It does." Lisa grabbed Michael's hand and led him to the couch. "Tell me about the job interview."

"The job was OK, but I didn't like Kansas City at all. Too bush-league, too cold. I don't know...I didn't pick up good vibes."

"Any other leads?"

"No, but I'm hoping the headhunters will have something when I get back to Houston."

Lisa grabbed his hand. "I've been thinking. We have a chance to start a business here, one both you and I can be involved in." Then she began the hard sell. As she talked, his hand flinched. Turning his head, he stared at the fireplace while withdrawing from her grasp. Lisa stopped mid-sentence, Michael's silence frightening.

He rose, facing her. "You just don't get it. That's not what I want to do for the rest of my life. Why can't you get that into your head? ... I don't fit in here. We should be planning a future where we'll both be happy."

Lisa wanted to explain all the warmth and love she had received here, the feeling of connectedness, how the intimate relationship with nature energized her, how.... Words failed. *Could I ever be happy again in my former life?*

Michael reached out his hand. "Please, you and the kids move to Houston with me. Let's start fresh. I know there's a job there for both of us."

Lisa ignored the olive branch. "It just doesn't make sense. If we do, it'll cost us a fortune to get settled. Then we'll probably be uprooted when you take a job somewhere else. We'll stay here until you find a job."

Michael rose, turned on his heel, and left.

Lisa's initial anger that Michael could not understand the disruption moving several times would cause, turned into downright depression. *What now?* She trudged into the bedroom, changing into her jeans and then washed the makeup off her face.

In the barn, she grabbed a hoe, shovel, and work gloves, then made her way to the mess of a vegetable garden. Viciously she worked out her anger on the budding weeds, thinking of Michael and his stubbornness every time she swung the implement.

She only stopped when Ellen called her name. Glancing at her Casio, she realized she had been at it for nearly two hours.

"Michael's left?" Ellen asked.

"He went back to Houston."

Lisa watched Ellen's trembling chin.

"He wants us to move to Houston…. I can't see it now. The kids are happy, I'm happy…I'm afraid if we move, we won't be there that long and have to move again when he finds a job…. We need to stay put."

Ellen moved in, embracing Lisa. "What can I do?"

"Nothing. It's something the two of us need to work out."

***

Ellen, Sam, and Carl sat around the kitchen table as Lisa laid out her plan. "Michael's still looking for a job, but we've got to get money coming in here until he can find something. I thought about a CPA practice, but it just doesn't make sense. In case we move from the ranch, I'd be letting the clients down. If we do the mini-cow thing and we move, I can just sell the cows. And, if we stay here, we have a solid business going."

Lisa then explained how she had calculated the number of cattle two hundred acres could hold, who to contact regarding sales, and feed required for natural beef.

"Have I missed anything?" Lisa asked.

"Well, Lisa, you sure got this thought out," Carl said. "The fence'll take lots of work. The little fellers might slip out, so we'll have to run another string close to the ground. Also, you got lots of weeds and mesquite in the pasture. If you want to stay natural, I don't know. You'll have to drag each of those mesquites out by the roots, I guess. The way most people kill it is to put a special poison on them. They are hard to kill. And it's close to $100 a gallon."

"My God," Sam said. "I've never heard of something so hard to get rid of. Maybe we should start with fifty acres. Then we could clear the other a bit at a time."

"I think that would be better," Carl said. "Come to think of it, we could use the cleared fifty acres for hay. Growing your own hay will save you money next winter. The cows can eat around the mesquite until we have a chance to clear the whole thing."

"Sam, the tractor—it works now, right?" Lisa asked.

"Doing good."

"Also, we need to buy hay for the cows to eat until the spring grass comes in. You'll need to cross fence to keep the cows out of the hay field." Carl paused and then added, "You're going to need a truck, don't forget."

"Oh, yeah." Lisa frowned. She had been putting off that purchase since she and Andrew could not agree on what to get.

"And come to think of it," Carl said, "We also could use a Mule."

"A mule? Why on earth would we need one? Are you planning to plow the fields with it?" Ellen asked.

Carl laughed. "No, Ellen, I didn't mean the animal, I meant the vehicle, Mule. You know, it's like a four-wheeler but seats two people and has a small truck bed in back to carry tools. Walking and carrying equipment over two hundred acres can be really tough."

Lisa giggled nervously. She had lots to learn. Scribbling copious notes, she said, "Carl, how many bulls do you think we need per cow?"

Carl grinned and chuckled. "I hope you don't mind me saying so, but this isn't going to be as easy as you think. You only need one bull. Put two bulls in with a bunch of heifers and you're going to see some bloody fights. Those tiny critters are sure to make the same fuss over the ladies as the big ones do. One will be enough as long as he does his business."

Lisa jotted on her pad and, looking up, said, "Carl, you're a lifesaver. You don't know how much I appreciate it. I'll talk with Dorothy and ask her to help me decide which breed to buy. I'm going to the office so I can get started on the business plan."

Ellen stood up and said, "I'm putting a roast on for supper. Let me know if you need anything else."

"Carl, if you could help me in the barn, I'd appreciate it," Sam said. "I want to see if I can get the posthole digger running off the tractor. Also, I need to inspect the fence line so I can figure out how much material we need to make repairs."

"I'd be happy to."

After an hour of pouring over her 401K balance as well as the price of cattle, Mules, and trucks, Lisa rose and ambled over to make some coffee. A new truck was not in the picture; Andrew was going to have to accept that fact. *Hopefully, I can get John to give me a bank loan for the cattle and withdraw a bit more from my 401K to get the Mule and fencing supplies.* She wanted to reserve some of her nest egg for emergencies. Offering to do contract work for some of the local CPA firms until the business got going was a possibility. Hopefully, that would tide them over.

A knock startled her.

"Yes?"

Carl stuck his head around the door. "Mind if I come in?"

"Of course not." Lisa motioned to the recliner.

He was carrying a small box which he placed on her desk.

"What's that?"

"It's for you."

Puzzled, Lisa looked inside. A rather large scrapbook sat at the bottom of the box. On top of it were several spiral notebooks that had seen their fair share of use. "What's this?"

"These belonged to Ruby. They're pretty personal. I didn't want to give them to you until I was sure you would respect them. Go ahead, take a look. That one first." Carl pointed to the album.

Lisa lifted it from the box and sat down, gently opening its red cover. Shocked, she carefully leafed through the pages which were becoming brittle with age. Pictures of her when she was born, with her father as she learned to ride a bike. Then, as she got older, newspaper clippings of her placing third in the one-hundred-yard dash at the eighth-grade track meet and graduating from high school with honors. Pictures of her wedding, baby pictures of her children, notices about her promotions.

"I know Mother said she'd sent a few things, but I didn't realize…"

"Your father was Joe's favorite. Joe and Ruby took it pretty hard when they learned they couldn't have children. Ruby had always wanted a little girl. I guess she just felt like you were their granddaughter."

"What's in the spiral notebooks?"

"Ruby's diaries."

"Have you read them?"

"No. I figure I know Ruby well enough."

"Why should I read them?"

"You don't know Ruby and Joe at all. This way, you'll know 'em like I do. Now, I got some work to do."

After Carl left, Lisa picked up the oldest of the notebooks and began to read. Ruby had met Joe while he was in the army and stationed in California. A whirlwind romance ensued, and, after his discharge, he brought her to the ranch. She disliked it at first. Bored and lonely, she thought about leaving. But Joe and the land grew on her. Ruby learned to love the stillness of the morning before the sun rose and the ferocious intensity of thunderstorms that periodically swept in from the northwest.

Lisa read greedily, taking in every word. *Ruby understood! That's what she was trying to tell me. It's hard, but you can do it.*

Lisa had never seen tough times like they did. They had barely survived the drought of the 1950s and had been forced to sell off almost their entire herd at rock-bottom prices. Slowly they built the place back with Carl's help.

Then Lisa's heart sank. Ruby was pregnant! She and Joe were ecstatic. They prepared a nursery in the room where Andrew slept while Ruby and her friends made a baby quilt. Then months went by without an entry. Finally, Ruby wrote a few short paragraphs. The baby was stillborn.

Lisa got up from her desk to find a tissue. She blew her nose and continued to read. They had buried Regina Lois Franks in the family cemetery. But Ruby, still grieving, took the quilt her friends had made as well as Regina's christening outfit and buried them at Julia's place in a small cedar box Joe made. Ruby frequently went to the place to be with her daughter.

Julia's place? Lisa glanced back through the notebooks but could not find any other mention of Julia's place.

The diaries ended about a year after Regina's birth. Lisa stored them and the scrapbook in her filing cabinet and then called her mother.

"I knew she had a stillborn child. Your dad said the two of them were just devastated. Apparently, Joe tried to get Ruby to adopt, but she refused."

Lisa chatted with her mother a bit, explaining what was going on, and promising to call later when she could talk longer.

Lisa quickly wrote a business plan to present to the bank. She was all in, now, no turning back. By the time she had finished this exercise and drawn up a strategy for tomorrow, it was nearing 5 p.m. Before closing her computer, she dashed off an e-mail to Michael informing him of what she was doing—she would not ask for permission because he would have a fit.

***

The next morning Michael piled his overcoat on top of the seat next to him and took out his iPad. He had a few minutes before his flight boarded. Seeing Lisa's e-mail, he immediately opened it, expecting an apology. He scanned, then reread, the missive. Buying damn cows! How ridiculous. He would never pry her off the place now. Furiously he turned off the machine and stood up.

Grabbing his coat and briefcase, he paced rapidly through the terminal to work off his anger. *How could she force me to choose between my family and earning a decent living? We can't live there and earn decent money. She can't do this to me, to us. We need to stay a family.*

His iPhone interrupted the agony. Pulling it out, he saw the call was from the ranch. He let it go to voice mail. After several minutes, he listened to the message. It was his mother, asking about his interview in Dallas and wishing he were there. Irritably he erased her communication and put the cell back into its clip on his belt.

Michael sat, watching a couple stroll down the concourse. Quickly, he fished Sharon's business card out of his billfold, picked up the phone, and punched in her cell number before he lost his nerve.

***

Jessica popped into the kitchen where Lisa and Ellen were chatting. "Hi, Mom, Granny Ellen. Whose truck is that outside?"

"It's our new truck," Lisa said. "Like it?"

"Yeah, it's cool. What did you do with your car?"

"I traded it in. I was lucky to get this truck for it."

Ellen put two cookies and a small glass of milk on the table for Jessica. As she ate her snack, she babbled happily about her day at school. Then she stood and stuck her hand in the cookie jar.

"Jessica, no more cookies. Two is enough," Lisa said.

"Oh, Mom, can't I have just one more?"

"No, you can't. Now go change and take Princess out. You both need some exercise."

Jessica stomped off, pouting. Both Lisa and Ellen sat in silence until her daughter and dog left the house.

"Lisa," Ellen said gently, "Don't be so hard on her. She's not that heavy."

"Well, yes, she is. And puberty will put more weight on her. You know childhood obesity is a problem, and I don't want her to turn into a balloon. She's halfway there already." Lisa paused. "And Ellen, could you try to give her some more nutritious snacks rather than cookies? I'd sure appreciate it."

Lisa didn't want to push too hard. Ellen was only trying to help, and Lisa cherished her presence. She continued hurriedly, "You and Sam have been lifesavers, you know that, and I love you being here. But I worry about Jessica, I really do."

Ellen sighed. "Alright, I'll watch what I fix. I guess all of us could eat a little healthier, couldn't we?"

Relieved, Lisa smiled. "We sure could."

The door opened and Lisa heard Andrew drop his books on the bench in the entryway before poking his head into the kitchen.

"Hey, Mom, Granny Ellen. Who's here?"

"No one, just us." Ellen got up to get Andrew some cookies.

"No, I mean the truck. Who's here?"

Lisa took a deep breath and then began, "It's our truck. I traded the Volvo for it."

"Mom, that truck is a piece of crap. I can't believe you bought it. It's not even new. You promised you'd let me help pick out the truck. I can't drive that thing around. I wouldn't be caught dead in it."

As Andrew raged, Ellen set the cookies on the table and excused herself, leaving Lisa to deal with the surly teenager. As she listened in horror, Lisa heard a spoiled, unappreciative brat. And, as her dismay grew, Lisa realized she and Michael had taught him to be that way. He had always gotten what he wanted. So had she and Michael, for that matter.

Rather than rave back, Lisa cried, her anger fueling tears. "Young man, stop this instant."

Frightened, Andrew shut his mouth and stared uneasily at Lisa.

"Let's both take a few minutes to calm down. When you feel you can carry on a civilized conversation, meet me in my office." Lisa picked herself up and left the house.

A few minutes later, a chastened Andrew poked his head into the tack room. Lisa motioned him in. He sat in the extra chair, saying nothing.

"Andrew, it's not your fault, it's all mine." Lisa fought back tears. "I've never taught you the value of money. But it's not too late."

For the next forty-five minutes, Lisa poured out their financial situation, explaining all options and showing him the account balances as well as clarifying the situation with the house in Raleigh.

"So, it's time to live in the real world. Life's not always fun or fair, for that matter. Right now, your father doesn't have a job, so you have to stay here and go to school. When he gets one, we'll see." Lisa sat silently looking at him, feeling guilty she had not taught him to respect what he had more. She continued, "I sure could use your help. Carl and your grandfather need to fence and clear the pasture. If you'll help, I'll see about letting you take driver ed so you can get a hardship license."

Andrew was distressed. "I'll think about it." He rose and walked out. When he was out of earshot, Lisa burst into tears.

***

Glancing at her friends, Lisa laughed. The weekly gatherings had been her salvation, a time when she could talk out her problems with sympathetic, level-headed women.

"So, Lisa, how's the work coming in the pasture?" Rachael asked.

"It's about to kill me. I'm sore all over. That mesquite is the damnedest plant I've ever seen." Lisa then began an in-depth narrative. She had broken down and hired a dozer with a root plow to dig up the fifty acres after realizing the enormity of the task. The plow had forged eighteen inches underground, churning up mesquite and cedar, leaving a chunky rutted mess in its wake. Everyone, Ellen included, had donned gloves and long-sleeved shirts to gingerly pick up the spiky plants which Andrew had eagerly burned along with the brush in several bonfires. Then Sam and Carl spent countless hours running the disc harrow over the area, eliminating clumps of soil, and smoothing out the ground. Finally, they planted native grass, which was coming up nicely.

"Looking at a fence," Lisa said, "You don't realize all the work that goes into it. But the good news is, we're all cross-fenced and have 150 acres ready for the cattle."

A cheer erupted.

"So, exactly when are they coming?" Dorothy asked.

"They're scheduled next week. Thursday, in fact. I expect them to roll in from West Texas around two in the afternoon."

"I'll put it on my calendar," Dorothy said.

Sometimes Dorothy seemed more excited about the cattle than Lisa. After much research, she and Dorothy had decided on Herefords. They were a popular breed line and could adapt to the hot weather. She had considered milk cows as well but building and equipping a dairy was just too expensive.

Edith poured Lisa another glass of the house wine and asked, "How are the kids?"

Lisa frowned, took a sip, and then said, "Jessica's still having trouble with her math even though she's working with a tutor. Math comes so easy to me. I just don't understand why she has such a tough time. And then, with Ellen here, she overeats. I swear, despite what I've done to feed her sensibly, she's put on a good five pounds."

"She doesn't seem so fat to me," Edith said.

"She will be if she keeps eating like she has been."

"Is she getting exercise?" Rachael asked.

"Well, not really, I guess. She comes home and plays with her dolls."

"Why don't you get her involved with the cattle? You know, let her have a couple as pets? She'll need to take care of them and feed them," Rachael said. "That's good exercise."

"But then I can't sell them. She'd never let me!"

"But you could let her show one," Dorothy said. "She could join the 4-H. We'll pick out a calf for her when they arrive. It'll be perfect. If she gets out and stays busy, she won't think about eating."

"Well, it's worth a try," Lisa said.

"And Andrew?" Rachael asked.

Lisa told them how Andrew had called Michael, wanting to stay with him. According to Ellen, Michael said it would not be possible until he got a job. "Since then, he's been helping with the fencing. He's rather enjoying driving the Mule and has gotten pretty good with the T-Posts. He's also hounding me because I said he could take driver ed. I signed him up, and he starts next week."

"You'll be glad," Edith said. "I was so relieved when my kids got to drive. I was tired of taking them everywhere."

"I know what you mean," Lisa said. "I've been spoiled because either Sam or Ellen takes them anywhere they want to go. That's about to end, though. Ellen told me she and Sam are returning home next week."

"Ouch!" Dorothy said. "I know they've been a godsend."

"Are you OK with that?" Rachael asked.

"Guys, I hate to admit it, but I'm a bit scared. I've depended on them so heavily. But I do understand. They've been down here since the middle of January. They need to get home and take care of things."

"What about Michael?" Edith asked.

Lisa grimaced. She was sure they were all dying to know the status of their relationship. None of them had met him. "I don't know. We haven't talked in a while. He's still looking for a job and has no intention of coming back until he has one."

The group sat mutely, sipping their drinks.

"Well, that does it, then," Rachael said. "You need some protection at home."

"You mean a burglar alarm?" Lisa asked.

"No, silly, a gun. You know there's nothing that puts terror into the heart of a trespasser like the noise a shotgun makes when a shell is pumped into the chamber."

"A gun, are you crazy?" Lisa eyed the women, but no one else seemed to think the idea was absurd. "Edith, you live alone. Do you have a gun?"

"Yes. I've got two. I have my dad's twelve-gauge shotgun and a small pistol I keep in my nightstand. Bought the pistol when that crazy railcar killer was roaming the state murdering people. They were looking for him on trains in Flatonia."

"Dorothy?"

"Of course. Everyone in Texas has firearms, especially out in the country. You may need to chase off the coyotes. I know they don't usually bother big cattle, but I don't know about the minis."

"It's settled then. We'll go shopping tomorrow. I have a day off," Rachael said.

"But I don't know how to shoot," Lisa said.

"What a whiny one you are. Have some more wine with that whine," Edith said. Lisa made a face as Edith poured the remainder of the bottle into Lisa's glass.

"We'll have shooting lessons next Friday," Rachael said, "for you and the kids."

"Does Jessica really need to join us?"

"You're damn tooting," said Edith. "Kids who learn to respect guns as dangerous weapons are safer than those who just think they're toys."

"OK, we'll be ready." Lisa finished the last of her drink and stood. "Gotta get home, ladies. It's been really fun. See you next week." Gathering her coat, Lisa headed out into the chill, damp night.

***

Meticulously Lisa reviewed the scant remains of her 401K accounts. She had been spending money faster than she realized. Carl had told her they had bought enough hay to tide them over, provided there was sufficient rain to produce copious amounts of grass this summer. He warned, however, that she would need to buy some for the winter months.

One thing for sure, Lisa absolutely refused to touch the money they had put away for the kids' college. Thank God they had funded the accounts sooner than later. After contacting area accountants, she picked up enough work to cover the basics—utilities, food, and gasoline. The savings accounts were now off-limits except for fence repair and equipment necessary for the cattle operation.

Lisa swiveled around in her chair, eying the box leaning against the wall. She could not believe she had spent good money on that thing. Even though Andrew had been excited, she had refused to remove the gun from the box until Rachael arrived. *Imagine—I've gone from toting a Gucci to toting a gun in a matter of months.*

The thought of her Gucci bag sparked an idea. Why not take all her high-end things stored in the attic to a resale shop in Austin? Hopefully, she could raise enough money to get the kids new clothes for the summer.

Back at the house, Lisa retrieved the kitchen chair and placed it under the fold-out ladder in the ceiling. A cord hung down that you pulled to access the ladder, but she had not been tall enough to reach it. After a bit of finagling, she fully opened the ladder and climbed up with a flashlight to inventory the boxes. While doing so, she caught a glimpse of something pushed tightly under the eaves.

Training the beam on the object, she realized it was an old chest. Curiosity got the best of her, and she carefully made her way over, balancing precariously on the beams. One slip would send her straight through the ceiling, and no one was home to help. *Oh, what the hell. I want to know what's in there.*

Finally, she squatted beside the footlocker. It was small and quite battered, exuding the odor of dust. The leather handles on both ends had long ago rotted off. The rounded top sported vertical wooden staves and seemed to have some type of embossed pattern on it. The front displayed three mechanisms to keep the lid closed.

Lisa struggled to position the heavy box so she could raise the lid. *What might be in there? A skeleton? Baby mice?* Taking a deep breath, she raised the top and trained the flashlight into its recesses. A few pictures, an old dress, some old books. Fascinated, Lisa gently let the cover down and considered how to get the treasure chest out by herself. Waiting for Andrew's help was the only option. Leaving the trunk, she eased her way back to the boxes of clothing and accessories and quickly surveyed them.

Closing the attic, Lisa headed into her bedroom. After a few minutes, she picked up a small leather pouch hidden under her brassieres and gently unrolled it. Inspecting her jewelry, she determined she could get another $10,000 for selling the pieces she would part with. Sighing, she eyed her Rolex. *I don't need it, do I?*

Lisa removed the Casio from her wrist and tried on her Datejust Special Edition. She hadn't worn it for some time. Its diamond bezel caught the sunlight streaming in the window and threw sparkling patterns on the wall. Lisa lay on the bed and shut her eyes.

This farm thing had been moving too fast. She had not realized what a challenge it would be. Owning a ranch should involve oil royalties, a foreman to care for the day-to-day details, a private plane, and homes in Houston and Raleigh—not such a big unbelievable mess. Her anger with Michael had kept her from admitting she might have been wrong; she had been plunging deeper into debt ever since. *Trading my Gucci for a gun? Is this what I want for the rest of my life?*

She missed Michael. Now that Ellen and Sam were leaving, panic fluttered within her; she had never lived without another adult. And now....

Lisa put on her coat and hurried outside, picking her way down the seldom-used path that wound past the vegetable garden and through a small copse of trees. She carefully opened the wrought iron gate that led to the family cemetery. Joe and Ruby shared a headstone near the entrance. Weeds that choked the rest of the plot had yet to reclaim the area around their memorial. Lisa sank to her knees in front of the grave and thought about the inscription:

The unity that binds us all together that makes this earth a family and all men brothers and the sons of God is love.

She wailed. "Uncle Joe, I know you put so much faith in me. But I can't do it. I can't live here."

Overwhelmed, Lisa leaned down and bawled. At the height of her anguish, a calm overtook her. Lisa sat back and closed her eyes. The rustling branches and the faraway cries of birds delivered a rhythmical lullaby. The earthy scent around her brought a promise of growth and renewal.

Reinvigorated, Lisa rose and set off to the house. Returning to her bedroom, she hid the Rolex in the drawer, determined to sell the other jewelry along with her clothes.

CHAPTER 10

Lisa heard a vehicle turn into the driveway. Looking at her watch, she guessed it was Rachael. Striding to the bedroom, she gingerly lifted the Remington 870 shotgun out of the box. At Rachael's suggestion, she had purchased a junior model because it was shorter and would be easier to control. Then, after much debate, they had chosen the twenty gauge rather than the twelve gauge. It was not as powerful, according to Rachael, but it would kick less. Killing stuff was not her goal, she merely wanted to scare the bejeebers out of anyone or anything threatening her family or herd.

With Andrew and Jessica in tow, she joined Rachael in the driveway.

"Oh, you look tough," her friend said. Lisa conveyed a dirty look and waved the rifle in the air, setting Rachael on a laughing jag.

The group set up behind the stock tank. The man-made structure entailed a large cavity scooped out of the earth. Piling dirt from the hole into the lowest area of the pit kept collected rainwater from escaping. The result was a steep outer bank on the deep end of the tank. As Rachael explained, the dam made a perfect backdrop because, if you missed the target, the bullets would go straight into the earth.

Safety was the first lesson. Lisa was relieved that Andrew was paying close attention as Rachael described how dangerous firearms could be.

"No pointing any weapon at anyone or anything, ever, unless you intend to kill. Also, when we are shooting, you never shoot until everybody is back from the target area and standing behind you." With that, she pulled out earplugs. "You can ruin your hearing. Never shoot without these."

Rachael patiently worked with Andrew, showing him how to load the gun and point it. While Rachel spoke, Lisa was busy setting up tin cans on a log. Once Lisa had returned and taken her position behind the firing line, Rachael pointed to Andrew. "Let's see what you got."

Andrew, sitting on the ground so he could steady his arms on his knees, pumped the gun once, flipping a shell into the chamber.

"Squeeze it nice and slow," Rachael whispered. "Don't jerk; don't move until the lead balls have hit their mark."

CRACK! Dirt flew below the first can to the left.

"Not bad. Is this the first time you've ever shot a gun?" Rachael asked.

"Well, I shot a few times at camp, but it was a BB gun, not a real one like this." Andrew's face appeared flushed with excitement. The lessons continued, and Andrew quickly hit the cans with ease. He then excused himself, saying he had homework to do.

"Fine, but when you finish, come back so I can show you how to clean the gun," Rachael said. "Alright, Miss Jess, your turn."

"Oh, I don't want to shoot. I don't ever want to use a gun. I love animals too much." Jessica appeared a bit on edge.

"Let's put it this way. If you saw a big, mean coyote coming toward Princess, would you fire a gun into the air to chase it away?"

"Yes."

"Well, then, just in case, you need to learn how to shoot."

Her lessons began. Because the gun was heavy for a youngster, Rachel had her lie down on the ground. Once comfortable, she fired away. After about fifteen minutes, Jessica felt confident she knew how to use the weapon although her shots were not always true.

After her daughter left, Lisa grabbed the shotgun, feeling positive that, if her children could master it, she could.

"Here, hand me the gun," said Rachael. Lisa obliged and Rachel put it to her shoulders. "I'm at my best when I have a reason to shoot. See that big pork and bean can? I just imagine it's my boss's fat ass and...." BAM! The can flew up into the air, landing several feet behind the log.

"Oh, allow me." Lisa took the gun and pointed it at the next can.

"Ooh, Michael, watch out," Rachael said.

BOOM. The can did not move.

"You're not pissed off enough. Give it another try. It can really be cathartic," Rachael said.

Lisa thought a minute, then her exasperation with him exploded. "Michael, you son of a bitch!"

BOOM. BOOM. Kapow! Cans flew right and left; up and down. Lisa lowered the shotgun, breaking out in a grin. "I do feel better."

Then Rachael put an empty plastic gallon milk jug on the ground not too far from where they were standing. Returning behind the firing line, she said, "Now make him dance."

"Huh?"

"Keep firing away at the son of a bitch. See if you can unload the whole magazine into him."

Lisa pumped the gun. She loved the sound the forestock made as it slid down and then back.

Pow! Kapow! Pow! She shot, pumped; shot again. With each hit, Michael's stand-in jumped this way and that, delighting Rachael.

"Awesome, totally awesome!" Rachel said. "Now, you need to get in some practice, but I'd say that's plenty for today. When you're real comfortable with that, we'll do the clay pigeons. That's fun."

They retired to the barn, where Rachael gathered the kids and showed everyone how to unload and clean the gun. All done, Lisa put the safety on.

Rachael glanced at her watch. "I have to go. I'm on duty tonight. The regular X-ray technician is sick. You take care. We'll talk later."

The children wandered away as well, but Lisa lingered, her mind drifting to the shotgun. *Never in a million years did I dream I'd allow the children to handle one.... But I'll feel safer when Sam and Ellen leave.* Her thoughts turned to Michael. *If he were here, I wouldn't need a firearm. But he's not.* She sighed.

CHAPTER 11

"My poor baby, you've had a time of it with the in-laws gone, haven't you?" her friend, Olivia, said. "What you really need is a day at the spa."

"Oh, that would be wonderful. Sometimes when I'm in my office working, I crave Hilda's strong fingers. And the time she stood on my back was exquisite. Are you still seeing her?" Lisa asked.

"I'm there twice a week when I'm in town. Lusting won't cut it. You need a massage."

"Well, I can't afford one, so there."

Silence resonated.

"Look at your calendar. What are you doing this weekend?" Olivia asked.

"Cleaning the house? Washing my hair? Drinking the house wine? What else is there to do out here?"

"The three of you just be ready by 5 p.m. Friday. Pack some nice clothes for yourself and outdoor clothes for the kids."

"We can't go anywhere. We've got the dog and—"

"Enough. Just do as I say and pack for the dog, too."

"Olivia, I just can't afford it right now."

"Not to worry. I just got a nice little check from Poo-Poo head, and I'm dying to get out of the house."

"Poo-Poo head?"

"My second ex-husband. That's my nickname for him. After I found out he was seeing someone else, I soaked his toupee in the toilet while he slept. The next morning, he put it on as if nothing had ever happened. I've always cherished the thought of him making love to another woman with a Poo-Poo head."

"Gee, remind me never to get crossways with you!"

"That's exactly right. You never know how I'll exact my revenge. So, you'll be ready, won't you?"

"We will."

After hanging up, Lisa danced a little jig. Though desperately loving her children more than anyone in the world besides Michael, sometimes she needed a break. What she would not give right now for a solid week of peace without having to scramble to take Jessica to 4H, sit through boring parent/teacher meetings, or host a bunch of giggling girls who would not go to sleep during the "slumber" party.

***

Lisa had the bags waiting. Andrew continued to gripe about going, insisting he could spend the weekend alone on the ranch. However, when the Hummer Limo pulled into the driveway, he changed his mind. Olivia stepped out after the driver, Roderick, opened the door.

"Oh, Lisa, I'm so glad to see you. I've missed you so much." She embraced Lisa and then turned to Jessica. "My little lamb, how are you? Are you ready for a weekend adventure?"

"Yes, ma'am."

"And Andrew, I have quite a busy weekend planned for you."

"Hmm. What are we going to do?"

"You just wait and see. Now, everyone, let's get going. Hop in."

White, with huge all-terrain tires, the tricked-out stretch Hummer sported neon lighting in various shades of purple in the interior. The bar was stuffed with soft drinks and snacks for the children. Olivia even had a water bowl for Princess and some dog biscuits.

"How cool! May I have a Coke?" Andrew asked.

"Help yourself. You too, Jessica. Roderick has some headsets so the two of you can listen to the media system in the back. I also have a few movies. Your mother and I will sit towards the front so we can chat."

"Olivia, this is too much, really. You shouldn't have," Lisa said.

"Dear, I wasn't born with money. I intend to enjoy what I've got. My goal is to have zero in my bank account when I die. So, please. No more of this. Let me enjoy myself."

By this time, Roderick had the bags loaded and was pulling out of the driveway. As he turned, Olivia asked him to stop. "Is that Carl, the dear man who helps you?"

Lisa peeked out the window. "It is."

"I want to meet him. Roderick, I want to speak to that man a minute, please."

Olivia exited; Lisa trailed behind. Upon seeing Olivia, Carl did a double take.

"Hello, I'm Olivia, Lisa's friend from Raleigh. We're going away for the weekend. Lisa's told me what a wonderful man you are, so I wanted to meet you." Olivia stuck out her hand, and Carl hurriedly shook hers.

"You ladies have fun. Don't worry about a thing, Lisa. I'll keep an eye out." Carl paused. "Where is Princess?"

"She's in the limo, too."

"Where you headed?" Carl asked.

"A secret," Olivia said. "But I can assure you, fun will be had by all."

The women, with Roderick's help, climbed back into the vehicle and, as it painfully bumped along Dog Run Road, Olivia scowled. "This road is horrible. We'll have to wait until we're on the highway to have a martini."

"Wow, you aren't wasting any time, are you?"

"I've been thinking about one for weeks but didn't have a good occasion. I read about a recipe using both Bombay Sapphire and Tanqueray. I can't wait to try it."

As soon as the chariot turned on the paved surface, Olivia began carefully mixing the juniper-infused concoction, topping off each with three olives.

"To us." Olivia held up her glass and then took a sip. "Ah, the wait was worth it."

About an hour later, the Hummer slowed and turned right. Glancing out, Lisa saw the sign *Hyatt Regency Lost Pines Resort and Spa.* "I had no idea this was so near the ranch."

"I hope you don't mind. Everything's planned out. We're getting the super spa package tomorrow. Two college students are in charge of the kids. They can do anything they want—kayak, ride horses, go hiking. Too bad it's so cold, they can't go swimming. The pool looks fun."

"Oh, Olivia." Lisa sniffed. "This is so wonderful I—"

"Enough of that. It's time to party."

The lobby was gorgeous; wood floors and arched ceilings accented with stone walls and cavernous fireplaces. To Lisa's relief, kids were everywhere. Outside, rocking chairs encircled a large fire pit where a group of children were busily roasting marshmallows.

Lisa's jaw dropped after realizing Olivia had rented the Litton House as well as a suite for the children and their counselors. Everyone had a private bedroom and bath! *Funny how I never appreciated not having to share a bathroom before now.*

"I can't believe they're letting Princess in this place," Lisa said.

"Money talks," Olivia said.

Dinner was a real treat. Lisa had a fabulous, planked salmon, and Olivia chose a spectacular white wine.

After dinner, the group went to the suite, amply supplied with snacks, movies, and video games, to meet the counselors. Lisa felt comfortable leaving the children under their supervision. After kissing the kids goodnight, she and Olivia then returned to the house.

"So, what's our schedule tomorrow?" Lisa asked. "I assume you've planned everything out."

"To the spa. We have five and a half hours of total luxury. I can't wait. We get a pedicure and manicure, too."

"Lisa glanced at her cracked, chipped nails. "I can use that, for sure." Lisa took in their surroundings. "How about a fire?"

"Lovely. Why don't you get it started?"

Lisa turned on the gas and instinctively pulled back as the flames erupted with a whoop. Olivia handed her several pine cones.

"Put these in. I bought them at a cute little gift shop before I left. They're supposed to make the fire have all sorts of wonderful colors."

Lisa tossed them in. "Nothing like gas logs to make life easy."

She gazed at the blaze while Olivia went into the kitchen to find a bottle of wine. She put a tray of fruit and cheese on the coffee table and poured out generous glasses of chardonnay. Olivia then settled back in the overstuffed chair next to the fireplace. "You look a bit distracted, dear."

Damn. She always reads my mind. She even looks like a fortune teller in that orange print kaftan and leggings. And her hair wrapped in that goofy headpiece. "Sometimes I miss my life in Raleigh: the good food, the massages. Money's tight right now. Not tight, non-existent. I'm going to have to figure something out to get more—and quick."

"You know, I've come to the conclusion that you never have enough money. I remember when my first ex and I were married. The two of us were bringing in $30,000 a year and thought we were rich. Then, we needed more stuff. A Corvette, a house on a cul-de-sac, a trip to Mexico. Before we knew it, we were $50,000 in debt. It's funny. I couldn't even make it now on $30,000 a month, and, if I only had $50,000 in debt, I'd be in hog heaven."

The wine mellowed Lisa's mood. Staring at the flickering flames, she verbalized her concerns about Jessica. "The child can't be serious about anything! She doesn't like math and won't try to learn it. The way she's going, she'll never graduate high school. She needs to be able to take care of herself and not depend on a man.

"And looks." Lisa trembled. "It's a well-known fact that fat people make less money than thin people. It's my job to protect her from all that, and I don't know what to do."

Lisa sat quietly, observing Olivia. Sighing, her friend took a deep gulp of wine and gazed intently into the fire. Watching warily, Lisa was afraid blurting out her worries was a mistake. But Michael didn't understand how important it was for Jessica to succeed in life. Surely Olivia, of all people, would understand. After all, she had had three husbands who dropped her for someone younger, more exotic. If they had not been so rich, Olivia would probably be working this very instant in Wal-Mart greeting customers on the graveyard shift.

Olivia rose. "One minute." She disappeared into the kitchen and returned with some Godiva chocolate. "I'm getting a bit tired of the cheese. Here, help yourself." She leaned over with the tray and served Lisa before setting them down on the coffee table. Then she grabbed another pine cone and threw it in, watching as green and red sparks soared up the chimney.

"How old is Jessica, anyway?" Olivia rocked on her heels, hands behind her and back to the hearth.

Irked, Lisa answered. "Ten." She hated the power play, Olivia standing, towering over her. The old negotiating tactic was working; Lisa felt intimidated. Framed in the firelight, Olivia took on the likeness of a wicked witch determined to weave a magic spell.

Her friend picked up her wine glass and roamed. "When I was ten years old, I used to ride my bicycle with the neighborhood kids to the corner store to buy Dr. Peppers in bottles and, if I were lucky, Mom would give me enough money to buy Hostess cupcakes. I liked the orange ones with the white squiggly on top and the cream inside. My brother wouldn't have anything but chocolate.

"We girls built castles in the nearby woods out of fallen branches so we could play Camelot. Some of us were horses—I personally preferred the role of horse to that of Queen Guinevere—and we galloped around the palace, watching for dragons. We were forever building more chambers. Can you believe? We'd take a broom and sweep the dirt bare of pine needles."

Stopping, she eyed Lisa inquisitively. "What did you do when you were ten?"

Lisa considered the answer carefully. She'd been like Olivia—going to the swimming pool every day, riding bicycles, and spending the night with her girlfriends. "But it's different now. It's a dog-eat-dog world.

There weren't as many things to master back then. Do you realize that when we were young, we didn't have to know much about computers? That's a whole new body of knowledge people need today. I'm afraid she'll never learn it all."

Olivia poured more wine and launched into a discourse about allowing children to be children. By the time the speech ended, Lisa was downright irritated and tipsy. Looking for empathy, she had found nothing but criticism.

"I don't believe in that nonsense. Kids need to be ready for the real world." Before Olivia could get a word in, Lisa hurriedly said, "Look, let's drop it. I don't want to talk about it anymore." With that, Lisa abruptly stood and headed to the bathroom.

Flushing the toilet, she turned the water on full speed and scrubbed her hands furiously. *Olivia is always so practical. I should have known better than to tell her how I felt. I'm so embarrassed.* Lisa blocked out the troubling thoughts of Jessica's future. Deep breaths and relaxing visions of the coming massage soothed her. *Ohmmmm, ohmmmmm.* Inhaling deeply, she returned to the living area. Olivia was still standing by the fireplace.

"Sorry," Lisa said. "When I'm real uptight, I start worrying about everything. You're right, as usual. I need to back off and let nature take its course."

"No, it's my fault. I shouldn't have come on so strong. The thought of you pressuring that sweet little lamb upset me. I was just trying to help."

"Let's just forget it. I'm going to bed."

***

Lisa awoke with a start, her head pounding unmercifully. *Where am I?* Remembering, she listened intently but could hear no movement. Going back to sleep was impossible; her throbbing cranium and cottony mouth demanded attention. Thank goodness she had quit smoking in college. Cigarettes and booze gave her an even worse hangover.

Her reward for struggling out of bed was a good thirty minutes in the shower. How awesome! Refreshed, she went into the kitchen, took a bottle of water from the refrigerator, and poured herself a cup of coffee. A note on the counter indicated Olivia had taken a walk. Lisa called to check on the children, delighted they were having fun.

Lisa toasted a bagel and slathered it with cream cheese. Sitting on the couch, she ate while gazing at the immaculately manicured lawn and gardens outside. The place was gorgeous, but so was JF Ranch, in a different, rugged way. Before she could get deep into thought, Olivia returned.

"The kids are having a fabulous time," Olivia said. "They're going horseback riding in about an hour. They should be well-occupied while we're at the spa. Princess is going to Bastrop to be groomed. I hope you don't mind. And I told the children we'd all have dinner together."

"Oh, fantastic! Princess was looking a little scraggly, wasn't she?"

Olivia nodded.

"When's our spa appointment?" Lisa asked.

"Whenever we want to go. They'll serve us lunch when we're hungry."

"I'm ready now. Let me get my jacket."

***

Later, relaxed and mellow, Lisa sat on the couch, marveling at how well her toes and fingernails looked. Weeks had passed without her having a manicure. It would probably last two or three days at most.

Olivia put down the phone. "How exciting! We're going to have a chuck wagon cookout. We're riding horses, unless you'd rather go by Jeep, to a campsite down by the river. The children get to help the cooks. In fact, they're already there."

"Uh-oh. Maybe we need to grab something to eat before we leave."

"Don't worry, we should be fine. I'm going to change. We need to be at the stables in about thirty minutes."

Lisa hurriedly put on jeans, a sweatshirt, and boots. She returned to the living room where she found Olivia decked out in a pair of tight-fitting blue jeans tucked into her red boots and a retro western-style shirt. Red with contrasting tan western yokes, the top sported pockets with piping and arrow designs. Sequins accented the embroidered running horses that highlighted the blouse. Red pearlized diamond-shaped snaps blinked sharply from the cuffs and down the front of the garment. An ornate horse-head belt buckle gleamed.

"Wow! Don't you look duded up." *At least she looks more normal than in one of her crazy outfits.* "What are those boots made of?"

"They're ostrich. Like the design?"

Lisa peered closer. Stitched into the upper part of the boot was an ornate decorative motif composed of three x's.

"X's?"

"To honor the three former loves of my life who made this outfit possible."

Lisa tried to keep a straight face. "When'd you get all this? I've never seen you dress like this before."

"Back when I thought I was going to meet Rick and Anita Perry at your place for cocktails, I flew over to Fort Worth and bought an outfit. I decided it was time to wear it."

"Ooh. Sorry. The kids and I aren't exactly their neighbors."

"Seriously, your neighbors are probably a lot more fun. Where else can you enjoy discussions of a pig carcass as you sip your morning coffee?"

Lisa made a face and climbed into the golf cart waiting outside which whisked them to the stables. She nervously surveyed the horse they had chosen for her—Honey Bee. Her golden coat shone, perfectly highlighted by a light mane and tail.

One of the stable hands brought over a stool for Olivia. Soon she was astride her mare, Tweetie Pie.

"Is she fast?" Olivia asked.

The cowboy chuckled. "The only time you need to worry is when you get close to the barn on the way home. Then she'll make a run for it."

Lisa tried to get her foot into the stirrup, but it was too tall. She relented and used the stool. Once astride her beast, the stable hand adjusted her stirrups. Then he gave them driving instructions. Pull back to stop. Lean forward and cluck to go. To turn right, pull the reins to the right. To turn left, pull to the left.

The aroma of horse flesh and leather triggered long-ago memories of Lisa's last horseback ride…. Uncle Joe holding Jack, the pony, and softly giving her guidance; her excitement and delight. She could feel the warmth of her uncle's smile as he watched her ride without help.

A jarring movement brought Lisa out of her reverie. Honey Bee fell in line behind Tweetie Pie and they were off into the deepening dusk. Lisa held onto the saddle horn tightly with one hand, scanning the trail for any holes or rocks that might make her splendid equine stumble.

About ten minutes of plodding brought them to the campsite. Before they could even see the chuck wagon, Lisa could hear Jessica chattering and Princess barking. A cowboy held her horse and, after instructions on dismounting, Lisa proudly slid out of the saddle and onto the ground without help.

She and Olivia entered the clearing. Ahead, she saw several men dressed in Western attire busy with an array of Dutch ovens, either hanging over or nestled in a liberal bed of coals. Andrew was helping stoke a bonfire where other guests were warming their hands. Several nearby picnic tables with red and white checkered cloths were set with tin dishes sporting blue and white speckles.

A woman dressed in jeans, a white shirt, and boots approached. "Ma'am? Could I offer you some cowboy coffee?"

"What's that?" Olivia asked.

"We dump the coffee into the water and the pot sits on the fire. When it's boiled a bit, we take it off and let the grounds settle. Then it's ready to drink. You can have it plain or with a shot of your favorite alcohol."

"If I have any more booze, I'll melt away into the sunset and won't be able to enjoy the party. I'll just have mine with some sweetener," Lisa said.

"Make mine straight black," Olivia said. "I'm too scared of falling off that horse."

Jessica came running, Princess at her heels.

"Momma, Momma I'm having so much fun. Can I get a horse? I love them so much!"

Lisa flashed back to the weeks and months after they had left Ruby and Joe's the summer her father died. She had pestered her mom for a horse something awful. They could keep it in the backyard; Lisa would feed it and scoop up the poop every day. They would never have to mow the grass again. The most Lisa could squeeze out was a dog.

"We'll see, we'll see. First, you have to learn all about them. We'll get Dr. Dorothy to teach you. They're a lot of work, you know."

Jessica caught the wave of another child in the group and, with a "see you later," she was gone. Lisa and Olivia sauntered over to the campfire to join the other guests seated on hay bales that formed a ring around the perimeter. The sky was turning dark, and a chill filled the air.

Lisa listened as Olivia quickly engaged in conversation with an older gentleman who had brought his grandchildren to the resort for the weekend. *Funny. Everything's so artificial. Olivia has spent so much money for us to be out of doors, eat good food, and visit people. I can do that at the ranch any old time. And this is so phony. Wait staff, stilted conversations with people you don't know.... Oh, but the massage! I really miss those.*

Then the most wonderful aroma engulfed Lisa. She looked around only to espy the cooks putting big, no—not just big—positively humongous—steaks on the grill. *I haven't seen a slab of meat that thick in months.* Fascination steered her straight to the man laboring over the pit, a pair of tongs in his hands.

Lisa peered into the smoke, the aroma of the marbled fat dribbling onto the hot coals tantalized her. Tiny flames whooshed and sputtered, creating sizzling sounds as the grease penetrated the depths of the grill.

"Oh, my God. I've never seen such a big steak in all my life! What kind of a cut is that?"

The cook laughed. "Looks good, doesn't it? We call it a cowboy steak. It's a bone-in rib eye two inches thick. It weighs about two pounds. I don't put a thing on it but a bit of salt and pepper."

"I'll never be able to eat all that!" Lisa would try her darndest, however. She had not had a good piece of meat in almost six months.

"Very few can. We usually just cut strips off the steak, and everyone helps themselves to as much as they can eat." He began to quickly flip the nicely seared beef.

Forgetting her resolve, Lisa wandered over to the bar area for a glass of red wine. She would never eat red meat without it. The velvety mouthful relaxed her. *Maybe I don't want to give up the good life.* A weekend apartment in the city would work, Austin, San Antonio, perhaps.

The meal was thoroughly enjoyable. Lisa pigged out on the beef, forgoing potatoes and even salad. Washing it down with wine put her in a heavenly mood. Even Andrew seemed to enjoy himself immensely.

The children made s'mores. Olivia and Lisa laughed as they watched Jessica wave her flaming marshmallow in the air to the chagrin of her counselor, who kept trying to coax her into producing a lightly browned version rather than a charcoal-riddled and shriveled one. This time Lisa did not interfere, her daughter was just having too much fun.

Cruising over to the dessert table, Lisa watched the staff spoon peach cobbler right out of the Dutch oven and top it with Blue Bell Ice Cream. Hmmm. Oatmeal cookies, bread pudding…. The cobbler was the standout, no doubt about it.

Bowl in hand; Lisa sat on one of the hay bales by the fire. Conversation with a couple from New York who were down for a week's vacation ensued. A glance at the dessert table revealed Jessica stuffing a cookie in her mouth with one hand and sliding several in her pocket with the other. Lisa excused herself and rushed over.

"Just what do you think you're doing?" Lisa reached into Jessica's pockets and unloaded the cookies.

"But momma, the man said it was OK if I had some."

"You already had s'mores. That's enough sweets for the day." Lisa dumped the cookies in a nearby trash barrel. Then she pulled Jessica off to the side, kneeling beside her.

"I love you; I really do. Too much sugar isn't good for you."

"Daddy would let me have them." Jessica put her hands on her hips and glared at Lisa.

"He's not here so you have to do what I say."

They stared at each other, neither backing down.

As Olivia approached, Lisa rose.

"Lisa," Olivia said, "Do you want to ride the horses back?" Jessica scurried off toward the group of kids who were playing nearby.

"No, I'm not up to it. Besides, I'm not too excited about a mad dash to the stables. Let's just take the Jeep."

About an hour later, Jessica and Andrew burst into the Litton House, followed by the barking red devil.

"Oh, Miss Olivia, I've had such a wonderful time," Jessica said. "Thank you so much." She ran up to Olivia and pressed against her.

"I have, too," Andrew said. "I wasn't expecting to get to do so much fun stuff. That was a great collection of video games. Marvel vs. Capcom 3 is awesome. I want to get that one."

"You two are entirely welcome. We'll certainly do it again. I also had fun," Olivia said.

A counselor stuck his head in. "Kids, it's time to go. Ms. Dunwhitty, we'll see you at breakfast around nine."

The kids and dog piled out, leaving the room silent except for the crackling of the logs.

"Olivia, I'm really tired. It's been wonderful."

Lisa rose, kissed her friend, and headed to her room. But she could not sleep. Jessica had truly upset her. And all the excess…. Did it really make any of them happier?

CHAPTER 12

The March wind, full of humidity, whipped around Lisa, sending chills through her body. Shivering, she wrapped her canvas barn coat tighter around her. Staring at the leaden sky, she listened carefully. *I hear it!* The whine of a diesel motor, barely audible, increased, replacing the reverberation of the wind crashing through the trees.

"They're here!" Lisa yelled to Dorothy, who was coming out of the barn. "They're here!"

Both scurried toward the road in time to see the rig painfully navigating the small driveway. The ruckus brought Carl out of his house and across the street. The cab and its long cattle trailer eased close to the eager women.

"Hi, I'm Pete Johnson," the man in the driver's seat said. "Where do you want to unload, ma'am?"

Lisa froze. Before, it was all a dream. Now, fifty cattle—her life savings—stood waiting for her to make a go of it.

Dorothy stepped up and said, "Hi, I'm Dr. Nichols. If you'll back over to the pen, we'll unload there. We're going to sort and examine the livestock before we let them in the pasture."

"Sure thing, Doc." Pete eased around the house and toward the barn, swinging to his left and pulling as far out into the yard as possible. Carl directed the endeavor with hand signals. Then Pete gradually backed up until the rear of the trailer was even with the corral fence.

As the men maneuvered the rig, Lisa got her first peek of the herd. The bull, T-Rex—one thousand pounds and three and a half feet tall—was easy to spot. Short, chunky horns that curved slightly toward his nose gave him a rather fearsome look. If he had not been so bite-sized, Lisa would have been tremendously terrified of him. Then, hooded brown eyes peered out from blond eyelashes, glaring at her insolently. They had deemed him gentle? *I cannot imagine what a mean bull would look like! As long as he does his job, we are fine. He better make lots of good babies to be worth the $8,000 I paid for his ass.*

Carl and Pete lowered the trailer's ramp and urged the weary herd into the pen. The Herefords were truly amazing. Coats the color of red Georgia clay contrasted with their white faces, bellies, and feet. The cattle milled around, checking out their new environment.

The group worked steadily through the afternoon, herding the bovines into a shoot that became extremely narrow until the animal could not move in any direction. Then Dorothy examined each creature, giving it an ear tag with the JF brand. When the doctor was satisfied, Carl released the beast into the pasture.

Carl shooed a small calf into the chute. She had beautiful curling hair and quirky ears, with delicate bits of white fluff growing from them. Her pink nose tilted up as if flirting with Dorothy.

"This is the one," Dorothy said. "This little beauty is perfect for Jessica."

Carl put a rope harness around the calf's nose and led her to a small pen built specifically for her. It contained a small loafing shed where the calf could find shelter from the elements.

When he returned, Carl said, "I believe I'm going to like these shorties just fine. They're a lot easier to work with than the big ones, that's for sure."

Once Dorothy assured the herd was healthy, Lisa signed the papers and, with much finagling, Pete finally got the rig turned around and left.

As Carl returned home, Dorothy and Lisa made a beeline to the house. After hanging her coat on a peg by the door and wrestling off her boots, Lisa sauntered into the kitchen and peered into the fridge.

"Beer?"

"Heavens, yes. What a workout." Dorothy peeled off her coat and sank into one of the kitchen chairs while Lisa used a bottle opener on the Shiner Bocks. They drank in silence. Lisa glanced idly at her hands. The manicure acquired at the spa was long gone. Dirt had lodged itself under her short nails and in the ridges of her cuticles. Keeping them clean was impossible. Michael had always complained about his dad's nails being filled with grease. Now Lisa grasped the difficulty of fingernail hygiene.

Dorothy retrieved another beer and swallowed this one more slowly. "So, are Sam and Ellen home yet?"

"They've been home awhile."

"And…." Dorothy looked at Lisa questioningly.

"And, what?"

"And how do you feel with them gone?"

How do you think I feel? Lisa wanted to shout. *Scared. Afraid. Can't sleep.* She was too embarrassed to tell Dorothy about hearing noises last night, pulling out that infernal shotgun, and crouching beside the front door for what seemed like hours. After deciding nothing was outside, she realized the gun was unloaded.

"Being alone scares me. The kids are here, but that's not like having another adult around. I've been thinking a lot about Uncle Joe, how much he missed Ruby. Dying here alone and all…"

"What do you mean alone?"

"I just assumed he was by himself."

Dorothy placed her bottle on the table and peered at Lisa. "Actually, Carl was there. John was called out as first responder and reached the ranch before the ambulance. My understanding is that Carl had been over here mending a fence when Joe had a massive heart attack. John said that when he arrived, Carl was cradling Joe in his arms. Joe was already dead."

"I didn't know."

Both sat silently. To Lisa, Carl was a complex man. What else did she not know about him?

Dorothy took another leisurely sip. "Well, I got to be going. Need to get back to the office. I have a few appointments this afternoon. The cows look good, though. Call me if you have any problems."

Lisa saw Dorothy out and then went to her office to get a little of the contract CPA work concluded before the kids returned from school. *How funny I feel sitting here in dirty jeans and boots, smelling like a mixture of cow manure and sweat, working on a tax return. If the folks at Benson Bart could see me now!* Mindful the work would most likely dry up after tax season ended, Lisa buckled down.

Sometime later the dull roar of the school bus drew her attention. *Strange how sound carries in the country.* Soon she heard the kids running up the driveway yelling for her. Guess they have seen the cattle. Lisa smiled.

When she walked out, she spied Jessica outside her calf's pen. She had dropped her backpack on the ground and stood, mesmerized. The pert little critter was small, no bigger than a large dog. Lisa glanced around for Andrew, but he had apparently gone in to put his things away and change clothes.

"She's cute, isn't she?" Lisa whispered. "What are you going to name her?" She could see Jessica's eyes were wide as saucers.

"She's so pretty—is she really mine? Mamma...you won't sell her, will you?"

"No sweetie, we won't sell her unless you want us to. She's all yours. Do you remember what Dr. Dorothy told you to do?"

"Uh, yeah, I think. She said to wear the same clothes every day and to stand quietly, moving closer to her every day."

"Don't forget you shouldn't look at her. Then what?"

"Dr. Dorothy said to sit in a chair inside the pen and read to her. Think she'll like *Charlotte's Web*?"

"She'll love it. Now run on in and change. You can spend the afternoon out here. Homework can wait until after supper." With that,

Jessica charged off, startling the calf. Lisa almost said something but thought better of it. Maybe, sometimes, she expected Jessica to be a little too perfect.

About that time, Andrew strolled up. "That thing looks like a shriveled-up Lab puppy. Glad it's not mine." He was wearing denim, roper boots, a vest, and a baseball cap.

Lisa gave him an irritated glance but said nothing. "Let's go down to the pasture. I want to show you the rest of the herd."

They walked through the fence, locking it behind them. The cows grazed steadily, keeping a wary eye on the intruders.

"Wow, that bull is awesome. Some cool horns," Andrew said. T-Rex glowered at them suspiciously.

"His name is T-Rex."

"Well, he's one cool dude. I've been telling the kids at school about these mini cows, but they think I'm putting them on. They say there's no way a cow can be that small. I'm going to take some pictures to show them I wasn't kidding." He pulled out his iPhone and snapped furiously.

"Is Eric coming over to see the herd?" Lisa asked.

"Don't know. Haven't talked to him in a while."

"Something wrong between the two of you?"

"No, he's just been busy."

As they surveyed the herd, Lisa felt closer to Andrew than she had in some time. His excitement was infectious, he genuinely seemed interested in being responsible for them. Carl had taught him how to drive the tractor and move hay into the pasture. The donkeys, whose task was to protect the cows from the coyotes, had been there about two weeks, Andrew watching after them. Lisa marveled at how much he had taught himself by researching the Internet. *I wonder if it has anything to do with the fact that he now knows things his father doesn't?*

When they returned from the pasture, Jessica was sitting on a small stool inside the pen, reading *Charlotte's Web* to the calf, which, by this time, was exploring her new home and giving Jessica little attention. Princess was curled up in Jessica's lap. *So far so good.* At least Princess was not chasing the calf all over the pen. She would have to pick up some treats for Jessica's new baby.

When Lisa announced a bit later that they were having leftovers for supper, a revolt started, accompanied by grumbles and moans. Lisa considered strong-arming the kids but did not have the energy. Anyway, she did not want any herself.

Piling in the truck, they drove to a local restaurant in town Edith had recommended. Lisa had not even changed! When they were settled in a booth, the waitress bought some tortilla chips and menus. She then took drink orders. Lisa relented, allowing the kids to have Cokes even though it was a school night. A method to her madness, she smiled and asked the server what kind of beer they had.

"We've got Bud, Coors, and Miller Lite. And there's some kind of beer back there with XX on it. Don't know what that is. Not many people drink it. Maybe only one or two of them left."

Lisa worked diligently to keep a straight face. "That sounds good. I'll take one of those."

The woman returned shortly with Dos Equis in a green bottle. Later, Lisa started to crack a joke about the fact that the waitress found the popular Mexican beer strange and exotic, but then stopped. *The kids won't understand, they won't think it's funny. Only Michael would appreciate it.* Her mood darkened.

Depressed, she scanned the menu, surprised that both Mexican and American fare was available. After ordering, the talk turned to what Jessica would name the calf. Finally, a name materialized—Precious.

"So, there you have it—Precious and Princess! What a pair!" Lisa said.

"Oh, Mom, that's so corny," Andrew said. But Jessica found it amusing.

"The 'P' pair!" Jessica said and made all the combinations of words starting with "p" she could.

The trio had a great time and even Andrew, for a change, was civil. When they returned home, Andrew took dibs on the bathroom while Jessica insisted on calling her dad and grandparents to tell them about the calf. Lisa relented and waited tensely while Jessica dialed Michael's number, but he did not answer. Next was a call to Sam and Ellen.

Lisa listened as Jessica gave an animated blow-by-blow description of meeting Precious and reading to her. God, that child could be an actress. At least you did not have to be a math wizard to act. When a pause came, Lisa motioned for Jessica to hand over the telephone.

"Hi, Ellen, how's everything going?"

"Fine, just fine. We got caught up on all the chores so there's not much to do here. I guess I was spoiled by the weather down there. It's too cold here."

"Well, we miss you, we miss you a lot."

"We miss you, too. Sam can't do much but sit around in his easy chair watching TV. I guess we're bored after all the excitement at the ranch."

An idea welled in Lisa's brain. It was so simple. Why had she not thought of it before? Sam and Ellen could move to the ranch. With 4,000 acres there was plenty of room for them to build a house nearby. Then they would not be on top of each other. She started to open her mouth—and then stopped. That would mean living here was permanent. And what would Michael say? Inviting his parents to join them when he did not care for his father? Was that the final blow to their relationship?

Rather than head down that path, Lisa said her goodbyes and then focused on getting Jessica bathed and her homework done.

"But I haven't called Granny S and Mel yet!"

"You can do that tomorrow. Besides, it's getting late. You haven't even done your homework."

After Jessica and Andrew settled in for the night, Lisa took a quick shower, fearful the hot water would run out. Back in the living room, she rapidly built a fire from the wood Andrew had brought in earlier and, once satisfied it was burning well, cruised into the bedroom and brought out the diary from the old trunk.

Curled on the couch, she leisurely examined the worn leather cover which had seen its share of abuse. The fly page of the diary had the name Julia Darby Kingston. Julia? Was this the Julia of Julia's place Ruby had talked about? Gently she thumbed through the pages. The handwriting was difficult to read; the ink faded. Lisa labored through the first page.

July 18, 1882.

Tragedy today. My heart aches. Elizabeth's little boy, the one she'd wanted for so long dead! It doesn't seem possible. We were working on a quilt when cries came up from out by the barn. Little James had crawled under the wagon just at the time Mr. Korff signaled the team to go. The wagon ran over him, crushing his skull. We took him inside to lay him out. It was so bad Big James went right ahead and buried him then and there. The preacher will be out tomorrow. I have the rest of her little ones here, poor girl. She and James need time alone to mourn. It will take all the strength the Lord can give for them to deal with the death of Little James. I don't think she's really ever gotten over Emily's death from the croup last year.

Lisa sat back, mesmerized. What a cruel world. Recalling how hard it had been just to clear the pasture with all the modern conveniences, accomplishing it with an axe, oxen, and brute force was unfathomable. And medical care. How frustrating it must have been being unable to offer more than a poultice or salve. She could not imagine.

Lisa froze; movement near her glass of water caught her attention. Gazing at the end table, she stared, horrified. A scorpion! A good two inches long! The light brown creature with stripes on its back waved its lobster-like claws at her while its tail curled tightly in a ball.

Lisa stood and backed away gingerly. Feeling safe, she ran into the bedroom to grab a shoe. Returning, she aimed. Whack! Whack, whack,

WHACK! Got him. And her glass, in the process, smashed on the floor, leaving a puddle with glittering shards.

Dropping the assault weapon, she sat on the couch, away from the obliterated remains. Heart beating wildly, she tried to calm herself. Andrew appeared, wondering what all the commotion was about. Lisa warned him to watch for the glass.

Peering at the beast, he said, "Good job. You fixed him alright. Carl is always telling me to wear gloves while I work because of the scorpions, but I didn't believe him. Now I do. It's the first one I've seen."

He went into the kitchen, grabbed a paper towel, and gingerly picked up the remains of the thing. "I'm going to take it back to my room and look it up on the Internet."

"Sure." Lisa was glad not to have monster disposal duty and relieved Jessica had not woken. She then began cleaning up the mess, removing as much water as possible from the carpet. The diary would have to wait for another day.

***

Michael grasped his glass of scotch, leisurely swirling it as he listened intently to Sharon speak of her day. He had enjoyed her company occasionally. Things with Lisa had been in turmoil for so long, he had forgotten how fun it was to relax and talk with someone who looked up to you—not being worried whether you were saying the right thing.

Michael felt his cell phone vibrate. "Just a sec." He lifted his index finger into the air while still clutching his glass. Setting it down, he pulled the telephone out—the ranch. Quickly he cut off the call and let the message go to voice mail. Now certainly was not the time to have a conversation with anyone there.

Dinner proceeded smoothly; both enjoyed the Cajun snapper with a crawfish-based sauce. The restaurant had been Sharon's selection, and a good one, too. After the waiter removed the dishes, Sharon excused herself and went to the restroom. Michael found himself lost in thought. *How'd Lisa and I get into this mess? I don't understand why she cares so much about that place. I've got to convince her she's wrong.*

As Sharon approached, his phone vibrated again. Reluctantly he checked the number. To his relief, it was his mother—his dad would never call. The two reminders of his other world were enough to bring on an attack of self-condemnation that sufficiently unsettled him. Michael ended their dinner on a cordial note. So far, he had arranged to meet her at places rather than pick her up at her house. Thankfully, that had been the case this evening.

Back at the hotel room, he grudgingly called his mother, not yet wanting to contact the ranch. Maybe she would know what was going on there. After a few minutes of pleasantry and questions, Ellen got right down to business. "Son, you know I've made it a point not to interfere with your life, but I'm concerned."

Michael sat silently, not moving a muscle. Yes, what she said was true, she had been about the best mother anyone could wish for. What seemed like forever passed.

"I'm worried sick about the children and Lisa, too, alone down there in the woods. I'm afraid something will happen, and they won't be able to get help."

Another round of silence.

"Michael, the kids miss you. Jessica called today, so excited about her new little calf. She went on and on. Precious is the name. She was so disappointed that she hadn't reached you to tell you about it. And Andrew, he's growing up, taking responsibility around the farm and all." She paused again and then continued, "I know, deep down, Lisa misses you, too. Both of you are too bull-headed to admit it."

Michael felt he was coming unglued. Sure, he was often out of town, but not for such a long stretch. Things were changing there so fast.... "Thanks, Mom, I appreciate your concern. So, how do you like being home?"

"Well, not as much as we thought. It's pretty slow here after all the excitement at the ranch—and cold, too." She told him about the forecasted weather. "I'm not able to tolerate the cold like I used to anymore…. Michael, your dad and I were talking about moving down to Texas to be nearer to you and the kids. What do you think about that?"

"But Mom, I don't know where we'll be living yet. I still haven't found a job. Don't you think this is a bit premature?"

"I think Jessica's found a permanent home; she loves it there. And, well, isn't it time you quit moving so much, at least till the kids get out of school?"

"Whatever you and Dad decide to do is fine with me." Michael squeezed the cell phone so hard he could feel the blood draining out of his hand.

"We're thinking about selling the house and buying a big travel trailer. I've always wanted to go on the road, and I'm tired of keeping up a big house."

"That's wonderful, Mom." Michael made his excuses, cut off the call, and threw the phone on the bed. Did anyone care about his feelings anymore?

After fixing himself straight scotch with a little ice, he flipped restlessly through the television channels, not interested in anything showing. Yet, his mother's words haunted him. *Stubborn, am I?* He resolved to return to the ranch and hammer things out.

CHAPTER 13

For the past thirty minutes, Rachael had been giving a blow-by-blow description of the fight between her and her significant other, Vivian. A new clerk at the grocery store had her eye on Rachael's woman. Rachael was furious! The two of them had gone to a concert in Austin—and guess *who* showed up! This thing/person Rachael described as a five-dollar hooker with an ass as wide as a barn and boobs that hung close to her belt. And Vivian, according to Rachael, was making goo-goo eyes at this freak.

Delighted, Lisa watched Edith and Dorothy, incensed at Vivian's behavior, let Rachael know it. Then Rachael dropped the bomb. The two fought on the way home. Near Smithville, she pulled onto the side of the highway, demanding Vivian get out.

"You didn't!" Edith said.

"I did!" Rachael replied.

"How'd she get home at that time of night?" Dorothy asked.

"Her brother picked her up, I guess. I didn't ask. She's been sleeping on his couch for the last few nights. I really don't care."

"Don't you think that's a bit juvenile?" Lisa asked.

"Oh, you with the mystery husband who is never here has good love-life advice, huh? I can't believe he doesn't make you angry." Rachael stared at Lisa, who began to twirl the contents of her wine glass anxiously.

"You're right. He makes me angry." Lisa looked away.

"Ooh," Edith said, "I like this. We're getting close enough to fight like sisters. Don't say anything else. I'll be back. I need to get some more queso dip."

Lisa scrutinized the swirling, burgundy-colored liquid while Edith disappeared into the kitchen. When Edith sat down again with the brimming bowl of Rotel-spiced cheese, she said, "OK, I'm ready."

"I'm sorry, Rachael," Lisa said. "I had no right to speak. I guess I haven't acted very maturely either."

"I'm sorry, too. It was a bit silly of me, wasn't it? After my last partner dumped me, I guess I'm a bit paranoid. It's not easy finding someone out here."

Dorothy, who appeared perturbed, hurried to change the subject. "Lisa, how's Jessica doing with the calf?"

Relieved, Lisa reported the progress. To their delight, she explained how Precious and Princess were becoming friends and how Jessica alternately brushed the duo. Princess was jealous that Precious got treats so Lisa had to buy extra dog tidbits for the red devil.

"She's so excited when she gets home, she forgets her snack most of the time, which is great," Lisa said. "She's been real good about putting out clean water for Precious and fresh hay, but I have to nag her to clean out the cow patties! Ah, the life of a pet! I think in my next life I want to come back as Jessica's calf."

Everyone laughed.

Glancing at her watch, Lisa realized it was time to leave. She debated whether to say anything about the fact that Michael was coming, but then decided not to. Just then her cell rang—the house.

"Excuse me a sec, the kids." Lisa jumped up and stepped into the store for some privacy. It was Jessica. Lisa listened intently, broke into a relieved grin, and returned to the party.

"Good news, everyone. Ellen and Sam called. They've decided to sell their house and buy a travel trailer. First stop in their wonderful adventure will be the JF Ranch!"

Whoops and cheers followed her announcement.

"A toast, a toast," Rachael said. They clinked their glasses together. "I'm sure relieved."

"You're not the only one!" Lisa said.

***

Michael savored the last of his café macchiato. *Today's going to be a good day, I just know it.* He grinned with satisfaction. The headhunter had set up an interview next week with a great company in Dallas. Michael was, for the first time in his job hunt, optimistic. Not only was the position a good one, but the pay was sufficient.

Glancing at his watch, he had just enough time to check out of his room and shop before heading to the ranch. Not wanting to feel like a duck out of water, he intended to do some chores, help with the cattle—anything to get back in Lisa's good graces. His mom had been spot-on, they made a good couple. If he played it right, she would give up this ranching idea and join him; she must be tired of playing cowgirl.

Sticking the newspaper under his arm, he policed his table and returned to the hotel. Later, at the sporting goods store, a wind suit, sweatpants, jogging shoes, and an Aussie-style hat with a chin string and brim that buttoned to the crown spoke to him. He changed in the dressing room.

Next, he ran the Porsche through the car wash. And, on a whim, he stopped by the grocery store and bought a nice bottle of wine and flowers for Lisa. Everything had to be perfect.

On his way to the JF, his mind drifted to Sharon. He enjoyed her companionship; the woman reminded him of his wife. He had mostly kept their conversations focused on her rather than him—and it had paid off. She seemed disappointed when he told her he would be in Dallas this weekend preparing for his interview. Naturally, he had failed to mention the stop at the ranch.

***

Hunkered down in her office, Lisa worked on a project due next week. Engrossed in her effort, the sound of a car turning into the driveway startled her. Looking at her watch, she realized it was almost 4:30. Was that Michael? *He's early.* Flipping off her computer, she stepped out of the tack room, watching as the scene unfolded.

In the yard, Jessica was jumping up and down by the driver's side of Michael's car. He stepped out and grabbed her, swinging her around in a circle. Jessica squealed in delight. Meanwhile, ever jealous, Princess barked at his heels.

Lisa's heart warmed at the sight. Michael put Jessica down and reached over to pick up Princess, cuddling the squirmy sausage under his arm. All the while Jessica was tugging on his wind suit, urging him over to Precious's palace. He followed her to the pen but seemed hesitant. Jessica opened the gate and urged him in. Putting down the dog, Michael took a step into the corral.

Lisa smiled nervously and called out a greeting as she neared the pen, giving Michael an excuse to remove himself. Neither offered a kiss.

"I'm glad to see you," he said.

Before she could say anything further, Andrew joined them. He seemed glad to see Michael and hugged him. By this time, both he and Jessica were fighting for Michael's attention. Lisa suggested Andrew drive Michael and Jessica around the property on the Mule to see the cattle. When they left, Lisa rushed into the house to freshen up.

After moving a few items into Jessica's room to free the master for Michael, she showered, fixed her makeup, and then ducked into the bedroom to dress, choosing a sedate cashmere sweater and a pair of clean Wal-Mart jeans. Then she daubed herself with Michael's favorite perfume, Clive Christian X. Did it stimulate him or remind him of the smell of money?

As she slid on her comfortable loafers, the crew entered the house. How wonderful to hear the chatter. In the living room, Michael and Andrew built a fire. Although it was unnecessary for warmth, it set the mood. Jessica, holding the flowers from Michael, asked for a vase. Lisa showed her how to cut the stems and add sugar to the water. Then they placed the arrangement on the coffee table.

Michael deposited a bottle of white wine into the refrigerator and, after asking where the liquor was stored, fixed them both a Crown and Seven. While Lisa prepared dinner, he and Andrew played the new Xbox game Michael had bought him. For once Andrew did not seem uptight. Lisa could see his newfound confidence.

She watched Michael carefully as he interacted with the children. He came across as unsure of himself, nervous. Not the Michael of old—the one who was confident, cocky, and full of himself. Her husband looked out of place in his wind suit and white running shoes. And that hat!

Thankfully, Jessica monopolized the dinner conversation, filling Michael in on her new friends and the school. And, he listened intently, asking questions; Lisa was relieved the jerkiness was absent. Her earlier reservations about the visit faded.

***

Later that evening, Michael followed Jessica into her bedroom and let her pick out a book, lying with her as she read aloud. He took his time, dreading being alone with Lisa. An uneasiness engulfed him. Being absent left him clueless about where household items were. The place had changed so much—the kids, too.

Finally, giving Jessica a goodnight kiss, he knocked softly on Andrew's door and entered, telling him good night, and returning to the living room.

Lisa turned off the television, and they sat silently, listening to the pop and crackle of the fire. Hypnotized, Michael stared into its flames, sweating profusely.

He looked at Lisa. "Hey, let's go for a walk."

"Sure, if that's what you'd like to do."

They put on their coats and noiselessly crept out of the house, wandering to the calf's castle, hands stuffed in pockets. Michael leaned on the fence railing and stared at Precious, curled in the back corner of the loafing shed.

"Jessica's crazy about that calf, isn't she?"

"Yeah, she's cute, you should see her. She's out here after school taking care of Precious. She even brushes the calf's hair every day, and the calf loves it."

"So those little critters don't get any bigger than what's out in the pasture?"

"No, wild, isn't it? I'd never heard about them before." Lisa then launched into a speech about miniature cattle and how she researched them.

Michael loved hearing Lisa's impassioned talk. It reminded him of her old days at Benson Bart when she would talk his ear off about a client and how she was streamlining processes.

"You know," Lisa said, "the kids and I are really taken with your dad. I don't understand why you don't care for him."

"He's so, you know, just like a fencepost. Most of the time he just sits there and doesn't say anything."

"That's only when your mother is around. She does the talking for both of them."

"Very funny. When I was a kid, he was never around. He'd never go to my school plays or baseball games. He didn't seem to care about me or what I did. All he did was work."

Michael gently took hold of Lisa's hand and led her past the barn, then down the trail to the creek where Jessica had been lost. That seemed like years ago. A full moon lit the path. It was as if they were walking in daylight. All he could hear was the crunching of their feet in the leaves and his heavy breathing. A slight breeze mixed Lisa's perfume with the tang of the damp night air, exciting him.

They reached the creek and stood, staring at the sky between the open patches of the forest. He had not seen stars so bright since his youth. Looking around, he noticed the trunk of a large tree that had fallen and guided Lisa to the sitting place.

"This reminds me of that camping trip we went on with my fraternity brothers," Michael said.

"That was some trip. I remember you and Johnson were discussing how to put up the tent. I kept trying to get your attention, but the two of you wouldn't listen. I knew how to put it up because I'd used one like it in Girl Scouts."

"Oh, I remember. You finally got our attention by raising your voice and stomping on my foot. I limped around for a week."

"If you hadn't had so many beers, maybe you would have paid more attention to me."

"Oh, but I did pay attention to you that night, remember? That's why I insisted on our own tent." Michael laughed. "I won't forget the look on Johnson's face while you were ordering him around. Hold this pole. Hammer the stake there."

"So, what happened to Johnson? Ever hear what he's doing?"

"About five years ago, I heard he took a job with a bank in Tucson…. I haven't really kept up with the gang."

Both sat in tranquility, gazing into the universe. Michael realized Lisa was his only constant in a rapidly shifting world.

Clasping her hands and turning to her, he said, "I'm so sorry. It should never have come to this. I miss you so much. You just don't know." He leaned forward and planted a chaste kiss on her cheek. "Let's call a truce, enjoy ourselves this weekend. I don't want to talk about the future; I just want to be with you."

Lisa said nothing but removed her hands from his and put them on his shoulders. Gently she pulled him toward her and gave him a long, leisurely kiss.

Despite his impatience, Michael unhurriedly caressed her, breathing softly into her ear, professing his love. When he could contain himself no longer, he loosened her bra, tenderly massaging her breasts. That instant they caught fire as they had in that tent so long ago. In no time Michael was easing Lisa down on top of his spread-out jacket. In a burst of passion brighter than the stars, he became one with the only woman he had ever loved.

***

The next morning Lisa stood on the porch and watched as the children walked Michael to his car. He kissed them and waved as he pulled out of the driveway. *Damn.* All her resolve had melted; she had given in. Her mind had said "no," but her heart had said "yes."

CHAPTER 14

Lisa was on a mental high for the first time in days. Andrew was spending the night with Eric while Jessica stayed with her new friend from 4H. Additional time to bond with the children gratified her, but being a single parent was exhausting. In Raleigh, she could come and go as she pleased, hiring sitters was affordable. But now… *A day out with the girls at the antique festival and a Saturday night alone is just what I need.*

Lisa listened to Jessica chat excitedly about what she and her friend planned to do today. Smiling, she realized they all needed a break sometimes.

They pulled up to a modest one-story house just north of downtown La Grange. Climbing out of the car, Jessica grabbed her Barbie sleeping bag and suitcase and skipped to the front porch. Lisa trailed behind, digging out a business card containing her cell number to give to the friend's mother in the event of an emergency. After exchanging pleasantries, Lisa returned to the vehicle.

"So, what are you and Eric planning this evening?" Lisa asked. She eased the truck away from the curb.

"Oh, I don't know. We may go over to Jason Hamachek's house. He's got a new Xbox game. Or maybe we'll just hang out and watch some movies."

"Fine, just be sure you check with John for permission before you go anywhere."

"Oh, Mom, you worry way too much."

"Well, you just mind what I say. Teenagers seem to have a knack for getting into things they shouldn't."

Andrew failed to respond, and they silently drove the last several blocks to Dorothy's house. Before they could reach the front door, Eric appeared.

"Come on, Andrew. Dad's got to run into Brenham. He says he'll drop us off at the movies while he runs errands."

Andrew's pace quickened, and he disappeared into the house before Lisa made it to the porch.

At the entrance, she called out. "Dorothy?"

"In the kitchen. Come on back."

Lisa found her friend sitting at the table, studying on her computer.

"Good morning. Just trying to catch up on my reading. It seems like I never have time to find out what's new in the animal treatment department. Let me finish this one article."

Pulling out a chair, Lisa sat and looked around. Small but comfortable, the room was the center of family activity. A built-in desk was piled with what appeared to be bills as well as other stacks of loose paper. Red gingham curtains with tiebacks framed the window over the sink, contrasting nicely with the white tile countertops. Dorothy had placed a collection of wicker baskets on top of the cherry-red cabinets. No state-of-the-art Viking stove, Sears appliances—in white—were the doctor's choice.

Lisa compared it to her sterile state-of-the-art set-up in Raleigh. That seemed so long ago—and so unimportant. Dorothy's kitchen could whip up food just as good—no, probably better—than the expensive one Lisa owned.

"Sorry about that." Dorothy checked the time. "Edith should be here any minute. Let me get my things. We can wait for her on the porch."

Both settled into comfortable rockers. Lisa was idly surveying the modest neighborhood when Edith arrived with Rachael.

As Lisa and Dorothy climbed into the back seat, Rachael asked, "Are you ready to shop till you drop?"

Laughing, Dorothy said, "You really mean that, don't you? That's why I wore my most comfortable shoes."

Lisa buckled her seat belt. "So, Rachael, are you looking for anything special?"

"Not really. I just won't rest until I've seen everything Warrenton has to offer."

Dorothy groaned. "That means we'll be there until it's too dark to see where we're walking."

"Well, you'll just have to hold your horses. We're having breakfast first," Edith said. "I need to be well fortified before I join the teeming masses."

Affirmatives rose from the others, so Lisa remained silent. Then Rachael said, "Lisa, I know this will ruin your diet, but once won't hurt."

"You don't have to inhale," Dorothy said.

"She won't be able to help herself." Edith snickered.

Before long, Edith pulled into a rutted gravel driveway, weaved around an 18-wheeler parked parallel to the highway, and came to rest facing a metal building fronted by a wooden porch badly in need of a coat of paint. A group of men sat at one of the stoop's picnic tables, gobbling their meals and taking long swigs out of large glass bottles of Coke.

Surprised, Lisa stifled a gasp. Workers in faded T-shirts, torn jeans, and dirty work boots filed in and out of the building. A man in slacks and a tie hauled a huge white plastic bag to his car. *I'd never stop at a place like this!* She started to say something but realized the rest of the group ignored the shabby, tired appearance of the restaurant.

"I've been dreaming about having a taco ever since we picked the date for our outing," Edith said.

She climbed out of the truck and the others followed suit, with Lisa trailing behind.

"The usual?" Edith asked. Rachael and Dorothy nodded and grabbed a table in the small dining area since seating was at a premium.

Motioning to Lisa, Edith directed her to the back of the line that snaked past a cooler filled with milk and soft drinks and ended in the seating area. "You can get what you want, but personally I like the combination taco. It has bacon, eggs, potatoes, and cheese. Can't beat it. And one is big enough for a good meal. We all generally have coffee."

Lisa quickly scanned the menu, noting dishes she was unfamiliar with such as menudo and barbacoa. "Make mine a combination, too. Coffee will do. Sounds good to me." Uneasily Lisa continued to take in her surroundings.

As they waited, Lisa listened to the chatter in Spanish and English. A small cabinet filled with Mexican pastries stood in the far corner, but customers paid scant attention to the conchas and empanadas. At last, it was their turn to place an order at the counter. While the server did not appear to be fluent in English, Edith articulated the request and, in nothing flat, the group reunited at a small table for four shoved under the mounted television tuned to a Spanish talk show.

Lisa unwrapped the glittering foil bundle placed on a Styrofoam plate hesitantly, only to find a large, steaming flour tortilla filled with goodies. Rachael shoved a small container of hot sauce over to her.

"This'll really open your nose. I love it."

Anxious, Lisa opened the pungent salsa, then dribbled a small amount on her taco and re-rolled it. If she was going to die of ptomaine poisoning at least she still had some good life insurance. A small nibble….mmmm…a larger bite…MMMM. The taco was excellent! Her earlier hesitation disappeared in the process of biting, chewing, and savoring the mixture of flavors.

"Oh, that's good," Dorothy said. "If I get another one, would someone split it with me?"

"Here, you can have mine," Rachael said. "I'm not really that hungry." She shoved the uneaten delectable toward Dorothy.

"Are you sure?"

"I'm sure."

Soon, stomachs satisfied, the group was back in the truck and on the way to Warrenton.

"Now, you need to understand that this fair has been going on twice a year for over forty years," Rachael said. "It started at the Rifle Hall in Round Top, run by a lady by the name of Emma Lee Turney and it just mushroomed. The show's going on in Round Top today, but we like the one in Warrenton better."

"How come?" Lisa asked. She knew that Round Top was a popular area for Houstonians to build second homes.

Edith chuckled. "Warrenton's the people's antique fair. You've never seen so many antiques, uh, junk, in your life. Sometimes I wonder who could come up with such crap. The Round Top merchandise is more high-end—and more expensive. One of my friends has a booth in Warrenton every year. She says the dealers from Round Top come to Warrenton, buy stuff, and take it to Round Top. Then they stick a real high price on it."

"Let's just say it's not as snooty in Warrenton. I'd say the difference is like going to a basement fire sale versus Neiman Marcus," Rachael said.

"Rachael, that's not quite fair. You can find some good deals on quality antiques in Warrenton if you know what you're looking for," said Dorothy.

"And look for deals we will. I'm determined to find an antique stove," Edith said.

"Stove? Whatever for?" Lisa asked.

"I want to update my apartment, turn it into more of a country look. I remember a stove my grandmother had and, if I see one, I'll get it. That's one reason I brought the truck. We need a way to transport our treasures."

The chatter continued as Lisa gazed out the window. Quiet pastures were occasionally punctuated with outdoor tables filled to the brim with bric-a-brac and glassware. Well-worn furniture, bicycles, and tools added to the clutter. Soon the truck slowed.

"It's going to be crowded today," Edith said. "We're still a half mile from town."

Cars were streaming into grassy fields confiscated for parking lots. Some eager shoppers alit with push carts and forged their way north toward the vast array of canopies that protected the merchandise from the fickle spring weather.

Patiently Edith maneuvered the stop-and-go traffic, allowing pedestrians to flow from one side of the highway to the other. Pickups loading or delivering merchandise pulled on and off the road. Booths lined the main thoroughfare as far as Lisa could see. A Fayette County sheriff on horseback directing traffic at a popular crossing startled her.

"We're going to go and park up where my friend 'Knobs' has her booth," Edith said.

"Nobs?" Lisa asked. "What kind of a name is that?"

Edith laughed. "She sells cabinet hardware. They call her the knob lady. She tells customers they can feel her knobs."

Lisa giggled.

Just past the convenience store, Edith nudged the truck to the right and followed a gravel road that wound through the displays. Eventually, they reached the parking lot and piled out. The still-cool air promised a wonderful day.

"Now," Dorothy said, "Let's synchronize our watches. I have ten. Sometimes cell phone reception is bad out here, so if we get separated, we're meeting at Zapp Hall for lunch at one."

"Let's shop!" Rachael said. The group responded with a cheer. Then the others set matching white straw cowboy hats on their heads. The crowns were high and decorated with a solid black band. The width of the brims was such that no sunlight intent on producing wrinkles could assault sensitive faces.

Lisa tagged along, speechless, as they rambled through canopies set out like big tops in a circus. Each vendor had specific merchandise jumbled on tables; excess product strewn over the ground. She stared in wonder at a collection of antique outboard motors. Red, orange, and blue engine covers in varying stages of deterioration contrasted with the chrome trim. Rust patches and streaks punctuated the blue one, denoting rough use. Surrounding the machines, Lisa spied old fishing poles and an extensive collection of fishing lures—several inch-long minnow-looking things with two or three sets of treble hooks. They came in every color from yellows and whites to reds and greens.

If man has made it, Warrenton had it. Slowing, Lisa eyed the display of Persian rugs critically, thinking of how one would look in her living room. After examining the price tags, her dire financial situation sent warning messages. Sadness welled inside her. *How I miss being able to spend without scrutinizing every penny.* She moved on reluctantly.

Looking up, she realized the white hats had clustered around a kettle corn vendor. Rushing forward, Lisa could smell the tantalizing aroma of freshly popped corn rising from the black iron vessel and see the vendor vigorously stirring the concoction with a wooden paddle.

Rachael stuck a bag under Lisa's nose and said, "Don't ask about the calories."

The sweet-salty flavor tickled Lisa's taste buds, and she quickly opened her purse to buy her own. Rachael waved her down, telling Lisa they could share. "Don't want to spoil our lunch."

As the group passed mounds of woven baskets, Christmas ornaments, silverware, candles, primitive furniture, bird houses, trunks, antique linen, dishes, cookie jars, necklaces, cow hides, water fountains, and yard art, Lisa took in the clamor. Laughing groups of shoppers made crunching noises as they meandered along gravel walkways. Vendors in earnest discussion with potential buyers added an air of excitement to the cacophony of sounds.

Around noon the group paused near a makeshift café with a seating area.

"I could use something to drink," said Edith. "It must be 5 p.m. somewhere on the earth."

"Indeed, it is," Rachael said. "Everyone, wait here."

The others took a seat while Rachael scurried off into the labyrinth of booths. In short order, she was back clutching four plastic champagne flutes. As she slid onto the bench next to Dorothy, she passed out the mimosas. "Nothing like a little bubbly to get the afternoon started!"

All touched their glasses together as Dorothy made a toast.
"To friends! The world would be a lonely place without them."
"Here, here!" The group cried.
"Now my turn," Edith said. Clearing her throat, she began,

"To my friends:
Friends we are today,
And friends we'll always be;
For I am wise to you,
And you can see through me."

Another rub of plastic on plastic and hearty laughs all around.
"Your turn, Rachael," Edith said. She eyed her half-full glass.
"Here goes…

Here's to you, here's to me…
May we never disagree.
But if we do, the hell with you…
Here's to me!"

Everyone laughed hysterically, the sweet potion adding a carefree air to the already festive occasion.
"My turn!" Lisa held up her glass. The others watched her expectantly. Looking from woman to woman, she put her glass into the air—then froze, shakily lowering it. "You guys just don't know how much this means to me, to be included in your group. It's been so tough, you know, and friends make it better…" Lisa bit her lip, trembling, trying to hold back the tears.
"No, you're the one who has blessed us," Dorothy said. She then patted Lisa's hand. "Frankly, we were getting a bit bored with each other. You've really livened things up."
Rachael put her arm around Lisa. "Dorothy's right. The others are boring."
"Speak for yourself!" Edith said. "I'm certainly not boring."

Their laughter gave Lisa a chance to shake off her sentimentality.

"Ladies, drink up," Rachael commanded. "We have about an hour left until our lunch break, and I intend to make every minute of it count."

The crowd was growing; most of the people had no doubt been coaxed out of the big cities because of the wonderful weather. Lisa was glad the trio was wearing those crazy hats because she could spot them; it kept her from getting lost.

While Dorothy was examining antique physicians' tools, Lisa spied an older woman with a stroller. Her children? Grandchildren? Curious, she sauntered around, peeking into the baby carriage. Shocked, Lisa stared into the face of a perfectly coiffed Yorkshire terrier. Pink bows held the vixen's bangs out of her eyes. Before Lisa could gather her thoughts, the white toppers were on the move. Scurrying to Edith, she relayed the bizarre scene.

Finally, the group found its way to Zapp Hall. Despite the late hour, the lines were long. Dorothy took charge. "Edith, you take beer orders, I'll get the sandwiches." To Lisa, she said, "Just bear with us. We get the same thing every year, you'll love it."

Rachael and Dorothy disappeared to order the food while Lisa helped Edith with the beer. After what seemed forever, Lisa and Edith, loaded with eight Shiner Bocks, found an empty spot at a shaded picnic table. On a nearby stage, an older man soloed, picking folk songs to the delight of the hungry shoppers.

The cold brew went down well, too well. Funny. She had enjoyed the resort, but this was fun, too. *It's not where you are, it's who you are with.*

Dorothy and Rachael appeared with their arms full.

"Here, you'll like this," Dorothy said. She pushed a wrapped bundle toward Lisa. Opening it, she discovered the strangest sandwich she had ever seen.

"BLT with shrimp?"

"Yeah," Rachael said, "And you'll never eat it any other way."

One bite and Lisa had to agree. She quickly devoured the mash-up cradled in homemade bread and washed it down with the second beer.

How she was going to shop, she did not know. Glancing at Rachael, she noticed her pal had eaten little of her sandwich and had balled it up in the wrapping paper. Just as Lisa felt a big burp coming, Rachael flipped open the lid of a Styrofoam container while Dorothy passed around plastic forks.

"Sorry ladies. In honor of waistlines, we are all sharing. You only get a few small bites. Now, don't be pigs." Dorothy glared at everyone and dug in.

"What is it?" Lisa asked.

"Only the best pie in Texas, maybe the world," Edith said. She stabbed her fork into the gooey creation.

"Come on, have a taste," Dorothy said.

Lisa was scared not to. One forkful hooked her.

"Wow!" she said as she waved her fork in the air. That is good. What is it?"

"Chocolate chip," said Ethel.

In double quick time, the pie was gone. Trash cleared; the shoppers plotted.

"We're going to have to get serious," Edith said. "I haven't seen a stove I'd be proud to have in my home yet—and it's already near three."

"Time's a wasting," Rachael said. "Look, I'm not feeling too good. I'm going to sit here a while and then you can come get me. Say, in about an hour?"

"We can go home if you're not up to it," Edith said.

"No. I insist. You continue. Your dream stove is somewhere nearby. I can feel it in my bones."

The group forged ahead, peaking in every booth just quickly enough to determine whether the desired antiquity was available. About an hour later, Edith let out a shriek. "Over here!" Gathering the team, she whispered instructions. "Dorothy, you go get Rachael. She's our best shopper. We can't move on it without her."

Edith and Lisa scanned the booths until Rachael arrived. Bright-eyed, she took command.

"Lisa, see the stove?" Rachael asked.

Lisa looked and quickly focused on a green and cream metal structure that appeared to be from the art deco era sporting a triangular-shaped oven and drawer pulls.

"Yes, I see it."

"Now, wander over there, nonchalantly, browse the other wares, and casually ask the price. Scope it out carefully and tell us how you appraise its condition."

Lisa nodded affirmatively. "Then what?"

"Come back over there." Rachael pointed to a booth around the corner, out of sight of the targeted merchant. "You can file your scouting report, and we'll decide how to proceed."

Lisa walked briskly to the booth while the others sauntered to the meeting place.

An inspection showed that the stove had a few rusty places, but the logo on the cream panel of the oven door was intact. Opening the top which commandeered the left side of the stove, Lisa found four gas jets. Unfortunately, someone had shut the lid while the burners were on, leaving two scorched areas. Inside one of the drawers, Lisa spied pieces of the Des Moines Register dated 1971 strewn with pieces of hay. Otherwise, the stove was in decent shape. Before she could ask the price, another shopper inquired. The vendor said, "$450."

After looking a bit more, Lisa made a beeline to the rendezvous.

After disclosing her findings, Edith said, "Hmm. It's a little steep, but we've been looking all day. I wonder if he'll take $400?"

"Nothing doing," Rachael said. "Besides, it has damage. Let's shop a little more."

Grabbing Edith's arm, she pulled the reluctant bargain hunter away from the area. Eventually, Rachael steered the group back toward the booth. Again, she barked orders.

"Dorothy, take off that hat and give it to me. Go over and see if the stove is still there. Inquire about the price."

Dorothy followed directions while the others waited anxiously. By this time, an exhausted Lisa was ready for a good hot bath.

An elated Dorothy returned about ten minutes later. The price is down to $225!"

"Excellent," Rachael said. "Now, here's the plan. Edith, you go in, offer him a check for $150. Tell him you have a truck and can haul the stove away."

"You're kidding, aren't you? Won't that be an insult?"

"Nothing ventured, nothing gained. Go! Now! Besides, if he outright refuses you can always offer more."

"OK, you're the shopping queen, but you better be right."

Lisa and the others browsed nearby while waiting for Edith's return. Time dragged. Eventually, a jubilant Edith, waving her cowboy hat, ran up to the group, ecstatic.

"I can't believe it! He took my offer!"

"I knew he would," Rachael said. "Just think. It's the last big weekend of the antique festival. If he halved his price, he must have been desperate."

"You're a genius. He told me he was from Iowa and that he'd gotten the stove out of someone's barn. He said his son would kill him if he brought that heavy thing back home and had to unload it."

Glancing at her watch, Dorothy announced it was nearly five. "Now it's time for happy hour. I declare the outing a success. We have what we came for. Let's get the stove loaded and find a drink. I'm parched."

As everyone trudged back to the truck, Edith called a quick halt. "We have one more purchase. Follow me."

Within minutes, Lisa found herself standing in front of the hat dealer, eyeing hundreds of white cowboy hats with black bands just like the others wore. Dorothy urged Lisa to try one on. When Lisa attempted to pay, Dorothy waved her off, saying, "My treat!"

Hat on her head, Lisa proudly followed the others back to the truck. Now she belonged. Laughing, Edith explained they only wore the fool things shopping at the antique festival and that if she ever saw Lisa wear it elsewhere, she would pretend not to know her.

Loading the stove was another matter. The vendor and two other men from the booth next door helped the women situate the appliance in the back of the truck. Edith tied it down with rope and bungee cords, although Lisa doubted the thing would go anywhere. It was just too heavy.

After discussion, the group decided to return to Dorothy's house since the good vet promised them a perfectly scrumptious pitcher of margaritas. The drive was tedious, however. Vehicles were streaming onto the highway. Easing into the southbound lane, Edith navigated the stop-and-go traffic, cursing everyone who tried to pull in front of her without waving for permission.

Edith said, "It's just un-Texan-like to cut in without motioning to be let in. I'd gladly let them in if they'd only ask."

As they picked up speed, the talk turned to how Edith was going to get the monstrosity out of the truck. "I just might not take it out. There's an antique appliance store in Houston where they refurbish. The more I think about it, the more I think I'll just run it up there Monday."

"What'll you do about the store? Who'll watch it for you?" Lisa asked.

Edith chuckled. "Didn't you know? Scotty's a great watch dog. I leave the key under a rock at the back door. My good customers get what they need and leave the money or write an IOU. If you give off bad vibes to Scotty—watch out!"

Dorothy pulled out her cell and called the Mexican restaurant, placing a large order to go. Edith dutifully swung by the eatery, and, after some haggling, Rachael got the honor of paying for the delectables.

The group settled in earnest around Dorothy's table, gobbling chips and queso as Dorothy fired up the blender. All agreed on salt, promising tomorrow would be the day to behave. Besides, every healthy eating guideline had been broken earlier.

Lisa went to the bathroom and, sauntering back, looked around, but could see no sign of the boys. Then, she remembered Andrew had said they might go over to Jason's. She thought about calling Andrew, but, upon hearing laughter coming from the kitchen, promptly forgot.

After one more round, Dorothy cut them off. "No friends of mine are going to be in a wreck." Then she fixed coffee, which they savored along with the sopapillas. As Lisa dragged the last of her doughy treat through honey, she thought about her friends through the years. This group topped them all.

"Everyone, I have something to tell you," Rachael said. The others eyed her expectantly. "I'm afraid this is going to be my last antique festival."

Lisa started to make a crack and then, sensing Rachael was about to cry, sat silently.

"What is it?" Edith put her hand on top of Rachael's.

"I have cancer."

Stunned, no one said a word. Finally, Dorothy said, "There are lots of good drugs around today—"

"It's pancreatic cancer. It's spread to my liver."

Sobbing, Edith took Rachael into her arms, causing Rachael to burst into tears.

"Does Vivian know?" Dorothy asked.

Rachael shook her head. "I haven't talked to her. I don't know how to approach her or what to say."

"How long do we have?" Edith asked.

"A couple of months, maybe."

CHAPTER 15

Lisa waited with the children until the bus arrived. She needed to work on some tax returns, but her heart was not in it. Rachael was on her mind. *What would I do if I only had months to live?* At first, Lisa had been angry about the loss of a new friend. Now, depression replaced outrage.

Lisa wandered back inside and sat on the couch, reflecting. Just when you are happy and comfortable, shit happens. Then you get restless, searching for ways to rekindle that feeling of pure joy and contentment. Eventually, you do, but somehow it always slips away. Sighing, she pulled out the old diary.

Julia, it appeared, wrote in it whenever she could. William, who must have been her husband, was out most of the day tilling, working the cotton crop, and Julia was solely responsible for the vegetable garden. Once a month the family did laundry, bathed, and washed clothes. Lisa could not imagine how the woman managed while pregnant with her third child.

> *October 14, 1883*
> *What a day yesterday! William left to deliver some cedar shingles he'd cut for Mr. Faison in La Grange and pick up some supplies. Since he'd be late, he said not to wait supper. I'd left chicken stew to stay warm by the fire and put the boys to bed early.*

I'd just gotten them down when I heard a ruckus outside. Sounded like coyotes and all. But then I heard something rustling in the barn. I got the gun and went to check, afraid some of those rascals had cornered one of our cows. I found a white woman! She was dirty and cold. Hair all stringy. Was hiding over in the corner, trying to cover up with hay. Said she'd been passing through with her husband but he'd beat her something terrible. She just ran and said she didn't know how long she'd been running. Then she fainted. I roused her and helped her into the cabin. I moved the boys into our bed and put her into theirs. Poor thing. I fed her some stew and wiped her face and arms with a warm wet cloth. She went to sleep, a restless sleep. She screamed out some. She's still sleeping this morning. Guess I'll need to wake her soon. She needs more nourishment.

How horrible it was for women back then. I'm so lucky I have options. The telephone interrupted her thoughts.

"Mrs. Dunwhitty?"

"Yes, this is she."

"Good morning, my name is Charles Hinze. I'm the assistant principal at La Grange High School. I have your son, Andrew, here in the office. It seems that he missed a few classes this morning. He's given me a note from you stating he had your permission to be gone. I was just checking to be sure that was correct."

Lisa froze. *Of course, I haven't given him permission. He's never done anything like this before.* "No, actually I didn't, Mr. Hinze."

"Hmm. Well, I see."

"Look, I need to come to town anyway, so why don't I just come up there, and we can get to the bottom of it."

Mr. Hinze sent Andrew back to class, and they agreed to meet in an hour. Lisa changed into one of her Tahari suits and slapped on some makeup. She thought about calling Michael but nixed the idea. He would press the move to Houston. *I'm so glad Sam and Ellen will be here soon. I guess I've been letting Andrew have too much time to himself. I can't believe he'd do something like that.*

She was in the assistant principal's office shortly, all ears. Andrew explained he wanted to get something else for breakfast. His first-period chemistry class was so boring he saw no reason to be there. He just left and came back—no big deal. Lisa nearly went ballistic when she learned he had borrowed Eric's truck to run into town.

"Aw, come on, Mom. You know I'm a good driver. You said so yourself."

"That's not the point, young man." By now Lisa could hardly contain her anger and frustration. "You were driving without a license and forged my name on your permission note."

Mr. Hinze said, "Well, Andrew, skipping school is a serious offense. I'll have to give you three days of detention. The rest will be between you and your mother." Then he stood. "Thanks for coming, Mrs. Dunwhitty. From now on the school will call when we receive a note giving Andrew permission to miss school, just to verify it's legit." To Andrew, he said, "You better get on back to class, now."

Andrew stole out with an irritated look on his face, while Lisa turned her attention to Mr. Hinze. "Please call me any time there is an issue with Andrew. I want to do all I can to cooperate with you."

"Well, that's refreshing, I must say. Quite a few parents these days side with the child and against the school. But, yes, if anything else happens I'll give you a call."

After the disturbing meeting, Lisa walked into the Laundromat with tubs of dirty clothes. She felt foolish in her work outfit and was getting a few odd looks. Fuming, she buried her head in the newspaper, trying to distract herself. Her cell phone buzzed. Michael. *He must be out of his interview.* Conscious of the eyes trained on her; she stepped outside to take the call.

"I've got it! I got the job!" Michael began giving Lisa a blow-by-blow description of the interview. "The headquarters is in Dallas, but they want me to open a new sales office in Houston. We'll be living there."

Lisa desperately wanted to tell Michael about Andrew, but she could not get a word in edgewise. When Michael said he was on his way to Houston to look at houses, her blood boiled.

"You don't care about anyone but yourself, do you? Andrew's in trouble because he skipped school and all you can do is talk about some damned job and money that's supposed to make us live happily ever after!" Noticing someone had taken her clothes out of the dryer and dumped them into a rolling basket, she hung up on him.

Hurriedly folding the laundry, her fury mounted at Michael for not listening. She had been trying to tell him she did not want to move, but he was oblivious. Anxiously Lisa checked her watch; time to pick up the kids. Climbing into the pickup in her suit with several baskets of laundry made her feel idiotic. *I won't be a doormat anymore.*

The trio rode home in silence. Lisa finally spoke, grounding Andrew for a week. No friends, no video games, and no driving practice. Additionally, if he got into any more trouble, he would not get his license. Andrew made out that he did not give a hoot. Was it an act for her benefit? Or did he just not care?

Back at the house, Jessica opened the door to let Princess out while Lisa and Andrew started unloading the clothes. Princess zoomed down the steps, sniffed them a bit, and then hurried to the garden area to do her business. As Lisa, basket in hand, was just about to kick open the front door, she heard Jessica scream. Turning around, she saw a large, beautiful bird diving straight toward Princess, who was squatting on the ground, unaware of the menace above.

The creature's wings and tail were striped black and white, its underside a rusty red. But the beak! An ugly, hooked bill loomed from below the ebony eyes, spelling danger. Lisa dropped her load and raced off the porch, her high heel catching between one of the wooden slats on the steps. She landed with a thud; spread eagle on the stone walk that led to the house.

Lisa lay, looking up, watching in horror. The evil aviator bore down on Princess, its talons open, ready to thrust its claws into the dog's silky red coat. Within feet of its prey, the bird hesitated and veered off, surprised by Andrew, who was running full speed, waving his hands, and yelling at the top of his lungs. A bawling Jessica rushed to snatch up the alarmed puppy.

Relieved, Lisa could now pay attention to the razor-sharp pain that was stabbing her right knee. The palms of her hands, reddened and skinned where she had absorbed a good part of the fall, also stung. Struggling, she rolled over on her left side to survey the damage—and damage there was. Her knee hitting the stone walkway had stained and shredded her skirt, her joint growing by the minute. Gingerly she sat, grimacing with every flex of her leg. By that time, Andrew and Jessica were hovering over her, expressing worry and concern.

"Mom, don't move anymore until we check things out," Andrew said. "And Jessica, put Princess back in the house. I'm going to need your help." Thankfully, Jessica did as Andrew asked. Andrew removed Lisa's right shoe and commanded, "Move your toes." When he saw she could comply, he confidently stated, "Good, no break."

Then, with the children at her side, Lisa fought to stand, the throbbing so severe she almost passed out. Once upright, she ordered the youngsters to help her to the car.

"Shouldn't we call 9-1-1?" Jessica asked. "Your knee looks awful."

Lisa thought a minute about the high deductible insurance she had just purchased because she had been struggling to pay the outrageous COBRA insurance premiums and shook her head. "No, we'll just drive to the hospital. It'll take too long for the ambulance to get here, and anyway, they need to save it for people who are seriously injured." She could not bring herself to tell the children the ambulance would cost too much; afraid they might later sacrifice their own care.

Limping to the truck, Lisa realized she could not drive, and had to depend on Andrew. *Great, his punishment hasn't even been in place for an hour, and I'm already making exceptions.*

She climbed into the vehicle, getting as comfortable as possible, and glanced over at Carl's place. His truck was outside. Looking at Jessica, she asked, "Would you like to stay here while we go into town? I can ask Carl to come over and the two of you can check up on the cattle and get the hay out. I don't think we'll be back early enough for Andrew to do it."

With those arrangements out of the way, Lisa and Andrew returned to La Grange. She sat quietly, trying not to concentrate on her knee that exuded pain with every bump in the road. *Every time I think I've got Andrew figured out; he surprises me. Sometimes he's a little kid—other times a man. He sure has more opportunities here to make a difference than he did in Raleigh. He's taken on so much responsibility and hasn't complained, either. Now I'm going to feel like a real bitch punishing him.*

"Andrew, I'm proud of what you did today, saving Princess from that bird and helping me."

"You're welcome."

"And just because I'm proud doesn't mean you're off the hook. You're still grounded." Lisa was expecting pushback, but Andrew said nothing.

The emergency room visit was routine. The good news, nothing broken. However, Lisa was on crutches and her knee in a brace, a bad sprain. When she and Andrew arrived home, it was almost eight. As they pulled into the driveway, Jessica came running out, Carl following her.

"Momma, Momma, are you alright?"

"Yes, I'm fine dear, just a bad sprain."

"Come on, I've got a surprise for you."

Carl inquired about her injury and said his goodbyes, promising to check on her tomorrow.

After Lisa had struggled up the porch and into the house, she inhaled a delightful aroma she could not place.

"Ta-da!" Jessica triumphantly gestured as she urged Lisa into the kitchen.

Immediately Lisa realized the table had been set, complimented by a small bouquet of wildflowers. Jessica hounded them to sit and then served. Lisa finally had a match for the odor that had welcomed her—chicken and dumplings!

Jessica set a small bowl of salad at each place and handed Andrew some cornbread. Then she dished up a generous helping of comfort food onto each plate.

"Jessica, how in the world?" Lisa said.

"Mr. Carl. Mr. Carl is so nice, Momma. He took me down to Zink's Corner and bought the chicken and showed me how to make the dumplings and cornbread. The salad was my idea. I know you want me to lose weight, so I thought we'd have salad, too." With a flourish, Jessica sat down and dug into dinner.

"Did Mr. Carl pay for the chicken?" Lisa asked.

"He wanted to, but Miss Edith wouldn't let him. She told him she'd settle with you later."

Lisa tasted the fare. "Yum! This is good. You're going to have to teach me how to make it."

"Yeah, it is good," Andrew said through a full mouth.

After dinner, to Lisa's amazement, Jessica and Andrew worked together to clean the kitchen and put away the leftovers. They went about their bedtime routines without complaint while Lisa sprawled on the couch. She then made calls to Edith and Carl, thanking them profusely and asking how she could ever repay their kindness. Carl said he had rather enjoyed cooking with Jessica and would be happy to share the recipe.

As they were winding down their conversation, call waiting clicked in. Lisa gave Carl a hurried goodbye and took the next call. Ellen was on the line.

"How are you, dear? I talked to Jessica earlier and heard all about the horrible bird and your terrible fall."

Lisa gave her an update.

"Anyway, I wanted you to know that Sam and I will be there by May 1st. We'll just park the trailer on the back side of the barn."

"I thought you were going to take a leisurely trip down and see the country? You don't need to hurry on my account. We're fine."

"Honey, it's no problem, really. We're missing the action there and can't wait to see those cute cows." Ellen paused. "Does Michael know what happened?"

"I haven't had time to call him yet. We just arrived home." Lisa then avoided the subject by telling Ellen about the wonderful dinner Jessica fixed. Hanging up, she leaned back on the couch and closed her eyes. *I'm so mad at him I don't feel like talking. I don't think he cares, anyway. He's just into his new job.*

Hearing Andrew enter the room stopped her contemplation.

"Hey, Mom, look at this. The bird that tried to attack Princess was a red-shouldered hawk." Andrew handed Lisa the picture he had pulled off the Internet. Sure enough, it looked just like the bird they had seen.

"And Mom, this is cool. Did you know that by the time they are five days old, they can shoot their poop over the edge of their nest? We need to look around and see if we can find bird mess on the ground so we can find their hangout."

Lisa grimaced. She did not really want to have anything further to do with that magnificent, but frightening creature.

After covering herself with a lap blanket and bunching the couch pillow under her head, she drifted into a light, unsettled sleep with the help of pain meds.

***

Lisa spent the next morning on the couch, watching TV. She needed to call Michael but could not summon the energy. Around ten her phone rang—Carl, asking if he could come over. She told him sure, just to let himself in.

He entered and took a seat on the edge of the recliner. "How are you doing this morning? Anything I can get for you?"

"Oh, Carl, I'm so worried about Andrew." Lisa explained the visit to the assistant principal's office. "I'm concerned whether the punishment I've laid out will get his attention."

"I believe you got more problems than just skipping class." Carl removed a small baggie from his shirt pocket and handed it over to Lisa. "I found this."

Lisa looked at the leafy contents of the bag and then opened it. The dank smell accosted her nostrils. She paled. "Where'd you get this?"

Carl exhaled. "I found it in my truck a couple of weeks ago. I always leave the keys in the ignition. I got in one morning and something seemed wrong. The seat appeared to have been moved. I started looking around and found that bag."

"You think it was Andrew's?"

"Yeah. I sat up for several nights. Sure enough, a couple of days later he got in the truck and left. He came back about an hour later."

"Why on earth didn't you tell me sooner?"

"Lots of people take family word over other people's word."

"Carl, you're family…. Oh, Carl, what am I going to do?" Lisa sniveled.

Carl rose and paced. Finally, when Lisa's tears ebbed, she asked, "Any idea where he's going?"

"I haven't a clue. The speedometer's broken so I can't tell how many miles he's driven. Doesn't seem to be much gas used."

"Any idea where he got the pot?"

"No…. Want me to confront him?"

"Let me think this out. I don't need the two of you crossways. With Michael not being here, he needs a man around who can give him some guidance. I need to catch him myself. Then he can blame me for anything that happens."

"If you think that's the way to go. I don't mind talking to him."

"Let's do this. You call me on my cell the minute you see him leave, and then we'll follow him. I want to know where he's going, how bad this thing is."

After Carl left, Lisa put in a call to Edith, who readily agreed to stay at the house for a couple of days—the cover being that Lisa needed to stay off her knee. Then Edith would be there to watch Jessica if Carl called.

That evening, after Edith and Jessica settled in for the night, Lisa limped into the kitchen and took some pain killers. Glancing at the clock, she realized it was after ten. Leaning back on the couch, guilt overcame her. She needed to tell Michael everything that was going on with Andrew.

Lisa dialed Michael's number. His cell continued to ring. Just as Lisa was about to hang up, the connection came alive. A female voice answered, "Michael's phone."

"Who's this?" Lisa asked.

"Who's this?" the woman on the other end asked sharply.

Stunned, Lisa put down the phone. She could hear the voice at the other end saying, "Hello? Hello?"

***

Michael washed his hands methodically, still boiling, replaying yesterday's conversation with Lisa. He had worked so hard to find a job and was so excited about finally getting everyone together—and she spoiled it. Sure, he was worried about Andrew, but getting him back to the city where he belonged would solve everything. *So what if he skipped a few classes? That was just part of growing up.*

Returning to the table, he gazed at Sharon. He planned to tell her their friendship was off, but Lisa changed all that. *At least Sharon listens…she understands… she cares.* A tingling sensation he had not felt in a long time for any woman other than Lisa intruded.

Michael settled in his chair and, quickly spotting the waiter, ordered another grand gold margarita.

"Your phone rang, so I answered. Whoever it was hung up."

As casually as possible, Michael raised his iPhone that lay next to the half-eaten basket of tortilla chips, glancing at the number. Quickly he shoved it into his jacket pocket.

"Who was that?"

"My mother… I'll catch up with her later." Trying to divert the conversation, he asked, "Any thoughts on a school for Andrew?"

"He's sixteen, right?"

"Yes. And bright. I don't think he'll have any problem getting into any of the private schools. In fact, he was in a private school in Raleigh and did quite well."

"One of my co-workers has a son about that age. I'll ask around."

"Hmm. I do need to find a school that will challenge him. He must be bored, or he wouldn't have skipped school yesterday. I'm going to try to find him a summer program to enroll in. He's probably behind the other gifted students because of his semester in La Grange." Michael chatted edgily, trying to focus on what Sharon was saying.

Meanwhile, the smartphone was burning a hole in his pocket. He and Lisa had not discussed their relationship since the night they had sex. But it was only sex. *We've drifted apart. I don't fit in. She's chosen a different path.*

Michael glanced at his watch. "Oh, Sharon, look at the time! I need to get up early in the morning. I've got lots to do before I start on Monday. Get out of the hotel, buy some new clothes, take my drug test."

While the waiter processed his credit card, Michael made plans for Saturday night. "Tell you what. You pick the restaurant and make the reservations. I'll treat you to the best time you've ever had."

A mischievous smile crossed Sharon's face. "Mr. Dunwhitty, you're on!"

The two walked to her car, laughing and talking. "Want me to drop you off at the hotel?"

"No, it's out of your way. I'll just take the rail."

As Sharon unlocked her door, Michael moved close beside her. After the lock popped, he gathered her into his arms and softly kissed her. She yielded. He pulled her close, erotically thrusting his tongue into her eager mouth.

Before he lost all control, he pulled away. "See you Saturday." With that, he strode off, not looking back.

***

Lisa gimped aimlessly around the kitchen; mind numb. A woman answering Michael's cell! She tried to pass it off as something innocent, but a nagging feeling would not let her. When Michael was jobless, she had a good excuse for staying at JF. But now…but now, he had work. *I'm out of excuses.*

And Andrew needed Michael. A boy needed his father. *Can I handle him? He's already taller than me!*

The next morning Lisa could not bring herself to think about either Andrew or Michael. A change of scenery might clear her mind. Hurriedly she packed her laptop and the diary, then impulsively arranged a late lunch in town with Dorothy. A trip to the library in La Grange might help her figure out who this Julia woman was.

"The Franks family? Julia Kingston?" the librarian asked. "Yes, I do believe we have some information on the family." The woman disappeared into another room while Lisa settled at a large wooden table. After propping her leg and crutch on a nearby chair, she spread out a tablet and pen, then started her laptop.

"Here you go, ma'am. We have a file on George Darby. He was one of the original settlers in Fayette County. Also, I think he was the father of Julia Kingston." Lisa took the folder and dug in. Embarrassed, she realized she knew next to nothing about the history of her home.

Amazingly, among the handwritten notes and photocopies of book pages, was a research paper dated 1964, written by a candidate for a master's degree in history at the University of Texas. Intrigued, Lisa carefully read the well-documented manuscript.

It turns out that George Darby had migrated from Tennessee in 1826 and secured a league of land in the area from Stephen F. Austin.

Lisa dug into her memory. The attorney had told her the league of land was family land. She now owned George Darby's land?

Darby had promised Austin he would build a grist mill. And, for that, he obtained extra acreage.

Turns out Darby did not marry until he was almost fifty. He then married Mary Collier who was only twenty. *The old coot.* Lisa cringed. That must have happened frequently back then. She could not see herself marrying someone that old.

Glancing at her watch, Lisa realized the time had gotten away from her. She was due to meet Dorothy in half an hour at Subway. Rapidly skimming the paper, Lisa hit gold. Julia was indeed Darby's daughter! Born in 1861, she was the youngest of three children.

Reluctantly Lisa stopped. The librarian promised to keep the papers waiting for her after Lisa expressed her intention to return after lunch.

She and Dorothy settled into a booth. "So, how's Rachael?" Lisa asked.

"She's trying to decide whether to quit work. The hospital told her she could work part-time, but Rachael said she doesn't feel up to it."

"Does she have enough income to tide her over if she isn't working?"

"I don't know. I'm going to run by her house after work and see what she needs us to do."

"Let me know. I want to do everything I can to help." Lisa opened her sub. "I don't understand. Isn't there something the doctors can do? Chemotherapy or something? This is just so sudden."

Lisa picked at her lunch. Her knee was aching, so she popped two more pills and washed the blue miracle workers down with iced tea. Then she told Dorothy about Michael's job and the woman. Dorothy asked a few questions here and there about whether Lisa had any idea who had answered Michael's cell phone.

"So, what are you going to do?" Dorothy eyed Lisa so severely that Lisa trembled.

"I don't know." Lisa stared at her half-eaten turkey sandwich. "I want Michael back in the worst way. I miss him, I really do. But I've got something here. I'm a piece of history. You know, growing up my dad died early. My mother eventually remarried. I was an only child. I don't know…. I never really felt part of anything. And then, Michael and I moved so often…. Every time I thought I had a place in this world where I could live forever…we moved."

"Aren't you upset about the woman answering the phone?"

Face crumbling, Lisa scrunched her shoulders. "I've got to get back to the library."

"I don't mean to stick my nose in your business but sounds like you're in denial."

Lisa sat silently, staring at her lap.

After an awkward silence, Dorothy eyed the time. "Sorry, I got to go. Call me if you need to talk. I'll let you know what Rachael says." Standing, Dorothy swept her trash into the plastic bag, patted Lisa's shoulder, and steered toward the exit.

Lisa took a few more bites before balling it up and throwing it away. Back at the library, she shut off the engine and sat in the parking lot. The nippiness of the morning air was long gone, leaving the weather pleasant. Carl had told her there would not be any more freezes and suggested they get the garden in as soon as possible. High clouds skidded across the big, blue sky. *Dorothy's right. But it's too painful to think about Michael now.*

She closed her eyes and imagined what it was like to live on the JF Ranch with no tractor, no pesticides to kill scorpions. It must have taken hours just to drive a wagon to La Grange! No wonder they shopped at Zink's Corner. She had heard how hot the summer could be and could not imagine living without air conditioning. Just the monotony of building a cooking fire every day and sewing your own clothes freed Lisa to see Julia in a new light.

Settling in the library, Lisa continued her research. Before leaving, she purchased a history book, *An Early History of Fayette County* by Weyland and Wade. *That'll keep me busy. Maybe I won't have to think about Michael, Andrew, or Rachael.*

***

Lisa, dressed in sweats, met the kids at the door. "Hurry up, change, and get the animals fed."

"Are we going somewhere?" Andrew asked.

"We're going to the family plot," Lisa said.

"Why?"

"We've got some cleaning to do."

"But Mom, I've got homework."

"No, this is important. I need you to load the weed eater and lawnmower in the Mule and come get me when you're finished with the cows."

"Do I have to go?" Jessica asked.

"Yes, you do, but you can bring Princess."

The kids scattered and Lisa sat on the porch, impatiently waiting for them. When the Mule rolled up, Lisa threw her crutch in the back and crammed in next to Jessica, who scooted closer to Andrew. As he complained about the lack of room, Princess squiggled and barked. Lisa's knee throbbed.

"So, what exactly are we doing?" Andrew asked.

"We're cleaning the family plot and looking for a grave."

"Why? Who cares about some old tombstones? We don't know any of those old people, anyway."

"Well, I do, and they're family. I'm looking for a particular grave for Julia Kingston. We might as well clean while we look," Lisa said.

"Whatever," Andrew said.

When they arrived at the gate, Andrew turned off the UTV, retrieved Lisa's crutches, and unloaded the lawnmower. Jessica let go of Princess, who sprang off the seat and eagerly sniffed her surroundings.

"Momma, are you sure you need to be walking around?" Jessica asked.

"Don't worry sweetie, I'll be fine." Lisa could feel her excitement mount. "Andrew, mow the back right first, where the older graves are.

Jessica, you pick up all the sticks and rocks, so Andrew won't run over them."

Lisa limped over to Joe and Ruby's grave, a small tombstone for baby Regina nestled behind. She studied it, lost in contemplation.

Andrew put in earplugs and donned safety glasses. After checking the gas level, he gave the lawnmower a crank and mowed a strip around the outside of the fence. Then he cut a path inside. Once he had an area clear enough for Lisa to walk, she struggled to the rear of the cemetery.

"Momma, over here!" Jessica waved excitedly.

There it was!

Julia Darby Kingston

1861 - 1921

Mother and Wife

Lisa hobbled as quickly as possible and, standing in front of the stained stone marker, wept.

"Momma, what's wrong?" Jessica fastened onto her hand.

"Nothing, pumpkin." Lisa pulled Jessica to her. They cuddled. The whining lawnmower passed behind them, giving Lisa a chance to choke back her tears.

"Isn't this exciting?" Lisa asked. "We have a family."

"But, Momma, we've always had a family. Me, you, Daddy, Andrew, Princess, and Precious… and Granny S and Mel and Granny Ellen and Papa Sam."

"You're right." Lisa hugged Jessica again. "But now we have lots more family. Go check on Princess, I don't want her lost."

After Andrew finished with the lawnmower, Lisa had him weed eat around the graves, giving specific instructions not to hit the markers with the cord. She visually inspected the fence to see whether any repairs were necessary. It needed a coat of paint.

Lisa tapped Andrew on the shoulder. He pulled out one of his ear plugs. "Why don't you stop? It's getting dark. You can finish tomorrow. Jessica, round up Princess."

Settling in the Mule, Lisa heard a blood-curdling scream, and looked around just in time to see Jessica and Princess bounding out from the edge of the clearing. Before they could reach Lisa, an obnoxious odor assaulted her. She gagged and wheezed.

"Gross!" Andrew said.

"Momma, Momma, a skunk!" By this time Jessica was crying and Princess was writhing on the ground, rubbing her nose with her paws, and foaming at the mouth.

"Just leave everything, let's get out of here," Lisa said.

Coughing, Andrew said, "She's not sitting next to me."

Lisa did not blame him one bit. "Put Princess in the back. Help Jessica in."

Dog and mistress loaded in the rear; Andrew roared off.

"Jessica, hold on," Lisa said.

The jarring ride sent searing pain through Lisa's knee. When Andrew stopped at the barn, the pungent smell akin to a mixture of rotten eggs, burned rubber, and garlic assaulted her with a renewed ferocity.

"You stink," Andrew said.

Jessica began to cry, and Lisa cast Andrew a warning look.

"Andrew, go in the house and get Jessica's robe and flip-flops. Jessica, we'll get those clothes off you and then you can take a bath." Lisa wanted so badly to physically comfort her treasured daughter and tell her everything was going to be alright, but an acidic taste erupting in her mouth kept her from getting any closer.

Clothes stripped and robe wrapped tight, Jessica ran as fast as her rubber-clad feet could carry her. Princess raced, too. "No, Princess!" Lisa was hysterical by this point. The dog would wreak havoc inside. "Andrew, get her."

"I'm not picking her up."

"Then just don't let her in the house."

Lisa watched as Andrew and Jessica tussled with Princess at the front door, the dog wailing. Lisa sobbed. Andrew returned and drove Lisa to the front door.

"What are we going to do with Princess?" Andrew asked.

"I guess someone will have to give her a bath."

"Who's someone?"

"Someone would be you. I can't bend over the tub."

"Aw, Mom, do I have to?"

"You have to. Get that tub in the barn and move it outside. I don't want that dog in the house."

Grumbling, Andrew hooked the leash on Princess and dragged her away.

Lisa settled into the kitchen, relieved when Jessica appeared. "Did you wash your hair?"

"Yeah. I washed it twice."

"Come over here."

Lisa took a hand full of Jessica's hair and a big whiff, fighting back the urge to regurgitate. "Uh, your hair still smells like skunk."

When Princess dashed into the kitchen, Lisa gagged. "Andrew, didn't you use soap?"

"Duh, Mom, I soaped her twice and rinsed extra-long. She still stinks."

"I can't go to school smelling skunky. The kids will make fun of me," Jessica said.

Lisa then called Dorothy for advice.

"Well, I suggest cutting their hair off. You can try tomato juice or vinegar or some other products on the market, but if they got squirted really bad, cutting is the easiest and quickest way to get rid of the smell."

"Can you make room for Princess tomorrow?"

"That should be fine. I'll ask them to do her first thing."

"What about a beauty parlor for Jessica? Who do you suggest?"

Dorothy was silent for a minute. "Why don't you just cut it off yourself?"

"I've never cut hair before."

"Just take some scissors and cut it straight across. You can take her to get a cute cut later. At least she'll be able to go to school in the morning."

"Thanks. See you tomorrow." Lisa hung up the phone and turned to Jessica. "Dr. Dorothy says we should cut your hair off. That way it won't smell so bad. Besides, summer will be here soon, and you'll be happier with shorter hair. Long hair is so hot."

Jessica whimpered.

"Dr. Dorothy knows what's best."

Wiping a tear from her eye, Jessica steeled herself and nodded in an affirmative.

Lisa and Andrew worked feverishly on the cut. After re-wetting her hair and combing it, Lisa took the big pair of scissors she had found in Aunt Ruby's sewing basket and began to chop. Andrew tried a ruler first and then a bowl to be sure Lisa's cut was true. Lisa gathered the hair in a plastic bag and ordered Andrew to take it outside to the trash. Then she washed Jessica's hair again in the kitchen sink, rinsing it with vinegar. A quick sniff by Andrew assured him no one would harass her at school.

"Just let me know if anyone messes with you. I'll take care of them," Andrew said.

With a little coaxing, Lisa convinced Andrew to fix sandwiches for dinner. She just could not stand any longer. As he was spreading the mayo, he snickered.

"What's so funny?" Jessica glared.

"It was just...just you and Princess running out of the woods, yelling and all! And the smell! It got to the Mule before you did! You should have seen Mom's face." Andrew screwed up his nose and twisted his mouth. Both Lisa and Jessica burst out in loud hoots. Just like his dad, Andrew had a way of seeing the bright side of a dire situation.

"Well, the two of you have a story to tell tomorrow at school, don't you?" Lisa said.

When Edith arrived, she took one look at Jessica and said, "Oh, I see you got a haircut." Jessica began a blow-by-blow description of the skunk escapade and had everyone laughing.

After doing the dishes and sending the kids to bed, Edith and Lisa sat in the living room.

"I really didn't want to say it in front of Jessica," Edith said, "but that is one bad haircut."

"I know. I just hope the kids don't tease her at school. I'm going to try to get her a decent trim as soon as I can."

Edith picked up a book. Lisa reviewed the photocopies she had brought home and dug into the area's history. George Darby died just after the Civil War. Lisa had not realized how desperate things were in La Grange during Reconstruction.

Darby had fought the Mexicans in 1836; he had even been at San Jacinto. She could not find any evidence he had fought for the Confederacy—probably too old. It turned out Julia had married a man by the name of William Kingston. After poring through the diary, Lisa finally figured out that Julia's brothers had died childless. Her oldest brother, Franklin, had joined Terry's Rangers and was killed during the war in Kentucky. The other, Enoch, died during the 1867 yellow fever epidemic. Lisa had seen Enoch's grave in the cemetery. Julia's daughter, Minnie, had married Joseph Franks Sr., who was Uncle Joe's father.

In what seemed no time, Lisa glanced at her watch. 2 a.m.! Edith had turned in long ago. Reluctantly she crawled into bed, determined to continue her diary readings. Amazingly, Lisa did not toss and turn. She felt a part of something—something wonderful.

Despite the serene start to her night, Lisa woke in a cold sweat. All that research had been an excuse to keep her from doing what she had to do—deal with Michael and Andrew. Glancing at the clock; 4 a.m. But sleep eluded her. Rising, she inched into the kitchen.

While preparing chamomile tea, she vowed at least to deal with Andrew. That was the major decision before her. He had somewhat redeemed himself by taking her to the hospital, but using Carl's truck and the marijuana thing was bad.

Lisa had tortuously searched the entire house and barn but could not find any traces of grass, drug paraphernalia, or incense. She had been watching Andrew closely for red eyes, but they seemed fine. *What if I can't catch him in the act? Then what? I can't wait forever to confront him.*

Lisa wrapped her terrycloth robe tightly about her and carried her drink out to the porch. The usual night sounds accosted her, a screech owl, insects chirping, and wind gently rustling the trees. The skies had turned overcast, hiding the stars.

Back and forth, back and forth. She rocked intently. *Andrew, Andrew, what's with you? Why are you doing all this? Have I failed you? What type of punishment is going to make you understand the seriousness of your behavior?*

When Lisa was young, her discipline had been separation from her friends; the one thing Lisa could not stand. But Andrew did not seem to care. Besides, breaking up Eric and Andrew's relationship might compromise her friendship with Dorothy. As for the weed, Lisa did not have any evidence, yet, that Eric was involved. And it was not Eric's fault that Andrew took his truck—Andrew was responsible for what had happened.

Lisa got another cup of tea and blew on it to ratchet down the heat, turning her thoughts to Michael. She wanted to believe a woman had not answered his telephone, but the woman had said "Michael's phone" and Lisa had used speed dial. Did Michael even know about the incident? Lisa decided to confront him.

The sky began to lighten in the east as she took her last sip. The sun peeked over the horizon, sending the birds into a frenzy of squawks, welcoming the new day. *It's time. I'll tackle Michael this afternoon.*

***

At precisely 2 p.m., after feverishly rehearsing the call and making an appointment with herself so she would not lose her nerve, Lisa picked up the phone.

"Michael?" Lisa was relieved to hear his voice rather than a female's. "Not only did Andrew cut school, but I think he's smoking pot." Lisa explained what Carl had said.

"I knew living there was a bad idea. You falling, Jessica sprayed by a skunk, and now this. Haven't you been monitoring his friends?

Skipping class is one thing, but drugs? You need to ground him, keep him from seeing that boy, what's his name…Eric?"

"I don't know whether Eric has anything to do with it."

"He must. Andrew's never done anything like that before."

Lisa did not like where the conversation was heading so she changed the subject. "I tried to call the other night, but a woman answered your phone." No sense in beating around the bush.

He hesitated. "Oh, she's just a friend." Lisa listened to Michael's voice intently, not convinced. "You hang out with a woman late at night and call her a friend?" Lisa continued to drive the spike deeper.

"What do you care, anyway? You don't want to have anything to do with me or this job. You're doing absolutely nothing to see that the family has any money to live on. You couldn't care less whether this family's safe and together. You don't care that Andrew is running with the wrong crowd or that the kids are getting an inferior education? You're just selfish!"

An emotional numbness swept through Lisa. She had been prepared to attack—not to defend herself. *What a manipulator!* As her fury mounted, her voice became shrill and grating. The two argued for another fifteen minutes until Lisa ended the standoff by hanging up.

Had her knee not been hurting so badly, she would have gone out for a walk to work off her indignation. All she could do was sit in her office and rage, feeling sorry for herself. Soon her heart hardened. She would make Michael be the one to ask for the divorce, so he would have to pay big time! *I'm not going down easy.* She would ask for eighty percent of everything. *I'll show him.*

Then, it hit her. *Everything? What in the hell do we really have?* A bunch of expensive furniture rotting in the barn, 401Ks that were practically worthless, and a house in Raleigh caught up in the bankruptcy of Harris Cardiac. And what good would any of that really do her?

Thunderstruck, she realized all they had to show for their relationship were the kids. *I'll mount an all-out custody battle*—Inner doubts intruded. *Was staying the best thing for the children?* Closing her

eyes and breathing deeply, she waited for a message from the heart....
"Yes." Digging in the drawer, she pulled out her sparkly Rolex, pressing
it against her chest, then, sighing, limped to her office in search of a
buyer.

CHAPTER 16

Just as Lisa was about to tell Edith not to spend the night anymore, her cell rang. Two in the morning. Sliding on a sweat suit and tennis shoes, she paused and then grabbed the shotgun and shells from the closet.

Lisa hobbled out to find Carl sitting in the driver's side of her truck. After putting her rifle next to his in the back seat, she climbed in. Once settled, she punched on her iPhone app for the GPS tracking device installed on Carl's vehicle. "He's headed towards Zink's Corner."

"Does he have much of a head start?"

"Some." Lisa continued to watch as the blue dot moved down Dog Run Road. She then showed Carl the screen.

"I'll be damned…look, he's turning left."

"Isn't that a dead-end road?"

"Sure is." Carl studied the screen intently. "He's turning into the old Pitney place. It's been abandoned for years."

Both watched as the dot stopped.

"Let's go," Lisa said.

They drove in silence, Lisa monitoring the stationary blip. As soon as Carl reached the turnoff to the deserted farmhouse, he pulled to a stop and switched off the ignition.

He whispered. "The house is about half a mile up ahead. I'll walk up there and see what's going on."

"I'm going, too."

"Not with your knee. You'll never make it."

"I'm going."

"Then walk behind me." They both retrieved their weapons and crept forward, keeping close to the right side of the gravel-strewn drive.

Jumping at every sound, Lisa was thankful for a full moon. Within minutes, her leg opposed the trek by emitting a dull, steady ache. A skunky odor intensified as they approached a gap in the woods to her right. As they crept closer, she peered in, catching a glimpse of waving rows of plants, watered by several hoses running from the nearby tank. Waves of fear rippled through her exhausted body, but she forged on, gripping the shotgun tightly. As they crept toward the house, beams of light and angry voices pierced the stillness.

Lisa saw a burly man with a beard pointing a shotgun at Andrew. Another had a spotlight shining on him. "What the hell are you doing here?"

A third walked up to her son and snatched something out of his hand.

"You little shit. You've been stealing our stash." He backhanded Andrew, whose lip burst. Blood dribbled down his shirt. Andrew put his hand to his mouth.

Lisa gasped.

Carl whispered, "Get behind the tree. Keep your gun pointed at the fat one." He then stepped into the clearing and said, "Hands up or I'll shoot." He pointed his weapon at the men. They hesitated. "I mean it. Now." He waved the barrel of his rifle in the air and fired a shot. The noise reverberated in the chill, damp air.

The stocky man carefully put his gun down and eased back.

"OK, mister."

"Andrew, get out of here. If you wasn't a Franks, I'd run you in with the rest of the scum." As the youngster dashed into the shadows, Carl called out to Lisa, "Get him out of here."

Frozen, she watched as Carl took out his cell phone. Regaining her composure, she yelled, "Over here," while flipping on the flashlight. The pair stumbled back to their truck. Once inside with the doors locked, Lisa glared at the teen. "You almost got us all killed. What were you thinking?"

Andrew pulled up the hem of his T-shirt and gingerly wiped the blood trickling down his chin. "How did you find me?"

"I put a GPS tracking device on Carl's truck."

Andrew stared at her.

"You're not the only technically savvy person in this family."

Lisa hurtled toward the ranch and pulled in just as sirens announced their presence on the rutted thoroughfare. After multiple vehicles sped past, Lisa struggled out, slamming the door, and hobbling into the kitchen, Andrew trailing behind. Edith appeared wrapped in a bathrobe, and, seeing Andrew's face, put some ice in a dishtowel and silently handed it to him. Then she put on coffee. The crew sat in uncomfortable silence, listening to the moans and creaks of the century-old farmhouse.

Thirty minutes later, Carl eased into the kitchen, gratefully taking the full mug Edith offered. Settling, he surveyed the solemn faces around the table. "Andrew, you're lucky those guys didn't kill you. That's the biggest pot find they've ever had in Fayette County."

"You need to apologize to Carl for taking his truck and putting him in danger," Lisa said.

"I'm sorry."

"And you're going to pay Carl back by doing chores for him for the next month. I don't know what your other punishments will be. Your dad and I will have to discuss it."

Edith looked at Andrew. "Was Eric involved?"

"No. One of the guys in my P.E. class had heard about the place. He pays me $100 for a big baggie. It sounded like an easy way to pick up some cash."

"What on earth do you need money for?" Lisa asked.

"Video games…. Stuff," Andrew said.

"Do you realize that makes you a drug dealer?" Edith asked.

Andrew hung his head. "I guess I didn't really think it through."

"Andrew, go to bed," Lisa said.

After he left, Edith said, "Kids have done worse and turned out OK." She patted Lisa's hand.

"I'm in shock. I just don't know what to say. And it happened right under my nose," Lisa said.

"I'm going to go. It's been a long night," Carl said. "The deputies want to interview me more thoroughly tomorrow. I didn't tell them you and Andrew were there. I just said I had seen a lot of traffic up and down the road and became suspicious. Hopefully, the dope dealers won't say anything. I told them if they did, I'd see they got charged with assault." Carl looked uneasy. "I won't cover for him anymore."

After Carl left, Edith rubbed Lisa's back. "Try to get some sleep."

But sleep didn't come. Visions of Andrew being denied jobs because he was a felon haunted her. *My fault. I've been too busy worrying about myself. I should've paid more attention.* He needs money? For stuff that isn't important…. *I can't blame him…. That's what we've taught him.*

CHAPTER 17

Lisa knocked on Rachael's door. When she finally answered, Lisa trembled. Her friend had lost so much weight already.

Rachael returned to the couch and lay down. "How's your knee?"

"It's fine…. How are you feeling?"

"Could be better. But hey, not much I can do about that."

"Aren't you angry?"

"Of course. I've been thinking a lot about how things aren't fair. But I finally realized I could keep on being mad as hell, but nothing would change. So why bother."

"Have you talked to Vivian yet?"

"No."

"Do you want to?"

"I don't know. I do, but I don't want her to see me like this. I don't want her to remember me this way."

"If I were Vivian, I'd be furious that you shut me out."

Rachael stared at the ceiling. "I don't know how to tell her."

"Why don't you let me talk to her? I don't mind, really, I don't." *If I can't straighten my own mess out, maybe I can at least help someone else.*

Rachael relented and gave Lisa Vivian's cell number. Then Lisa began to put together a shopping list.

"What do you feel like eating?"

"I'm not really hungry."

"But you've got to eat something. What sounds yummy?"

"I don't care. You choose."

"Fine. You get a nap, and I'll be back in a while."

Lisa parked outside the nursing home and waited. She knew Vivian's shift would be over at three. Soon she saw her exit with a group of women. Lisa got out and waved. Vivian walked over.

"Viv, I need to speak with you."

"If it's about Rachael, I'm not interested. I'll never forgive her for how she treated me."

"Please, we need to talk. It's important. Let's take a walk."

Vivian reluctantly agreed and put her things in her car. Then she joined Lisa as they strolled to the nearby park. Lisa directed Vivian to a bench; they both sat.

Looking into Vivian's eyes, Lisa said, "I don't know how to tell you this, but Rachael is dying."

Vivian gave her a strange look. "What is this, some kind of bad joke?"

"No, she has pancreatic cancer. It's already in her liver. The doctors say there's nothing they can do about it."

Vivian stood and rapidly walked up the path. Lisa started to follow, then thought better of it. She sat, studying the nearby meadow. Wildflowers peeked through the grass, but Lisa was not in the mood to contemplate new beginnings and growth.

Eventually, Vivian returned, eyes red, and sat down next to Lisa.

"Rachael wants to see you, but she's afraid," Lisa said.

"Afraid of what?"

"I think she's afraid you won't see her, afraid you'll hate her, and afraid you'll remember how she looks now than remember how she used to look."

"What do you mean, look?"

"She's lost a lot of weight. She's not looking so good."

"I don't care. She needs me."

Lisa felt relieved. "I've got some shopping to do for Rachael. Then I'm fixing her dinner. Why don't you just go on over? I'll be there in a bit."

They both stood, and Vivian turned to Lisa, who held her tight.

"Thanks for letting me know."

"I'm glad I could help."

As Vivian walked away, Lisa sat, toying with her phone. She rolled last night's scenario through her mind, still trying to grasp the enormity of the situation. She needed to tell Michael but knew he would blame her for everything. Eager to avoid another confrontation, she sent a text briefly outlining what happened.

Lisa perused the aisles before deciding on comfort food. A mild meat loaf, macaroni and cheese, green beans. Nothing spicy. Then, on a whim, she decided on banana pudding for dessert.

Arms loaded with bags, she let herself in the back door. "I'm back."

"We're in the den," Rachael said.

Lisa unpacked the bags and joined them.

Rachael was lying on the couch with her head in Vivian's lap. Vivian was stroking her hair.

"Thanks. I know I'm a hard-ass sometimes," Rachael said. "Now that Viv's with me, I can face what's coming."

Since the cancer started, Lisa had felt helpless, not really knowing what to do or say, but now thankful she had helped her friend in some way. "I'm going to get dinner started," Lisa said. She returned to the kitchen fighting back tears and vowing that Rachael would not spend her remaining time alone.

***

Later, Lisa dished up fast food fried chicken for herself and the children, too exhausted to cook another meal. Just before they finished, Andrew's phone rang.

"Let it go to voice mail," Lisa said.

"It's Dad," Andrew said.

"OK." Lisa continued to eat while listening to one side of the conversation.

"I know. I told you it won't happen again. I learned my lesson…I don't know, Dad. I guess…Sure…. I love you, too."

"What was that all about?" Lisa asked.

"Dad says I'm going to come live with him when school starts."

Lisa almost choked. "He what?"

"He says I can't stay here anymore because of all the trouble I got into."

Lisa's anger flashed. *How dare he? How dare he decide about where Andrew was going to live without consulting me?*

"You're not going anywhere. You're staying right here."

"What if I don't want to? This is a stupid hick town, and all the people here are stupid. You never let me do anything fun. I'd rather live with Dad."

"Enough. You aren't doing anything fun because you got in trouble. Besides, you'd be grounded at your dad's, too…. What about Eric? We said you could see him, but you haven't in quite a while."

"He's a stupid dweeb. I don't like anyone in Texas!"

"Momma, Andrew, stop!" Jessica closed her eyes, put her hands to her ears, and started humming loudly.

Lisa glared at Andrew, said nothing more, and removed the remains of dinner. Jessica eventually stopped droning but failed to finish her meal.

"Jessica, go get your bath," Lisa said.

Andrew rose from the table, brought his plate to the sink, and then stomped out of the room. Stewing, Lisa scoured the plates with a soap-filled scrubber.

The truth was that Andrew was old enough to decide where he wanted to live. She could never prove Michael was abusive or that living with him was detrimental. In fact, the blame for Andrew's behavior would shift to her. And Andrew wanted to move. Listlessly, Lisa filled her glass of wine and crumpled onto the couch with Julia's diary.

March 2, 1884

Today is real cold. The wind's tearing through the trees, but at least the sun is out. With William gone to Zink's Corner and the kids at school, I am able to have a bit of time to myself. Lord knows I need it. I got a hunk of bread and some cheese wrapped in a dish towel with me for later. I don't expect William home too early. Today's Texas Independence Day. The whole town is celebrating and I'm sure William will have a mug or two of that German beer. He's not a drinker, bless him, but can't blame him for wanting to take a nip or two every once in awhile.

I love this place. I got momma's old horsehair carriage blanket over my shoulders and I feel quite warm and snug. I'm sitting at the base of a young cypress tree and watching the small waterfall dance and gurgle. The water drops sharply and forms a small pool. I don't know if William knows about my place. Hate to keep secrets from him but I need something all my own.

I'm going to quit writing now and do some thinking about life.

Lisa put her glass down and re-read the passage carefully. *This is it! Julia's secret place! I have to find it. I need a place to get my act together.* She thought about asking Carl to help her but hesitated. *I want it secret. Just me, Ruby, baby Regina, and Julia. If I ask him for help, he'll find out about it. It won't be ours anymore.*

***

The next morning, Lisa propelled herself out of bed around five and, wrapped in her terrycloth bathrobe, hustled into her office. The morning was cool, but Lisa knew the chill would not last. With some effort, she located a topographical map of the area on the Internet. She would take the trail from the house to the creek that led through the mini-cow pasture then head west along Zink's Creek.

An hour later she was back in the kitchen preparing breakfast for the children and eagerly seeing them off on the bus. That chore out of the way, packing for her journey began. Hmmm. Bread and cheese.... Yuck, no, twenty-first-century food—granola bars and a plastic water bottle—would have to do. She would have to be back by one anyway for a conference call.

Lisa grabbed an old backpack of Andrew's and loaded it with provisions as well as her camera and a stake to mark the place in case she found it. Then, the thought of getting lost alarmed her. *Should I leave a trail of breadcrumbs to help find my way back? How stupid.... I'll just follow the creek. No way I can get turned around.*

As Lisa moved along the pasture trail, the morning dew soaked into her lightweight hiking boots. Spider webs sprang up throughout the pasture, sparkling like crystals as the strengthening sun hit the water-soaked tangles. Several hundred yards from the creek Lisa became entangled in a huge web strung between two trees, only to come face to face with a large spider.

The fat creature had a light gray head while its body consisted of white dots and bars on its brown back. Black-tipped legs flayed as it frantically scampered up the silken rope that anchored its snare to a nearby tree. Lisa screamed and then pulled at the web, whose center had a heavy zigzag pattern, the same mark Zorro's sword would make.

T-Rex, who had been following her, gave her a mean look, putting her a bit on edge. *Sure glad he's small.* Web off, Lisa continued her trek. At the creek, where the trail ended, she stopped to catch her breath. The shade was welcoming but could not really fend off the building heat that, along with the humidity, was causing her to sweat mightily.

Critically Lisa studied her surroundings. The brush was heavy around the creek bed. No other path was discernable. Peering into the water, Lisa could not see the bottom. Walking there would be easier than pressing through the undergrowth.

She soon found a long stick and poked into the creek to gauge its depth. The pole slid quickly down several feet, then hit the bottom. A push, however, sent the pole deeper. Lisa sighed. Just as she thought. The bottom of the creek was muddy, like the pond near the house.

Tossing the branch, she began to push through the dense foliage. Brambles caught her jeans and mammoth vines of poison ivy climbing huge oak trees unnerved her. The green-leafed ivy was so beautiful—until you knew its ugly secret. Thankfully, Andrew had shown her pictures of it on the Internet.

After about thirty minutes, Lisa was wishing for gloves and a long-sleeved shirt. *At least I've got sturdy shoes.* Stopping, she took a big slug of water, her cotton shirt clinging to her body. She wiped her forehead on her arm and continued, determined not to turn back empty-handed.

As Lisa entered a small clearing, something moving caught her eye. A snake! Stifling the urge to yell, she froze in her tracks as Carl had trained her. The creature was exquisite. *"Red and yellow kill a fellow. Red and black friend of Jack."* A coral snake, a member of the cobra family. Its venom was exceptionally poisonous. But the snake was unable to strike like a rattler, it had to chew. Getting to the skin between your fingers or toes to unleash its terrible toxin was difficult. Backing up, Lisa was relieved when the reptile slithered into the brush.

Soon she became conscious of all the sounds around her—feet plodding, twigs cracking, labored breathing, branches brushing against her legs and arms, the caws of crows, an occasional rustle of the underbrush caused by a rabbit or armadillo. And then, a gurgling sound. The noise captivated her, faint but distinct. Her chest swelled; a new urgency propelled her onward.

About a hundred yards further, she was there.

Zink's Creek rolled off a pile of rocks, falling about two feet. Below the drop-off, the creek widened into a small pool before narrowing to continue its journey to the Colorado River. Dragonflies darted and Lisa spotted a ladder-backed woodpecker noisily searching for breakfast.

The cypress tree still stood. Lisa sank against its trunk, releasing all tension. A powerful sense of belonging overwhelmed her, a true bond with the women who had come before her. She did not see any marker for baby Regina's belongings, but felt her presence, nonetheless.

I'm not sharing this with anyone. Listening to nature and watching the clouds flit over the sun, Lisa's face softened. An inner strength flowed with every deep breath.

Idly, she glanced at her watch, the real world intruding. Lisa hurriedly ate her granola bar and finished the water. After pounding in the stake and tying her red bandana around it, she reluctantly began the trip back.

While fighting the dense underbrush, Lisa decided to bring clippers to cut a trail next time. The entrance, however, would stay well hidden.

CHAPTER 18

The wind had been blowing mercilessly from the southwest for three days, drying the pastures and turning vegetation into crackling tinder. Gusts, up to thirty miles an hour, whipped the trees into submission, forcing them to bow to the path of least resistance.

Lisa sat in her office, brooding. The whistling seemed to send an ominous message. Cloudy skies made her little shrine to solitude dark and gloomy like her mood.

The negotiations with Whole Foods to buy her organic beef were progressing but at a glacial pace. Their marketing department was toying with a name—The Chicken Ranch's Other Meat. The name did not enamor her. Her friends let her know, in no uncertain terms, that Fayette County residents did not appreciate references to the Chicken Ranch. The community was apparently still trying to live down the infamy of being the home of the brothel immortalized in the musical *The Best Little Whorehouse in Texas*.

Again, she worked the numbers. *Damn. I'll have to counter.* They were not giving her enough profit margin. Hay and cleaning the pasture without herbicides had been costly. Then, too, Lisa owed Carl thousands of dollars. The man continued to insist he could wait until her first check from Whole Foods, but guilt about not paying him nagged at her. Without him, she would be ankle-deep in prickly cow patties without boots.

As Lisa concentrated, the tang of acrid smoke tickled her nose, reminding her how the fireplace smelled when the wind blew exactly right and forced gray plumes back into the living room. A peek out the door revealed nothing unusual. Restless, she returned to her desk and redid her calculations.

Carl called as she was pushing her e-mail's send button on a counterproposal.

"Lisa, we better go down to the back corner of the property. We got big problems." Anxiety edged his voice, Lisa's skin crawled.

"What's wrong?"

"Fire. It's a fire. It's got the whole corner of the property back there. An electrical pole fell, and sparks lit the grass. Then all that dead wood just exploded."

Paralyzed, all she could envision was a huge wall of flames barreling down on the recently cleared pasture—consuming the cattle and donkeys, then the house.

"Lisa, Lisa?" Alarm tinged Carl's voice. "I'll come get you. Don't worry. The La Grange Fire Department's on it, and they're the best around."

"I'll be outside."

Within minutes, Carl rolled up in his ancient vehicle. By this time Lisa could see towers of black smoke billowing out of the southwest. The stink of burn was becoming ever so strong.

"Lisa, get all the water and ice you can grab. I've already called Edith, and she'll meet us there with more."

Lisa scrambled, gathering everything Carl had demanded, and hopped into the truck. He then hit the gas and they began a tire-screeching wild ride down Dog Run Road. Turning south on Highway 71, Lisa swore only two of the tires had hit the asphalt. Several miles down, Carl pulled off the highway and drove along a dirt road. All Lisa could see in the distance was chaos and confusion.

John, in his capacity as the Assistant Fire Chief, had set up a command center off to the right. Another firefighter was busy directing the fire trucks and tankers. A deputy sheriff shooed them off the road, not allowing them to get any closer.

"Sorry, Carl, this area's only for the fire trucks. Just called out Muldoon and Schulenburg. Fayetteville and Ellinger are already here. They're even thinking about calling Columbus. Haven't seen it this bad in years."

Carl left the truck and approached the command post with the ice and water, Lisa in tow. Lisa watched, dumbfounded. A large tanker was emptying water into what appeared to be an immense plastic swimming pool. As fast as the water emptied, a smaller fire truck Carl called a grass truck was loading water into its holding tank. Once filled, the grass truck set off, but not before getting the coordinates they were to report to from John.

Carl tugged at her arm. "They got a map over there showing where they're working." Lisa turned to observe.

"See here, they're going to try and bulldoze a fire line right through here. That's why those Forest Service dozers are here. Hopefully, that'll keep the fire from getting too much closer to the house."

Lisa focused on the chart. To their right, much of the area was charred, with piles of logs smoldering. Gasping, she tried to control her breath. "Can't they put it out?"

"Nope, it's too hot and there's too much fire. Best way is to starve it out, leave it with nothing to eat. Fires need to have fuel to keep on burning." Carl paused. "I always worried something like this was going to happen. Too much dead wood."

"Carl," John said, "Can you and Lisa get a rest area set up? Some of these guys need a break."

"Sure thing." Carl hauled out a canopy from the fire commander's SUV. He motioned to Lisa, giving her instructions. In no time they had it set up and began hauling in ice chests that the Red Cross and various community members had delivered.

Lisa opened a Gatorade and stuck it in John's hand. He took it without even looking at or acknowledging her.

Edith backed her truck to the relief station. "Deputy says I got to move as soon as I unload." Without another word, the trio began removing not only drinking water but snacks and bags of ice.

As Lisa moved supplies, she watched the activity swirling around her, an overwhelming sense of dread building. The clerk at the La Grange meat market stood inside the aid station. He must have come straight from work. Even though it was not warm outside, sweat dripped down his face, mixing with ash and grime. The man shed his helmet and jacket and, tilting his head, finished a bottle of water in one gulp, wiping his mouth on his sleeve. Then, noticing his re-filled grass truck, he grabbed his gear and returned to the front lines.

Edith walked over to Lisa, putting her arm around her.

"Honey, we better get back to your house. The kids will be home soon. The bus may not let them off with the smoke and all." She gently guided Lisa toward her truck and eased out of the area. As soon as Edith vacated her spot, EMS pulled in.

As they drove, Lisa monitored the heavens. Billowing black clouds of smoke were blowing northeasterly, darkening the sky. Despite the rolled-up windows and running air conditioner, a bitter stench now hung heavily in the truck cab.

When they reached the intersection of Dog Run Road, a blockade stopped their progress. Edith slowed, turned off the highway, and leaned out the window.

"Tom, what's going on?" Edith asked.

"The emergency coordinator's real worried that this fire isn't going to be under control for some time. We really don't want residents back in there, it's moving too fast."

"This is Lisa Dunwhitty. She lives at the JF. We're expecting her kids home on the school bus."

Tom lumbered over to his squad car radio and then quickly returned. "They've taken the kids over to the KC Hall in La Grange. The Red Cross set up a shelter there. The bus driver is staying with them until someone can pick them up."

Lisa climbed out of the truck, stood on the running board, and looked over the top of the cab. Worst-case scenarios ran through her mind. "Sir, can I go to the house and get the dog and at least my daughter's calf? If something happened to that little heifer she'd just die."

A pit formed in Lisa's stomach as she watched the deputy in deep concentration. A pained look crossed his face. "I'm not supposed to do it. Promise you won't stay back there more than thirty minutes at most. Just keep an eye out."

"Thanks, Tom," Edith said. Lisa swung back in, slamming the door.

As Edith flew over the washboard road, bumping and squealing her tires, Lisa made a quick call to Dorothy who volunteered to retrieve the children.

"Dorothy said we ought to open the pasture gate and let the cows move up around the house if they need to. The cattle guard should keep them out of the road and hopefully, the rest of the fence will hold. Think we can get Precious in the truck?"

"We'll have to. I knew you should have gotten a trailer."

Lisa started to argue, then shut her mouth. She had no business raising cattle when she was so unprepared for anything that could happen.

Edith backed the pickup to the cattle chute and killed the engine. Running into the house, Lisa grabbed Princess, then stopped, thinking about the few remaining pieces of jewelry. Hesitating, she ignored the valuables and grabbed the diary as well as an armful of towels and sheets. Meanwhile, Edith had cobbled together two stout wooden boards, fashioning a walkway from the end of the chute into the bed of the truck. Coughing because of the pungent smoke, Lisa shoved Princess into the car and approached Precious in her pen. By tempting the calf with a few range cubes, she managed to harness her.

She led Precious into the corral and up to the chute's entrance. Edith stood nearby with additional cubes and a handful of hay. The heifer eyed them guardedly. Nervously Lisa glanced at her watch, twenty minutes wasted.

Edith cooed softly to the bovine, telling her how much her Momma Jessica loved her and wanted to see her. Precious eased forward, tongue swirling, attempting to snatch the tasty treat from Edith's outreached fingers. Edith eased back until Precious was totally in the narrow passage. Lisa promptly shut the gate.

"OK, girl, that deserves a cube." Edith allowed Precious to swipe the greasy pellet from her palm. Edith took hold of the halter rope. "Now, you ease in behind her and gently push that little red booty."

The plan was working until they got to the planks. The calf took one step onto the shaky ramp and planted her hind feet firmly in the dirt, refusing to budge.

"How hard can this be? This damn cow isn't any bigger than Scotty," Lisa said.

Edith grimaced, shaking hay at Precious. "Heerre, cowie, cowie, cowie. Come on."

Lisa burst out laughing. "She's not a cat!"

Precious began bucking and pulling away from Edith. "Lisa, grab her rear! Push!"

"Are you nuts? She's kicking!"

"OK, OK, back off." Edith loosened the halter rope and spread a trail of cubes from the bottom of the ramp into the bed of the pickup. Precious settled, and, after glowering at the two, began to greedily gobble the easily reached snacks.

"To the side," Edith whispered. "On three we slap her on the rear flank and then grab her halter and jerk her into the truck. One…two… three…GO!" POP!

In a flash, Edith and Lisa collared the startled calf and threw her into the back of the pickup. Precious turned, giving them the evil eye. Edith quickly slammed shut the tailgate.

"Lisa, get in there and settle her down. See if you can get her to sit." Edith wrestled a small square bale of hay while Lisa hefted herself into the back of the pickup. They spread it along with the sheets into the truck bed, making a comfortable nest for the heifer. Lisa stroked Precious and talked to her. Edith squeezed into the cab, slapping at

Princess to keep her from escaping. As the truck started to move, Precious went down to a sitting position. Lisa anchored her arms around the beast's pudgy neck, settling in for the ride. The earthy aroma of the animal, tinged with the foulness of wood smoke, mingled with her perspiration, jarred her. *If only Olivia could see me now.*

This time, Edith drove deliberately, taking back roads to Dorothy's office. All the while, Lisa tried to stay positive. Her thoughts roamed to Michael. She longed for his comforting arms; a sounding board, a partner to handle the horror.... *Forget it; he's not here.* About five minutes into the ride, a large aircraft droned overhead, dropping a load of water over the JF Ranch. Her spirits soared.

Jessica, Dorothy, Andrew, and Eric were standing outside the clinic when they arrived. Dorothy guided Edith with hand signals to a ramp they could use to unload Precious. Before the truck could come to a halt, the others peppered Lisa with questions.

"Is Precious OK?"

"Where's T-Rex?"

"Didn't you get Princess?"

By this time, Lisa was in a tussle with the calf who became excited after hearing Jessica's voice. Dorothy climbed into the back of the pickup and helped Lisa guide Jessica's baby down the ramp. At the bottom, her daughter clamped her arms tightly around Precious, who stood still, absorbing all the attention.

Andrew tugged on Lisa's sleeve. "Mom, where's T-Rex?"

"Couldn't bring him, hon. He's too big. We left the pasture gate open so the cows could wander up to the house. I'm hoping the firefighters can at least keep the house from burning even if they can't save the pasture."

Lisa could see the look of concern in Andrew's eyes.

"The others will be fine," Dorothy said. "They'll run from the fire, that's for certain. I'll call John and ask him to be sure the firefighters cut a hole through the fence in case the fire gets up to the house."

Andrew did not respond but tended to Princess; a frazzled-looking Edith had unceremoniously dumped the dog in his arms.

202 | TOUGH TRAIL HOME

"Eric, take everyone to the break room. I'll be in as soon as Jessica and I get Precious settled in a stall. I've got some other patients to see and then I'll join you."

Wearily, Edith and Lisa dropped onto the couch, their smoky aroma magnified inside the clean, sterile interior. She was glad to be out of the danger zone, but her shaking hands betrayed frayed nerves. Exhaustion pummeled her body. Would they have a home to return to? *I didn't realize how much that old house means to me.*

Eric put some snacks on the table.

"Mom thought you all might want something; she thinks eating is a great stress reliever."

Edith and Lisa soon had their mouths full of chips. The boys grabbed a soft drink and disappeared into the barn to check the bovine, leaving Princess under Lisa's supervision. At least Eric and Andrew are talking. *What a relief.*

Edith glanced around, then made her way to the cabinet below the sink. A few seconds later she pulled out a locked metal container.

"What's that?" Lisa stuffed another chip in her mouth.

"Uh, the secret stash—for emergencies." Twirling the numbers, she quickly popped open the box and drew out a fifth of Maker's Mark.

"Oh, My God! How'd you know it was there?"

"Well, sometimes when Dorothy has a bad day or loses an animal, she takes a shot or two. I lost my dog before Scotty, and we came and knocked back a few. She told me the combo—the La Grange area code."

By this time Edith had poured each a large tumbler of Mark and Coke, short on the Coke. Lisa took a satisfying gulp; tired of holding it in, focusing on keeping it together. The fright of the fire and the fear of going home to a vast pile of rubble destroyed the barriers she had so carefully erected over the past few weeks. Uncontrollable sobbing ensued. Alarmed, Princess scurried over and climbed onto her lap.

As the tears continued, Edith silently searched the kitchen for tissues. Finding none, she gave Lisa a wad of napkins. "Honey, it's just stuff out there. You're safe. The kids are safe. Everything will be fine."

Lisa continued to wail. After a few minutes, she wiped her nose and took another long drink of the soothing concoction. "It's not just the fire, it's a lot of things. Michael wants Andrew to live with him in September and go to school in Houston."

"Oh."

"And Rachael. I can't stop worrying about her."

Edith came over and sat, gathering Lisa in her arms. "Honey, I wish there was something I could do to ease your pain. I don't know what to tell you. I keep thinking about Rachael, too. Why her? What did she do to deserve cancer?" The two sat, as Lisa, head on Edith's shoulder, continued to softly cry.

Soon, eyes drying, Lisa untangled herself from Edith's comforting arms and leaned back onto the couch. They sat, speechless, nursing their drinks, and listening to the barks and yelps of Dorothy's patients.

Dorothy popped her head in. "Have you seen the boys?"

"No, I haven't," Lisa said. "She immediately picked up her cell phone and called Andrew. He did not answer.

Then Dorothy dialed Eric. "Where are you?" She listened a minute and then said, "Hold on." She put her iPhone on speaker and sat at the table. She motioned Edith and Lisa over.

"Now say that again."

"We're about three miles from Andrew's house on the old Jacob's Trail Road." Eric started coughing. "It's real smoky out here. Anyway, I couldn't see and ran off the road and into a ditch. I couldn't back out so Andrew's checking to see what the problem is."

Lisa huddled over the phone. "What are you doing over there?"

"Andrew wanted to save T-Rex. Without him, there'll be no cattle to sell."

Dorothy pursed her lips. "You need to get out of there, now."

"Let me call you back."

"No, you stay on the line. I'm going to call your dad." Dorothy hit the "add call" button but John did not respond.

"Edith, call dispatch at the sheriff's office. Tell them we need to speak with John, it's an emergency. Tell him to call me immediately."

"Eric, what's happening?"

All they could hear was coughing over the line. Lisa had never seen Dorothy so rattled. A sense of dread settled in the recess of Lisa's stomach.

Dorothy's phone signaled an incoming call. "Eric, stay on the line. Tell Andrew to get in the cab."

Dorothy switched over. John was on the other end. She explained where the boys were and put the calls together.

"Eric," John asked, "will the truck drive?"

"No, I tried to back up but—"

"You boys listen very carefully. The fire is only about a mile from you, moving fast. I want you to leave the truck running, the AC on, and the windows up. Put the AC on recirculation. Close the air vents. Then I want you to get on the floorboard and cover your mouth and nose with whatever you can and stay down."

"Shouldn't we try to outrun the fire?" Andrew asked.

"NO. Stay in the truck." John's voice was beginning to break up. "You have the best chance there. You stay on the line. I'm going to get off now and see if I can direct one of the helicopters to drop some water around you. Whatever you do, don't get out."

The three listened in horror as the boys settled onto the floorboards. The hacking increased.

"Andrew, are you OK?" Lisa asked.

"Mom, I'm sorry, I was just trying to help—"

"We'll worry about that later. Just do what John said."

"Mom, it's getting awful hot in here," Eric said. Lisa could detect fear in his voice.

Dorothy kept talking to the boys in a calm, deliberate manner, telling them they were going to be fine, to just stay in the car.

"The fire's all around us!" Andrew yelled.

All Lisa could hear was static and crackling.

"Eric, can you hear me?" Dorothy yelled.

"Mom, we're OK. The fire passed over us. I can hear the helicopter."

John came back on the line.

"Are you boys OK?"

"We're fine."

"Get out of the car and stay on the road. I'll send someone to get you as soon as I can."

"Mom, my phone battery's running low," Eric said.

"Have Andrew call every fifteen minutes just to let us know you're OK. Call us when someone picks you up. I love you," Dorothy said.

Hands trembling, she ended the call and leaned back in her chair.

"We almost lost them. If they'd been about a mile further up the road in the wooded section, they would have probably died."

Emotionally spent; Lisa's tears would not come. No matter what happened to the JF Ranch or the cows, she had her son—for now.

Finally, Dorothy glanced at her watch. "I have a patient waiting. Let me know if anything bad happens to the boys." She rose to her feet and pushed in her chair. "I've never felt so helpless in my whole life. You raise a child. You take so much time and care. And they can be gone in an instant."

About an hour later Dorothy returned. "Just talked to John. One of the crews should pick up the boys in the next fifteen minutes. He'll have someone from the sheriff's office drive them back to the house. He's confident they can keep the house from catching fire. They've got a good containment line built and think they can save the pasture as well as all the land around Zink's Creek. Bad news is it looks like a good five hundred acres is burnt to a crisp. He says you should stay in town for the night. He doesn't want you to go back home until they're completely sure they have it out. I've got one more dog to see and then we'll go to the house."

"Wow," Edith said. "What a relief! Look, I'm going to head back to the site and see if they need anything more for the mop-up crew." To Lisa, she said, "Give me a call in the morning, and I'll come pick you up and get you home."

"Thanks. If you hadn't been here, I don't know what I'd have done."

"You're quite welcome. We're going to look at used livestock trailers this weekend…. I've got to go home; my back is killing me. You owe me big-time!" Edith grinned impishly and grasped Lisa's shoulders. "Seriously, don't worry about anything. Andrew's safe, the house is fine. The fire was probably good for the place, anyway. New growth timber will be a big seller for you."

Andrew called as they neared Eric's house. Lisa, Dorothy, and Jessica waited impatiently on the porch. As the boys climbed out of the cruiser, Lisa and Dorothy rushed off the porch and gathered the boys in their arms. Jessica ran up and put her arms around Andrew and Lisa.

"Mom, I'm so sorry," Eric said. "The truck is toasted. Burnt to a crisp."

"We were just trying to save T-Rex," Andrew said. "It's all my fault."

"We have insurance for the truck," Dorothy said, "But nothing can replace the two of you. I'm just so glad you're both in one piece."

The group walked into the house, and Dorothy told the boys to take a shower. She turned on the cartoons for Jessica in the den while she and Lisa sat in the kitchen.

"I'm so mad at those boys, I could spit," Dorothy said. "What a dumb thing to do."

"It was dangerous," Lisa agreed. "But I just can't see punishing them. They were trying to help. I do think, however, Andrew should do chores at your office to help repay you for the truck's deductible."

"I'll talk to John and see what he says and let you know. Hopefully, they've learned their lesson."

"I hope so." Lisa leaned back in her chair and watched as Dorothy rose to start dinner.

"How's Rachael?"

"Vivian has finally agreed it's time to start hospice. They're coming in the morning."

Later, Lisa, scrubbed clean and wrapped in Dorothy's robe, watched as Dorothy put hamburger meat in the skillet, browning it. *Such drama, but the mundane humdrum of life goes on.* Replaying the events of the day, a realization jolted her core. *Every moment we have with loved ones is something to cherish. Nothing else really matters.*

***

Lisa had insisted on tidying the kitchen after breakfast since Dorothy had agreed to drop Jessica off at school. Just as she was stowing the last of the dishes in the dishwasher, her cell rang.

"Lisa, it's Edith. Some bad news. The fire burned a bunch of electric poles. Doesn't sound like we'll have any electricity for at least a week."

Taking a lungful and steadying herself, Lisa fought back the tears. "You and Carl are out, too?"

"Yep, it was a rough night, that's for sure. I've got a generator set up in the store to try and keep at least one cooler running, but I had to get up a couple of times last night to fill it with gas. Carl said he'll come get you if you want. I've got to stay here. You and the kids may not want to stay out there without any lights."

Lisa could not impose on Dorothy anymore and the costs of a hotel room…. "Just tell Carl to come when he can. Thanks."

Lisa sat at the kitchen table, head in hands. *It's just one thing after another. At least I have a house and kids. Living without electricity can't be that big of a deal, can it?*

Several hours later Carl, pushing a loaded shopping cart, followed Lisa to his truck. Wal-Mart had everything Lisa needed to last through the week. The two had vigorously discussed the pros and cons of getting a generator. When Lisa realized the cost was around five hundred dollars, she quickly vetoed the idea. They would just tough it out.

As they pulled into the driveway, Lisa was relieved to see that everything appeared normal. She could still detect the lingering odor of smoke, however, even when she opened the front door.

After putting her bags on the kitchen table, she tried to raise the window over the sink.

"Carl, the window won't open. Do you mind trying it?"

Carl set his load down and tried, but it would not budge. Frowning, he explained that Joe had gotten central air and heat just a few years before Ruby went into the nursing home. The workers must have

208 | TOUGH TRAIL HOME

painted the wooden sashes and sills at the same time, sealing them together.

"I'll go get my tools. I'll have to run a knife around the windows to break them apart."

Lisa propped open the front entrance. For the first time in her life, she could appreciate screen doors. At least a host of annoying bugs would not bother them. Rummaging through the purchases, she extracted the cute little lantern for Jessica and several kerosene lamps.

Next Lisa salvaged what she could from the fridge. Most of the things would have to be thrown away. In no time she had a large garbage bag full of ruined food. A hundred bucks down the drain.

While filling the lamps with fuel, she heard Carl working on the window and walked over to check on his progress. He had removed the screen and was busy banging away at the paint seal.

"See if you can pull it up now." Carl motioned.

Lisa got the window started, and Carl helped her lift it all the way. As soon as they both let go, it banged shut.

"Drat," Carl said.

"Why won't it stay up?"

"The windows have rope and a weight attached to them so that they stay up when opened. The rope's probably rotted. I'll just get a piece of wood to hold it open for now." He climbed down the ladder and disappeared around the corner.

Lisa took a paper towel and wiped the sweat from her face. The house was suffocating, yesterday's winds long gone. Being comfortable without the air conditioning was going to be a challenge. At least they could have a warm bath.

Lisa helped Carl with each window until they had all of them propped open and the screens secured. One screen had a hole. Carl told Lisa to just stick a wadded-up paper towel in the opening.

"Lisa, I need to get back to the house. I got animals to feed. You call if you need anything."

"You're a dear. Thanks so much." Lisa hugged him.

"Here. Give me that trash. I'll dump it on my way out."

After he left, Lisa fixed a sandwich and sat on the porch to eat. A text crossed her phone from Michael, irate about Andrew's brush with death. The ranch is too dangerous, her husband ranted. Flippantly she texted back: so is Houston. Murders, rapes, traffic wrecks

Appetite ruined, she ditched lunch and wandered into the office. One look at the computer reminded her of the tax returns promised by the end of the week. She would have to take her laptop to the library and work there.

Restless, Lisa, accompanied by Princess, strolled down to the tank and sat against the trunk of a tree. Gathering the dog in her lap, she watched dragonflies flit and dip over the water's tranquil surface as her thoughts roamed. Sleeping with the windows open made her nervous. Visions of that macabre pig in Carl's tree flashed through her mind. *Thank God pigs don't fly... or do they?*

Entertaining the children was going to be a challenge. What would they do? Read by lamplight like Abraham Lincoln? Play cards? Maybe they could learn that game Mexican Train Edith was always talking about. No, the kids always fought when they played anything, especially Monopoly.

A large splash startled Lisa. Turning her head, she saw circular ripples expanding, disturbing the reflections of the nearby trees generated by the pond's glassy top. A turtle must have slid off a log and disappeared.

Movement to the left caught her eye. A vulture landed on a hump about four feet from the shore. Lisa shooed Princess off her lap and moved closer to the mound, sending the nasty creature fleeing. Unable to identify exactly what it was, she climbed down to the shoreline to get a better look.... A deer! A deer in the tank. And it was dead. Not moving. Its head and feet were underwater. A faint pungent odor wafted from the carcass. Lisa fought the urge to heave, then turned and ran, scrambling up the embankment and shoving the complaining canine into the house.

Lisa yelled as she ran toward Carl's place. He was on his porch by the time she reached her front gate.

"What's wrong?"

"A deer. It's dead. In the tank." Lisa was breathless.

"It's not the end of the world. I'll go look." Carl disappeared and then, with a straw cowboy hat on his head, followed Lisa back to the pond.

As Lisa stayed at the top, Carl edged his way down. Peering into the murky water, he said, "Well, I'll be. It's a buck. A big one. See the horns?"

"Yeah, I see." Lisa, however, had no intention of getting any closer than necessary. "What do you think happened?"

"I don't rightly know. Maybe the fire scared him and sent him running, maybe he got burned or something."

"Now what?"

"Well, we probably need to pull him out. Doesn't look like he's been dead too long."

"How do you know that?"

"Well, first off, the smell's not too bad. Don't see that anything's been nibbling on him."

Lisa nodded.

Carl joined her. "I'll get the tractor."

Lisa stared at the lump. Was that the same beautiful deer she saw at the first of the year? *I hope not.* Soon Carl backed the tractor next to her.

"Now, I'm going to just drop this loop around his antlers and pull him up."

Lisa watched as Carl waded into the water and secured the noose around the animal's horns. Keeping it taut, he made his way back to Lisa's vantage point. All Lisa could hear were his footsteps as the mud oozed off his boots.

"I'm going to need your help." Carl looped the free end around the back of the tractor, tying it off. "You keep the rope tight until I tell you to let go. I'm going to go real slow, I don't need any of that deer coming apart on me. You watch it real close and signal me if there's a problem."

Carl climbed into the seat and moved systematically ahead. Lisa held the rope firmly, allowing no slack. When Carl nodded, she let go and scrambled to a safe spot to watch without encountering the rotting flesh. Soon the head emerged from the water. The antlers! Gorgeous. Abruptly, sadness overwhelmed her. A life extinguished too early. *Rachael…baby Regina…I'm so blessed Andrew wasn't hurt…. Why is life so unfair?*

Carl worked the tractor, maneuvering the carrion, first to the edge of the tank and then as far as he could from the house. Lisa watched him unhook the rope.

"Aren't you going to bury it?"

Carl grinned. "I promise you that in twenty-four hours there won't be much left of that poor feller. I am, however, going to call the game warden. Look."

Carl pointed to a spot on the deer's side where blood had congealed. "He looks real healthy. I'm not seeing anything wrong with him that would be caused by the fire. Probably got wounded by some poacher and then just ran till he died."

Lisa shivered. "Thanks again. As usual, you've saved my life. How can I ever repay you?"

"There is something you can do for me. I've been craving a fish dinner. You mind if I do some fishing? The perch in this tank are the best I've ever tasted."

"Better than that. What if we all fish? I still remember fishing with Uncle Joe. And I still remember how good they were when Aunt Ruby fried them up."

"Sounds like a lot of fun. It'll be better than us all sitting at home. I've got a propane burner. We'll just fry'em outside and have a picnic. I'll go get some poles ready. And Lisa, I'm going to do all the cooking—fixings and everything."

When Andrew arrived, he demanded to see the deer. Intrigued, Jessica wanted to, as well. After the children changed into their old clothes, the trio loaded into the Mule. Andrew slowed as they detected the odor emanating from the decimated deer.

When they neared, Lisa noticed the legs of the animal were now sticking straight out and the belly was a bit more distended. A few buzzards were circling overhead.

Andrew looked up. "Is that what's going to eat them?"

"I guess so," Lisa said. "I don't know what else would."

"Gross," Jessica said. "I want to go back."

By the time they returned to the barn, Carl had arrived, his truck full of poles.

"Alright," Lisa said to Andrew. "Let's see you catch a grasshopper."

Andrew strutted behind the barn, wading in the grass. To Lisa's dismay, he quickly nabbed one.

"See, it wasn't so hard after all." Andrew waved the mottled brown creature tightly secured between his finger and thumb.

"How'd you learn to catch them?"

"I read about it on the Internet after you said it was so hard. I've been practicing. They got lots of eyes. You have to move slowly to grab them."

Lisa felt a surge of pride. "Good for you. Now, let's catch some fish. I'm hungry."

Carl handed Andrew a pole. "Take the hook through the grasshopper's back and come up just in front of his head." While Andrew worked, Carl swiftly strung one on another line and adjusted the red and white bobber. He then threw it out and motioned to Jessica.

"Take hold of the pole. Watch that cork real careful. When it goes under, jerk as hard as you can." Then he prepared one for Lisa.

"Uh, Carl, I'd appreciate a little lesson on how to cast."

Beaming, Carl demonstrated. Just as Lisa's bobber hit the water, Jessica screamed.

"My cork! It's gone!"

"Reel it in, pull back." Carl moved next to her, holding his hands over hers and helping her haul in the line. Abruptly it went limp. "Sorry, sweetie. It must have jumped the hook." He instructed Jessica to reel the line in. Sure enough, the bait was gone.

He put another grasshopper on the hook and tossed it out. "Now, Miss Jessica, just be sure you wait until the cork goes down all the way. Then jerk hard." He handed the rod back to his young pupil.

Then he turned to see how Andrew was doing. "Next time cast right over there, in that bit of shade."

Andrew's line had just landed when the bobber vanished; he jerked and furiously rolled in his line.

"Let the pole down. Now, pull up, reel." Carl gave firm, decisive instructions. Both Lisa and Jessica turned to watch the battle. The fish surfaced and then dove. Carl scurried over to his truck and found a net, returning just in time to ease the webbing under the monstrous creature as Andrew lifted it out of the water.

"Well, I'll be darn. A largemouth bass. Must be all of three pounds." Carl wrestled the whale of a fish for possession of the hook. Then he gave the net to Andrew. "Hold this while I put some water in a bucket. That fish is going to be good eating."

After securing his prize catch, Andrew insisted Lisa take pictures of him and the fish, proof of his tale of a whopper. Grinning, he scampered into the grass searching for another insect.

By this time Jessica was almost in tears. "How come I haven't caught anything?"

"Well, while you were fussing, your cork disappeared." Carl pointed to the water. "Guess you better reel it in."

Excited, Jessica tugged on the line, spinning the reel handles as fast as her chubby little hands allowed. A mid-sized sun perch popped into view. "Oh, it's so small."

"Your fish may be small, but it's better tasting than that big old thing your brother caught."

"Really?"

"Really."

Now Jessica was all business, impatient for Carl to re-bait her hook.

"Jessica," Lisa said, "Why don't you learn how to catch a grasshopper and put it on yourself? Mr. Carl wants to fish, too."

At first, Jessica protested, then allowed Carl to teach her the art of the grab. With some coaching, she had it on her hook and in no time her line was back in the water.

As twilight enveloped the ranch, the group paused in their endeavors, having secured plenty of fish for the evening meal. Carl took Andrew with him to clean them while Lisa and Jessica went inside.

"Jessica, go take a bath, you're covered in nasty fish juice." Jessica didn't argue. Lisa grabbed a flashlight, making her way to the bathroom and lighting the kerosene lamp. "Be careful. Don't hit it. It'll break and start a fire. I'll bring you some clean clothes. Wash your hair, you're all sweaty."

Lisa then went to the kitchen where she gave her hands, arms, and face a thorough scrubbing. She gathered some clothes for Jessica and put them in the bathroom. "I'll be outside. Come on out when you finish."

"What about the lamp?"

"Just leave it alone, it will be fine."

Stepping outdoors was a relief, the house remained stale and stuffy. Taking a deep breath, Lisa looked over to the barn. Carl and Andrew had set up a table and covered it with the red and white checkered oilcloth. Carl was showing Andrew how to filet the fish by lantern light while a huge pot heated atop a propane-powered burner.

Lisa's heart broke. Carl was so good with Andrew; his children and grandchildren were missing so much love. *He's giving it to my family. How can I ever repay him?*

Lisa sat on the porch waiting for Jessica, thinking about what life throws at you, the unexpected twists and turns. She always thought she would live happily ever after.

"Momma, I'm hungry." Jessica burst out of the door carrying a flashlight, Princess trailing behind.

"Lead the way. Let's see what Mr. Carl's got cooking." Lisa fell in beside Jessica who walked toward the barn, flicking the beam from side to side.

"Point the flashlight on the ground. I can't see where I'm walking."

"Sorry." Jessica concentrated the illumination just below their feet.

As they entered the circle of light, Carl said, "I'm glad the cook is here. Jessica, I need you to bread the fish." He showed her how to dip the fish in milk, then in a cornmeal/flour mix. When Lisa tried to extract the exact ingredients, he refused. An old family secret.

Lisa wandered to the pot where Andrew was frying potatoes and hushpuppies.

"Did you have fun today?"

"It was awesome, particularly the big fish."

"More fun than surfing the net?"

Andrew paused. "Not more fun, but fun. I like learning different things. I wouldn't want to do it every day, but I'd do it again."

How ironic. A bump in the road has made my son better-rounded. He's learning things he'd never learn in an elite high school. Maybe there's hope, yet.

Soon they were sitting down to a scrumptious meal. Carl had thought of everything. Lisa did not care for coleslaw, but Carl's was delightful. After some fear of swallowing a bone, Jessica wolfed down several pieces of fish and more hushpuppies than Lisa felt prudent.

After dinner, Lisa sent Andrew and Jessica to the house to get ready for bed while she helped Carl clean. The water bucket atop the burner was steaming, allowing ample hot water for the dishes. Pouring part of it into a dish pan and adding liquid soap, he saved the rest for rinsing. Lisa washed while Carl dried.

"Carl, I've been thinking. I'd like to help you find your children."

"Would you? I've always dreamed of seeing them again…. But they've been gone so long, I don't know how you'd ever find them."

"I'd like to try anyway…. Why don't you give me their names and dates of birth? Let me see what I can do."

"Sure. They're written in the family Bible. I'll bring it over tomorrow."

Both worked silently. Lisa struggled to clean the large fry pot while Carl loaded the burner and propane tank in the back of the truck and disassembled the makeshift table.

After extinguishing the lanterns, Carl started his pickup. "Lisa, I enjoyed tonight so much. Thanks for having me over."

"The pleasure was all mine." Lisa waved to him and, at his insistence, walked back to the house using the truck headlights. Once on the porch, she turned and waved, watching until Carl pulled into his driveway.

Lisa entered the house, finding it eerily quiet. She peeked into Jessica's room only to find her daughter had fallen asleep while reading a book with her flashlight, the precious puppy out cold. No need to walk the little devil. Giving her daughter a peck on the cheek, Lisa turned off the beam and set it on the nightstand. She started to pull the sheet over Jessica but changed her mind. It was just too hot.

Tiptoeing to the door, she tapped lightly and entered after Andrew gave permission. He was also in bed with a flashlight and book.

"I don't see how they did it in the old days," Andrew said. "It's only nine and I'm bored stiff. No TV, no video games. It's even hard to read."

"Now you know why Benjamin Franklin said, "Early to bed, early to rise, makes a man healthy, wealthy, and wise.""

"Aw, Mom, that's so stupid."

Lisa smiled and leaned over, kissing Andrew on the forehead. "Don't stay up too late." She returned through Jessica's room, leaving the door open. Hopefully, the air would circulate and cool the house.

After a quick bath, Lisa extinguished the lanterns and climbed into bed. Sleep eluded her, however. Her mind raced. *How am I going to locate Carl's children? Why, they must be grandparents themselves by this time.*

Lisa soon fell into a troubled slumber…in the barn, cold and shivering…the coyotes baying and snarling…. The din grew louder. Something touched her shoulder, rousing her. The room had grown cool and was pitch black except for a flashlight beam trained in her eyes. Startled, she threw her arm over her face to shield it from the intensity of the light.

"Momma, I'm scared," Jessica said.

Lisa was awake, but the sound of coyotes didn't stop. It was not a dream!

"Jessica, go get your brother." Lisa pulled the sheet back and climbed out of bed.

"I'm too scared."

"We'll both go." Holding hands, the pair threaded their way to Andrew's bedroom. Lisa shook him as Jessica nailed him with the spotlight. Pushing the flashlight down, Lisa said, "Get that out of his face."

A groggy Andrew opened his eyes and looked questioningly at Lisa. "Listen."

Andrew became animated. "Wow!" He climbed out of bed and groped for his flashlight.

The trio filed through the bedrooms and to the living room window, listening tensely. Andrew aimed his beam through the screen but could see nothing.

"It's coming from over there where the dead deer is," Andrew said. "Should we take a closer look?"

"Absolutely not." No way was Lisa going out there, gun or no gun.

A screech pierced the air. Lisa and Jessica screamed.

Andrew laughed.

"What's so funny?" Jessica asked.

"Think about it. We've never slept with the windows open before. That kind of stuff must go on out there every night. We just never hear it. Nothing's happened to us before so nothing will happen now."

The logic wasn't making Lisa feel any better.

"Do they really have wolves around here?" Lisa asked.

"I don't think so. I think they just got lots of coyotes. I guess we'll have to ask Carl," Andrew said.

"Well, it's cooled off now. I'm going to put the windows down so we can go back to sleep." Lisa lowered them which did indeed have a muffling effect on the growls and yips. Then, looking at Jessica, said, "Want to sleep with me?"

"Mom, Jessica's not a little baby anymore. She can sleep by herself."

"Mom's afraid. I'll sleep with her, so she won't be scared," Jessica said.

"Thanks, Jessica. I'd really like that."

After Andrew disappeared into his room, Lisa took the shotgun out of the closet and laid it on the dresser. She did feel better with the Remington by her side. Then she and Jessica settled in.

"Thanks for sleeping with me. I am a little scared," Lisa said.

Jessica kissed Lisa, then cuddled by her side. "Don't tell Andrew, but I'm scared, too."

Lisa chuckled softly and pulled the covers up under her chin. Soon the pair were fast asleep.

***

Lisa heard banging in the kitchen and glanced at her clock. Dead. Groggily she picked up her iPhone and squinted to see the time. Still thirty minutes before the kids needed to be up for school. Easing out from under the covers, Lisa donned her robe and slippers and went to the bathroom. Andrew had already lit the kerosene lamps.

"Why are you up so early?" Lisa asked.

"I want to see what's left of the deer."

"Ugh. Before breakfast?"

"On second thought, I'm going to have a peanut butter and jelly sandwich and then go out." Andrew busied himself scrounging through the ice chest, pulling out milk and jelly.

"Why in the world do you want to look? What if the coyotes are still out there?"

"Well, I'll take the Mule and the shotgun. Besides, I've read all about vultures. I want to see them in action."

"I don't want to hear about what the Internet has to say about them."

"But it's really neat. Apparently, if the dead animal's hide is too thick, the birds just wait until the bigger predators have their fill. Then they move in." Andrew went into the bedroom and came out with the shotgun. "Want to go?"

"You leave me no choice. I'm not going to let you go down there driving and holding the gun at the same time."

Andrew handed Lisa the weapon as well as a big flashlight. Outside, light was winning its battle with dark though the sun had not yet peaked over the horizon. She settled in the passenger seat, resting the stock on her leg with the barrel pointed outwards and up.

Andrew gently pulled away from the house and eased toward the desecrated deer. As they rounded the corner of the tank, Lisa almost gagged. Andrew began coughing. The stench of death ran to meet them. He put on the brakes.

"Breathe through your mouth. That's what Eric said." Andrew panted.

Lisa stared. The corpse had been violently savaged; the ugly black birds finishing it. Andrew took out his cell and began snapping pictures. Then, taking his foot off the brake, he inched forward.

Lisa elbowed him. "This is disgusting. Take me back."

Andrew drove to the house and turned off the engine. "Amazing. Nature sure knows how to clean up a mess. Did you know that those birds gorge themselves until their crop bulges, and sit, sleepy-like, to digest their food? They have real corrosive stomach acid so they can eat rotten meat without dying. They can also use their vomit as a defensive projectile if you threaten them."

"Too much information." Lisa rushed inside, put the shotgun away, and woke Jessica. "I'll drive you to school today. I'm going to stay in town. There's no way I can work here without any electricity."

***

Lisa settled in at the La Grange Internet café, consuming a delightful mocha while running through her e-mail. Flashbacks of dozens of buzzards waiting their turn to finish that poor deer crept into her thoughts. *Yuck! I wish I didn't know what went on after sundown.* Being oblivious was not always such a terrible thing…. Her thoughts turned to Carl and his children. She could not wait to start the hunt for them.

Switching to her work, she closed out one tax return, then decided to stretch her legs. Strolling around the nineteenth-century town square and browsing the local gift shops was a welcome distraction. A book entitled *La Grange* caught her attention. Curious, she purchased a copy, quickly immersing herself in times gone by.

Scouring the paperback gave her a new appreciation for Texas in the eighteen hundreds. No wonder Texans love their guns. Their ancestors had fought Indians, Mexicans, Yankees, and each other. Local legend said the town's founder coerced one son-in-law to kill another. A prominent citizen quarreled with a physician and stabbed him with a knife. After posting bond, the accused promptly took a seat on the Texas Supreme Court. Hangings, cattle rustling, duels, and bank robberies seemed routine.

Then there were the drunks and prostitutes. The old jail had a hoosegow to lock up inebriated citizens overnight. Lisa was acutely aware of the Chicken Ranch, but not the fact that "soiled doves" had been operating in the area well before the establishment of the famous bordello.

Looking at the nearby Muster Oak, a new-found respect filled Lisa. The 175-year-old oak tree had served as a rallying point for local citizens eager to fight for their beliefs. Military recruits from six conflicts gathered under its branches before going off to war. Julia's brother, Franklin, full of bravado and swagger, must have once stood under its out-stretched boughs, raising his rifle, and threatening to kick the Yankees' asses from here to kingdom come.

Lisa walked to the courthouse which sat in the middle of the town square. The towering three-story stone structure described as Romanesque Revival had entrances facing each side of the square with a clock tower above the main entrance. Inside, a sunken atrium and fountain graced the center of the structure. Descending, she came face to face with a statuesque deer.

The county had purchased an iron statue of a red stag in 1882 to decorate the courthouse grounds. Over the years, extraordinary abuse occurred; its antlers had been repeatedly broken off, replaced with real ones. Shooting the poor sculpture with small-caliber bullets was common. Finally, the county refurbished the bedraggled beast, giving him a pair of native white-tail deer antlers, and placing him inside, away from the clutches of vandals.

And I thought the deer in my tank had problems!

Settling on a bench, Lisa closed her eyes. Listening to the gurgle of the fountain conjured images of what it must have been like in 1891 when they laid the cornerstone for the courthouse. Julia was surely there. She could just picture the woman, dressed in her finest, lining up with the other ladies to fill her plate with barbecued beef, mutton, and pork. Was her William one of the men who rushed the food, causing a free-for-all?

Outside, Lisa surveyed the sedate square, observing citizens going about their daily routines. Imagining the old days and the eleven barrooms where residents relaxed with their beer boggled her mind. History was intriguing but thank God she lived in the twenty-first century.

***

After a bite of lunch, Lisa went to her shift at Rachael's. Dorothy had mobilized everyone to help while Vivian was at work.

Lisa let herself in the back door, made her way to the bedroom, and sat in a chair next to the bed. Edith had fixed some soup and was trying to coax Rachael into tasting it.

"I'm not hungry," Rachael said.

"Well, you need to eat something," Edith said.

"I just can't. Food tastes gross."

Edith sighed and took the tray back to the kitchen.

"I know Viv wants me to eat, but I just can't," Rachael said.

Lisa reached over and patted her hand. "Don't worry about it. If you don't want to eat, don't. It's OK."

Leaning back, Rachael closed her eyes. When Edith returned, Lisa told them the story of the demolished deer and the night creatures, leaving the women howling with laughter.

"I've got to get back to the store," Edith said. "Rachael, let me know if you need anything at all." She leaned down, kissing Rachel's forehead. "Bye." Edith waved as she left.

"Thanks, it felt good to laugh for a change," Rachael said. "What's up with you and Michael?"

Lisa sighed. "I don't know…. We're so far apart now…."

"That's what I thought about Viv, but it's not too late. That's what you told me…. You know, they've got me so doped up, I can't think."

Lisa smiled. "Why don't you take a little nap? Viv will be home soon." She helped Rachael get comfortable.

As Rachael slept, Lisa's thoughts wandered to Michael. *What's the answer?* Upon hearing the door open, she glanced at her watch. *Must be Vivian.* Lisa stood and leaned over, kissing Rachael on the forehead. They had so little time left. Would this be the last time she saw her friend?

***

Anxiously Lisa peered out of the tack room, thrilled to have the electricity restored and thankful that Ellen and Sam would arrive any minute. They had stopped in Austin overnight and purchased a fifth-wheel camper. Lisa had insisted they could have her bedroom, but they would hear nothing of the sort. As Ellen had explained, there was plenty of room for the two of them to have some privacy. Then, if they got restless, they could go on a little trip.

Lisa had used the last of the funds from her prized Rolex to have a water and electricity hookup placed several hundred yards from the house in a nice copse of trees. Additionally, she bought them a picnic table and some nice lawn furniture.

Back at her desk, Lisa stared at the telephone numbers on the screen. The search for any of Carl's children was proving to be harder than anticipated. A friend of hers in Raleigh who worked in human resources had given Lisa some tips, leading her to concentrate on the youngest son because of his unusual name, Melvin Leonard Turner. The other boy's first name was John, just too common. Now she had the telephone numbers of five Melvin L. Turners who were just about the right age and lived in Texas. The calling began.

Looking at her watch indicated enough time to make one more call. A man answered the phone.

"Hello, my name is Lisa Dunwhitty, and I'm looking for a Melvin Leonard Turner who was born in Fayette County, Texas in 1965 to Rebecca and Carl Turner."

"What is it you want?"

"I am a friend of Carl Turner's. Mr. Turner has been looking for his children for years. I told him I would help him." Silence ensued.

"I'm not interested—"

"Please, Mr. Turner, just give me a chance. You are Carl's son, aren't you?"

"Yes."

Lisa inhaled deeply. "I met your father about five months ago when I moved in across the street. He's wonderful. I've never seen anyone work so hard in all my life. He's—"

"You can save your breath. He was never around when I was little. I don't know that I can forgive him for that."

"He told me your mother took you away. She told Carl she didn't want to live in the country. She didn't tell him where she was going. He searched for you. He said he spent one whole week driving the streets of Houston just hoping to see her car."

Lisa sat silently. Finally, Melvin spoke.

"That's not how my mother told it."

"Mr. Turner, I don't know what really happened. That was a long time ago. The point is— the man longs to see his children. If I didn't think so highly of him, I wouldn't have tried to track you down. Please, just give him a chance. Once you know him like I do, you'll be glad you did."

"I'll have to think about it. Give me your phone number."

Lisa exchanged information with Melvin and then hung up the phone.

The whining gears of a truck coaxed Lisa out of the office. She saw Carl directing Sam into the driveway. The trailer was huge! After parking the rig, Sam and Carl worked to level it, hook up the utilities, and extend the slideouts. Then Sam cranked open an awning.

Surveying the interior amenities, Lisa was amazed. The well-equipped kitchen had a three-burner stove, microwave, and a double-door refrigerator while the bathroom tub/shower sported a skylight!

Ellen beamed. "What's so wonderful is that there's not much to clean. And there's so much storage. Look!" Motioning to the master bed, she pulled out a large drawer underneath. Their tour continued, with Lisa and Ellen planning a trip to the grocery store and Wal-Mart to outfit the new digs. Ellen had sold most of her belongings at a garage sale before leaving. A new beginning, she explained, was important to her.

They climbed down from the trailer only to find that Sam and Carl had arranged the patio furniture under the awning and were testing the chairs. Carl had been filling Sam in on the fire.

"It's so good to have y'all back," Carl said. "We got so much to do, Sam. Those durn hogs have been in the pasture again. We're going to have to trap them, I guess. Don't know what else to do."

Lisa froze. "Why?"

Carl said, "They're big—and nasty. They dug a couple of holes in the back and trying to mow is a problem. T-Rex is a tough little man, but I don't think he's a match for one of those big boars."

Lisa settled into a recliner, idly listening to the chatter. Sam and Carl were deep in discussion about the art of trapping. Carl thought they could catch the smaller ones and fatten them for sale. Lisa smiled. Thoughts of offering wild pork—certainly organic—to Whole Foods emerged. She would let them call it La Grange's Other White Meat.

Her mind drifted to Michael. How much better she would have felt had he been with her during the fire.... *But I survived just fine. With friends, I can even thrive.... Still, I miss him.* Her thoughts roamed to Rachael.

Lisa examined her arms, running a finger over the gashes on her left forearm that had yet to heal. While checking on the cows, she had located a drooping piece of barbed wire. While pulling it as tightly as possible, she lost her balance and fell into the fence. The scratches and bruises earned while wrestling Precious were still visible.

How life had evolved…. Working out was unnecessary—she obtained sufficient exercise tending to the herd and vegetable garden. That you could buy a tomato for under a dollar amazed her. *I've never worked so hard in my life.*

After getting nowhere trying to clear the plot by hand, Carl suggested they burn the area to rid it of the remaining briars, weeds, and poison ivy. Then, she attacked the scorched earth with Dorothy's motorized tiller, jarring her teeth and leaving an annoying buzz in her ears. How did Julia manage with mules and a plow?

Then, more money. Mushroom compost, cages for the tomatoes, and stakes for the rows of plants. Carl had insisted on erecting a fifteen-foot-high fence around the patch to keep wildlife at bay. All that expense before even buying the plants!

On hands and knees, she and Jessica had sowed seeds beneath a string stretched between the stakes. The line helped distinguish the plants from the weeds. Lisa worked, envisioning zucchini, turnips, yellow squash, tomatoes, bush beans, potatoes, watermelon, carrots, jalapenos, and green peppers, a riotous array of colors and various tastes to satisfy the most discerning palates. Shortly Jessica quit with the excuse of checking on Princess. Soon Lisa's eyes stung from dripping sweat. Her immediate payback: ant bites and a pile of dirty, stinky clothes.

Within days, weeding and destroying ant beds had consumed her. One day, barehanded, Lisa jerked out a small intruder with feathery white tentacles emanating from its leaves and a small yellow flower. The bristly plant quickly got even, shooting a burning sensation through her arm. *Shit!* The evil invader's punch rated twice what the biggest scorpion could deliver on her pain meter. Lisa stumbled into the house trying everything to alleviate the burning.

Later, after complaining to Carl about the difficulty in finding something to ease the discomfort, he chuckled, explaining there was one home remedy for the nasty nettle's poison. Lisa perked up. This would be important if she ever encountered the wicked weed again. After some prodding, Carl explained it was urine! *URINE!* Easy for the men. They could spray wherever it hurt. Women always had it hard....

And the bugs.... The first time Lisa discovered large, jagged holes in the tomato leaves, she screamed so loud that Carl came running. Then the tedious work of spraying an organic mix containing seaweed extract consumed her. Nothing took care of the grasshoppers, however, which were quickly becoming a nuisance. Edith finally convinced her to spray the perimeter of the garden with insecticide. Only the actual garden, her friend stated, had to be chemical-free to qualify as organic. Lisa, too tired to argue, capitulated.

"Lisa, how's the garden going?" Ellen asked, bringing Lisa out of her reverie.

"Just great. In fact, we need to pick some zucchini today."

"Yeah, the garden's great if you like to fight the bugs all the time," Carl said. "Lisa insists we don't use any poisons. It'll be a miracle if it makes it through the summer."

"Oh, Carl, shush!" Lisa laughed. "Actually, Ellen, I was thinking we could spare a few zucchini for dinner tonight. I was sure hoping you would cook us a good meal."

Ellen grinned. "Tired of eating your own cooking?"

"What cooking?" Lisa asked.

"I'd love to. Carl, you'll join us, won't you?"

He nodded.

"Wonderful!" Lisa responded. "Let's pick the vegetables, and I'll drop off what we don't need at Zink's Corner. I've got quite a following over there." Lisa and Ellen walked to the vegetable patch, leaving Carl and Sam to their plans to defeat the dastardly swine.

Jessica burst into the house as Lisa was peeling squash. Ellen had removed a batch of Jessica's favorite sugar cookies from the oven, their delicate aroma overpowering the other odors lingering in the kitchen. Squealing, she threw down her books and jumped into Ellen's arms, all the while chattering like a squirrel. After asking about Papa Sam, who was working in the barn, she sat down to eat her snack. Lisa bit her tongue, allowing Jessica to snarf up an extra treat.

After changing, Jessica took Ellen to see Precious and explore the RV. About twenty minutes later, Ellen and Sam returned to the kitchen, having left Jessica to tend her pets.

"Where's Andrew?" Sam asked. "I was going to get him to take me on a pasture tour and show me the herd."

"Oh, he's been spending quite a few weekend nights with Eric lately. It's good to see the two of them are friends again. He promised he and Eric would come back tomorrow morning and help you clean out the barn."

"Sounds good. He can help me build that durn hog trap Carl talked me into. Carl and I are also going to work on the Bush Hog. He thinks we may be able to get several hay cuttings off the field this year since we've had some good rain lately."

"Extra hay would be wonderful. If we didn't have to buy any this winter, we could sure save a bunch of money."

Lisa and Sam, joined by Carl, were soon into deep conversation about the ranch finances and what to do about the burned swath of earth. She shared the details of the recently finalized contract with Whole Foods, and they discussed plans for delivery as well as a future expansion of the herd.

Lisa sipped wine while listening to Carl explain how some of the burn areas could easily be converted into useable, healthy pastures. Lisa realized how much she had missed Sam and Ellen. *They support me unconditionally.*

The night passed swiftly. Around nine, Sam and Ellen retired to their trailer, telling Lisa they planned to cook their breakfast and would not be over until they saw her and Jessica stirring. And Jessica, with Princess in tow, crawled into bed with a book.

Lisa was flying high, elated to have family near—but not on top of each other. Pouring another glass, she settled back on the couch, determined to read a few more pages of Julia's diary.

October 14, 1890

At last! A wonderful baby girl. I've wanted a little girl for so long. She's beautiful and has all her fingers and toes. I feel like she's giving me a wonderful contented smile as she yawns and stretches. I've named her Minnie. I got my hopes put on her. The boys don't want anything to do with the farm. I hope she does. I hope she can find a good man to help her with it. Eli got him some good farm land up in Oklahoma during the land rush. Seth, I don't know. He headed east. He wrote last year saying he wanted to work for some man named Eastman who invented some kind of new camera. Not sure what he ended up doing. Haven't heard from him in awhile. My heart aches, I miss him so much.

Lisa frowned, taking another sip of chardonnay. Julia had had some tough times; she seemed down. Maybe it was postpartum depression. Lisa read on.

My William, he's a wonderful man. But he and the boys couldn't see eye to eye. Guess they needed to make their own way in the world.

Shaking her head, Lisa realized boys and their dads have been clashing since time began. She lowered the diary on her lap, then, closing her eyes and leaning back, fell into a soothing, contented sleep.

***

The next morning Lisa woke early, dabbling in the flower bed by the house while Jessica slept in, a rare weekend luxury. Ellen ambled over mid-morning with a mug of coffee.

"Why on earth are you out here? Haven't you spent enough time gardening lately? This flower bed can wait till next year."

"Actually I'm, uh, kind of spying. Have a seat." Lisa pointed to a rocker on the porch. Let me get something to drink, and I'll explain." Lisa wiped her dirty hands on her jeans and then hurriedly went inside to grab a glass of water.

As she returned, a blue car pulled into Carl's driveway. Lisa sat down and pointed to the car. "Watch."

An older man climbed out of the automobile and knocked on the door. Within a minute, Carl opened it and stood in the doorway, listening to the visitor. Then he invited the man in.

"What's going on?" Ellen asked.

"His son. I found Carl's son. Carl hasn't seen him in years. I owe that wonderful man a lot. I hope this pays him back some."

"I don't understand."

"Carl's wife left with the kids, and he lost track of them. I managed to find his youngest son, Melvin. I had to do some hard and fast talking. Melvin had always thought his father had abandoned the family. When I explained what had happened, he softened and agreed to see Carl. I just left it a surprise."

Ellen leaned over and squeezed Lisa's hand. "What a wonderful gift."

CHAPTER 19

Michael rolled over and stared at the clock. Groaning, he fumbled with his cell phone. His head ached from the copious amounts of wine he and Sharon had drunk with dinner.

"Yeah?" He fell back on his pillow.

"Son," his mother said, "It's Andrew. The sheriff's office called and they're holding him at the county jail."

Michael tried to focus, not registering what his mother was saying.

"Michael! Your son is in trouble. He needs you!"

"Uh, Mom, sorry, I was sound asleep. In jail? Are you serious?"

"Yes, I am. Lisa and your dad are going there right now."

"OK, I'll be there as soon as I can."

Michael slid on a pair of old jeans and a T-shirt, secured his wallet and keys, and was out the door in less than three minutes. As soon as his Porsche was on the freeway, he called Lisa.

"What the hell's going on?"

"I'm not sure. Andrew told me he was going to spend the night with Eric. Eric told Dorothy he was spending the night with Andrew. We all thought the kids were safe. Next thing you know, we get a call from the sheriff's office. The boys are at the jail. Sam and I are on our way."

"How irresponsible can you get? Who's Dorothy?" As Michael's anger mounted, he pressed down on the accelerator, unleashing the auto.

"What do you mean? Me? Irresponsible? You're hardly ever here, you—" Sam snatched the phone from her.

"Son, we don't know what's going on, so let's all calm down. I know Eric; he's a nice young man. Remember, he was working on the tractor with us when you were there. His mother, Dorothy, is the local vet. Good as gold. You know, once kids get to be that age, you can't control them anymore. You just hope to God you can influence them, and they'll listen. We'll call you as soon as we find out anything. Are you on your way?"

Taken aback by his father's forceful speech, Michael said, "I'll be there as soon as I can. Where's the jail, anyway?"

"Take the 77 exit in La Grange. It's off to the right about a mile."

During the drive, Michael rolled down the window and rode in silence. The dank, tepid air bathed his face and arms. The drafts billowing into the car functioned as white noise, giving him time to think.

Andrew was going to live with him, but not until fall. He did have a good excuse—Michael worked late, and Andrew would be home alone. But deep down, Michael feared he would do no better at keeping the teen out of trouble than Lisa had.

His thoughts turned to Sharon. *What do I see in her, anyway? She just reminds me of Lisa. There's no way I could continue a relationship with her and care for Andrew. Something's got to give.*

Michael turned off the highway as the eastern sky brightened. He parked next to his wife's pickup and entered a conference room occupied by anxious people. Lisa introduced him to Dorothy and John. "Son, we're waiting for the deputy. He should be here any minute. Could I get you some coffee?"

"No thanks, Dad." Michael slumped in a chair, listening to the worried discourse. Everyone knew each other.

A young, slender man wearing the nametag "Tom Seekatz" and dressed in a brown short-sleeved shirt entered and greeted the others by name.

"Tom, this is Andrew's father, Michael," Lisa said.

"Y'all have a seat, please." Tom pulled out a chair, turned the back to face the conference table, and straddled the seat. "Here's what happened. Your two young men went to a pasture party the Hamachek boys threw. There was beer, a big bonfire—the works. Afterwards, they decided to do a little mudding."

"Mudding? What's that?" Michael asked.

"They drove Eric's truck through a pasture, tearing it up, running through puddles, that kind of stuff…. Sorry this took so long. I finally reached the county judge. He agreed I could release them, but they're due in county court Monday morning at 9 a.m. Underage drinking and destruction of property's serious, so I'd suggest you be sure they show up."

All promised to comply. With that, the deputy remanded the boys to their parents' custody.

"Let Andrew ride with me," Michael said.

"My pleasure," Lisa said. "We'll be along shortly. I need to discuss how we're all going to handle this with Dorothy and John."

A tired and somewhat dirty Andrew dropped into the passenger side of the Porsche. Buckling his seatbelt, he reclined the seat, closing his eyes and crossing his arms over his chest.

"Sit up!" Michael said. Startled, Andrew did as told.

Michael shifted the car into gear, trying to remain calm. He clutched the steering wheel tightly as if that action would give him the control he needed.

"Whatever were you thinking?" Michael asked.

"What do you care, anyway? You're never here. Why do you care what I do?"

"I do care. I care a lot. I want the best for you. If you're not careful, you'll ruin any chance of getting into an Ivy League school."

They rode in silence. As he neared the entrance of the JF Ranch, Michael said, "Andrew, I love you. Let's get some sleep. We'll talk about this later when we're not so tired."

Andrew stared out the window. When the car came to a halt, he climbed out and slammed the door behind him, stomping into the house. Another bang. Michael sat in the car, studying the early morning sky. He hoped the promised sun would dry out the damp darkness that had descended upon him.

Rather than go inside, Michael wandered into the barn and leaned against the wall. He heard his dad and Lisa arrive and enter the house. His mind raced. *I've turned into my father. And what have I done? I haven't been there for Andrew. I'm too busy looking after number one, concentrating on my new job.* Finally, it hit Michael. He was one unhappy bastard. Kicking the wall, he sobbed uncontrollably.

After regaining his composure, he sauntered out and over to the pen where Precious was nibbling hay. He watched, listening to her snorting and chewing, the whiff of fresh cow patties tickling his nostrils.

Something touched his arm. Michael jumped. Looking around, he found Jessica in her pajamas. She leaped into his arms, kissing him. "Oh, Daddy. I've missed you so much. We were so worried about Andrew. I'm glad you're here. Don't ever leave again."

Michael squeezed her hard, reality smacking him. What he had always wanted, what he had ever wanted, was right here, his wife and his children. He lowered Jessica to the ground and distracted her by asking questions about Precious. She told him about the cattle operations and pointed out T-Rex. Michael looked closely. Yes, she had slimmed down. Must be all the outside activity. *The ranch has been good for her. She's happy.*

"Honey, let's go in. You need to get out of the pj's, and I'm mighty hungry. Has Granny Ellen started breakfast?"

Jessica laughed and skipped ahead. "Yes. And she's fixing something called grits."

Michael entered tentatively, peering into the kitchen. Ellen was setting the table, Sam was drinking coffee. With relief, Michael noted Lisa was absent. Both looked at him, Ellen saying, "Could I get you a cup of coffee?"

Michael nodded, easing into a chair next to his father. Ellen said nothing but continued bustling around the room. Both men sipped the strong brew. The bacon sizzling and the slight knocks of eggshells on the side of the bowl punctuated the silence.

"Andrew's a good kid." Ellen concentrated on her preparations. "He's had a tough time adjusting, you know. It's all so different for him."

Sam said, "He's as smart as or smarter than you. He knows his way around a computer and a tractor. He'll make a fine adult one day."

About that time, Jessica reappeared in a red T-shirt and shorts, chatting nonstop. "Papa Sam, Precious needs more hay."

"Honey, why don't we let her in the field to eat some fresh grass? She can join the others for a play date." Sam patted her hand.

"Ooh, I'm scared she'll get lost or that she won't want to come back to the pen…. Or the coyotes will get her. I'm scared I'll lose her."

"You won't, sweetie. She loves you. She knows who gives her range cubes." Sam sighed. "Someday everybody's got to let their babies make it on their own. If it'll make you feel better, I'll help you watch over her while she plays."

"Would you, Papa Sam? You're so wonderful." She ran over and clutched him around the neck, plopping a big wet kiss on his cheek. He cuddled her back, obviously delighted.

Raising his eyebrows, Michael regarded his father. Relaxed, confident. Jessica adored him. Fighting back envy, Michael wished he were the one who was helping Jessica watch over her pet. *But I haven't been here and don't really know what's happening in her life.*

"Honey, get you some milk. Breakfast's ready," Ellen said. She stirred the last of the eggs.

"Want me to get Mom and Andrew?"

"No, sweetie, let them sleep a little. I think they need more rest than food right now."

Everyone dug in, Ellen explaining to Jessica how to butter her grits. They ate quietly, the adults in deep contemplation.

After Sam helped Ellen with the dishes, he took Jessica to halter Precious and lead her to the pasture.

Ellen gave Michael a refill and then wearily sat down, staring at the plastic tablecloth dotted with small red apples. The aroma of bacon hung in the air.

"I've never seen Dad so happy," Michael said.

"He loves those kids to death. He's having the time of his life."

"So why didn't he ever take time with me?" Michael asked.

"Honey, he was a product of his times. He was so worried about not being able to provide for us that he spent every waking hour trying to earn money. Why some months we wouldn't have made it if he hadn't done all that overtime."

Michael, startled, looked at his mother. "We had financial difficulties?"

"Yes, Son. Your dad was too proud to let on. He wanted you to have everything—a new baseball mitt, a trip to summer camp—all the things he never had."

Scenes from childhood ran through Michael's mind. He could not remember ever going without physical things. Now, his kids had everything but his attention—and he had sworn that would not happen. *But one can change.* Flashes of his father tenderly talking to Jessica about Precious rushed through his mind.

"Don't hold it against him. He loves you deeply. He'd do anything for you, you know that."

Putting down his cup, Michael stood. "I need to rest. I've had a tough day. I'm going to run into town and get a hotel room. I'll be back this afternoon after I've cleaned up. Tell everyone I'll be back, please."

Michael swung by the store and bought toilet articles as well as jeans and T-shirts; a pair of tennis shoes that were not too hideous rounded out his purchase. After checking into a local motel, he cleaned up and lay down to an agitated sleep.

***

Lisa stayed in bed until she was sure Michael was no longer in the house. Pulling on shorts, an old T-shirt, and hiking boots, she crept into the bathroom. Then, steeling herself, she entered the kitchen where Ellen was working on a crossword puzzle.

"Good morning. Can I get you something?" Ellen asked.

"I'm not really hungry. I'll just have cereal."

Lisa poured coffee and fixed a bowl of Cheerios topped with a sliced banana.

"Michael went into town. He said he'd be back this afternoon."

Lisa continued to eat, ignoring Ellen.

"Lisa, look, I know it's none of my business but—"

"You're right. It is none of your business. This is between me and Michael." Lisa turned and put her hand on top of Ellen's, "I know you mean well, but this is something we've got to work out for ourselves. I'm going to take a walk. I need to do some thinking."

Lisa rose and washed her cereal bowl and spoon, depositing them in the dish strainer. Then, as she left, she leaned over, kissing Ellen's cheek. "Thanks for understanding."

Lisa stopped by her office, stuffing two bottles of water and several granola bars, as well as a pad and pen, inside the backpack. Then she walked briskly down the path through the pasture. Sam and Jessica were visible in the distance, watching the privileged bovine dancing and skipping along with the other new calves. A smile crossed her face. Soon she became oblivious to everything around her, reliving her actions at least a hundred times, the self-reproach overwhelming. Her occupation with Rachael had left little time to focus on the kids. *I trusted Andrew a bit too much, got too comfortable…. I've been a bad parent…. I should've seen this coming.* Upon arriving at Julia's haven, she was beside herself.

Leaning against the old cypress tree, she closed her eyes and listened to the water trickle over the rocks, willing herself to clear her mind and relax. Then, when sufficiently calm, she opened her eyes, taking in her surroundings. The day was warm; the beads of perspiration that had formed between her breasts during her hike had soaked her T-shirt. Her legs, once glistening with the sheen of sweat, were now plain dirty, the grime clinging tightly.

Lisa removed her boots and socks, easing her feet into the creek and, cupping a handful of water, rinsed her grubby face. Drying her hands on her shorts, she sat back against the tree and guzzled a bottle of water. Rested, she began to write the pros and cons of each decision.

Divorce Michael—stay at JF and get Andrew some help

Divorce Michael—move somewhere where she could get Andrew help

Try to make things work with Michael—move to Houston and get Andrew help

Putting down the pen, she balled up the piece of paper, irritably throwing it into the water. How stupid. *This isn't an accounting problem; this is my life.* The yellow-lined sheet caught in the current, swirling around the rocks. Finally, saturated, it disappeared into the murky depths.

Tears flowed; she used the hem of her T-shirt to wipe her runny nose. Eventually the outpouring of grief slowed, leaving her numb and depleted.

Her mind and heart were at war. Competing desires battled within her, trying to gain the high ground and proclaim victory. One voice told her Andrew needed counseling to help him see the destructiveness of his behavior, another proclaimed he was a typical teenager; he would grow out of it. But he needs a father…. No, he has plenty of loving adults around.

She thought about the woman who answered Michael's cell. *Can I overcome my anguish? Can I ever trust him again?*

Swiftly she rose, hoping to chase the voices away and give her instincts a chance to kick in. But nothing came. Exhausted, Lisa sat and closed her eyes. Head dropping, she jerked awake. A peek at her watch confirmed it was getting late. Grudgingly, Lisa hiked back to her office.

Sitting in her chair, feet propped up on the desk, she sipped a glass of cold-brewed iced tea while wiping off the sweat and grime with a paper towel. A quick text informed Ellen of her return.

***

Around three, Michael woke to the ring of his iPhone. Sharon. Taking a deep breath, he answered, speaking with her for the last time.

An hour later, Michael arrived at the JF Ranch. The afternoon sun was promising a long, sizzling summer—the kind he had heard about in Texas. Ellen was standing on the porch as he climbed out.

"She's in her office." His mother disappeared into the house.

Michael braced himself and walked straight to the barn. Swallowing, he tentatively knocked, then pushed the door open a bit. "May I come in?"

Pausing as possibilities swirled through her mind, Lisa said, "Sure. We have lots to talk about."

Michael approached and went down on one knee. "I'm sorry I've been such a jerk. Everything will be fine if we can work things out." He reached for Lisa's hand and turned it over, studying the calluses and broken nails. "I want to get back together. I've never wanted anything so much in my life." He looked up at her. "I love you."

Lisa sat wordlessly, staring into Michael's eyes. "I want to believe you mean it. I don't know…so much has happened."

Michael sighed deeply. "I'm coming back whether you want me to or not. I have children who need me."

Another silence ensued. "Andrew needs you, but he needs a father, not competition."

Michael stiffened. "I'm willing to work on that if you work on easing up on Jessica."

"Point taken." Lisa leaned in. "So exactly what are you proposing?"

"We'll start slowly. I'll stay here every Friday evening and leave Monday morning. If you want, I'll stay at a hotel in town. In the meantime, I'll see if I can find work closer, in Austin, maybe."

Lisa observed Michael carefully. He sounded sincere enough. *Will he break my heart? Should I chance it?* Her thoughts roamed from her children to Rachel and Vivian…the fragility of life…. Closing her eyes, she inhaled, a feeling of exhilaration overwhelming her. "I'd like that, I'd like that a lot."

THE END

Also by Marie W. Watts

RiRi's Advice to the Grands

Rapture by Revenge: Warriors for Equal Rights

Only A Pawn: Warriors for Equal Rights

The Cause Lives: Warriors for Equal Rights

La Grange (Images of America: Texas)

An American Salad

Discussion Questions

1. What are your experiences with nature? Would you have moved to the JF Ranch? Why or why not?

2. How do you cope with being out of your comfort zone? Learning new things? Do you fear failure?

3. Lisa contemplated money. "Sometimes she hated the thought of money; but you needed it. *And it does make me happy.*" What are your feelings about money? Do we ever have enough?

4. Have you ever lost a job? How did you feel? What are the stressors surrounding it? How do you believe it affected the Dunwhitty family dynamics?

5. Are you aware of your family's history? Is it important to your sense of self? Why or why not?

6. Michael mistakenly believed his father was an uninterested parent rather than someone who was working to make ends meet. Should you share financial situations with children? If yes, then when?

7. Most friends are not forever. We—or they—move, drift away, or die. How do you make new friends and nurture the old ones?

8. Have you ever coped with difficult situations by avoiding taking action as Lisa did? Is there value in providing emotional distance before acting?

9. How would you have handled Andrew's behavior?

10. Do you believe Lisa and Michael will be able to repair their relationship? Why or why not?

I am available to speak with book clubs.
Please contact me through my website:
http://www.mariewatts.com

About the Author

Marie W. Watts, author of the award-winning trilogy Warriors for Equal Rights, brings her life experiences as a mother and grandmother, wife, friend, divorcee, and human resource specialist to explore what matters in life.

Her works encompass both fiction and non-fiction, including co-authoring the best-selling textbook *Human Relations*, 4th edition. Additionally, her work has been published in the *Texas Bar Journal* and the *Houston Business Journal*, as well as featured on *Issues Today*, syndicated to 119 radio stations, NBC San Antonio, Texas, and TAMU-TV in College Station, Texas.

She lives on a central Texas ranch with her husband, volunteers at a historic house, and hangs out with her grandsons.

Follow Marie and her blog, *Stories About Life* at
www.mariewatts.com.

Note from Marie W. Watts

Word-of-mouth is crucial for any author to succeed. If you enjoyed *Tough Trail Home*, please leave a review online—anywhere you are able. Even if it's just a sentence or two. It would make all the difference and would be very much appreciated.

Follow Marie and her stories about life at:

Website
https://www.mariewatts.com/blog
Newsletter Signup
https://mailchi.mp/8eec9d6c8b15/newsletter
Bookbub
https://www.bookbub.com/profile/marie
Facebook
https://www.facebook.com/mariewattsbooks/
Instagram
https://www.instagram.com/mariewattswriter/
Mewe
https://www.mewe.com/i/mariewatts4
X (Twitter)
https://twitter.com/MarieWattsBooks

Thanks!
Marie W. Watts

We hope you enjoyed reading this title from:

BLACK ROSE
writing™

www.blackrosewriting.com

Subscribe to our mailing list – *The Rosevine* – and receive **FREE** books, daily deals, and stay current with news about upcoming releases and our hottest authors.
Scan the QR code below to sign up.

Already a subscriber? Please accept a sincere thank you for being a fan of Black Rose Writing authors.

View other Black Rose Writing titles at www.blackrosewriting.com/books and use promo code **PRINT** to receive a **20% discount** when purchasing.